WILD IRISH WITCH

BOOK 6 IN THE MYSTIC COVE SERIES

TRICIA O'MALLEY

LOVEWRITE PUBLISHING

TO MY FRIENDS — WHO ARE ALL PART OF MY TAPESTRY.

"You know what the problem with this world is? Everyone wants a magical solution to their problems, and everyone refuses to believe in magic."
– Alice in Wonderland

CHAPTER 1

"*D*on't go," Fiona whispered as she pressed her hand to John's cheek. She could all but feel the bristle of his beard under her hand, just as it had felt the last time she'd touched him. Two days out from a shave, his eyes a laughing blue, and his dark hair just long enough to curl.

They were always young in her dream. Well, it was the only way she'd ever known John. Young, full of life, yet tender-hearted and gentle with her in their most intimate moments.

He'd been coming to her in her dreams over the years, but they'd increased in frequency as of late. Even though a part of Fiona knew that she was curled beneath worn flannel sheets in her cottage, in her mind she dreamt of her happiest moments. After all these years, the loss of John still stung. Fiona wondered if she would ever get over the grief, but it had been almost half a century since she'd last felt his lips against hers, and the sting of loss had yet to go away. It might have dampened a bit, but it had never truly left her.

Fiona shifted as the dream slipped away, taking her beloved with it. She let out a soft sigh of loss, and stayed still for just a moment longer. In her mind she was still young, agile, and full of zest for life. As the years crept on, Fiona felt a bit bewildered by the chasm of time that separated her from the last time she had spoken to John.

It shouldn't have been this way.

And yet, it had been the only way it could be.

Fiona knew without a doubt that John wouldn't have begrudged her the choice she'd had to make.

But the pain had never faded for Fiona. Perhaps that was just her cross to bear. Shifting once more, she rolled over and forced her eyes open. Ronan slumbered at her feet, her constant companion. Though he was technically Keelin's dog, when Keelin had moved over the hill to Flynn's he'd decided to stay with Fiona.

She'd never admit how secretly pleased she was by his choice.

"Come on boy, we've got a big day ahead of us," Fiona said, and Ronan popped his head up to look at her.

"It's Thanksgiving! Come on, come on, sure and you know we've got to be helping in the kitchen."

"I CAN'T BELIEVE I'm cooking a Thanksgiving dinner! This is my first Thanksgiving," Fiona pointed out as she followed Keelin's carefully printed recipe card for preparing bread stuffing. Fiona had crossed the hills, blustery with November wind, to help Keelin prepare for her favorite holiday. Ronan had raced beside her, barking into the gusts and chasing away imagined intruders.

"Maybe it's dumb of me to try to continue the tradition in Ireland. I'm the only American here, really." Keelin bit her lip, her pretty brown eyes scrunched in concern.

"It's never dumb to get the family together for a nice dinner," Fiona said with a smile, winking at Flynn as he ducked his head into the kitchen, Baby Grace cradled in one arm.

"I've got a fire started. It should help ward off some of that chill," Flynn said.

"How's Gracie doing?" Keelin asked, her hands deep in a bowl of cranberry sauce.

"She's fine. You know how much she loves me," Flynn said as he left the room, at ease with being a father. Grace shot them both a look over his shoulder. Fiona winked at her, and sure and the baby didn't wink right back.

"It's true. I've never seen a baby take such a shine to her father quite so quickly," Fiona chuckled as she sliced an onion.

"Yes, well, you'd think she'd love her mother. I'm the one who gave birth to her, aren't I? Yet she cries like a banshee half the time that I hold her."

Fiona bit back a laugh. She'd known since the day Baby Grace was born into this world that she was going to give Keelin trouble. The baby was major magick, after all. "We'll just have to wait and see what sort of gifts this little one gets. I expect she's going to give us all a run for our money very shortly here. I'm sure her crying around you has to do with her trying to communicate something that you aren't understanding yet."

Keelin's head shot up.

"You think? Really? I've been worried that I'm missing out on something. I just don't know what she's trying to tell me."

"All in good time, dear. It'll work itself out," Fiona said gently, warmth racing through her at Keelin's concern. She was a good mother, surprisingly so for not having been raised with siblings or around other children. Fiona was proud of how she'd navigated her first few months of motherhood.

"I just keep worrying that I'm doing everything wrong," Keelin admitted as she checked on the turkey in the oven.

Fiona pulled a bowl of cream from the refrigerator and began to whip it, focusing on the repetitive task as she thought about her words.

"I don't think that ever goes away," Fiona admitted. "As a mother, you're going to constantly question whether you're doing things right. Sure and you'll never stop worrying, either. But I always feel that, so long as you come at your decisions through love, it will all work out. The best you can do is give your child love and direction. As they grow and change, you'll need to step back and let them make their own decisions. Even if it means failing. You think the crying is hard? Wait until she walks out the door and starts to make decisions on her own. It only gets more difficult from there."

"Like my mom. When she left you alone," Keelin said softly.

Fiona shrugged.

"Yes, but what do you do? You can't force a grown

adult to listen to you," Fiona said as she tapped the whisk on the side of the bowl. "Now enough about that. Pull out the whiskey I brought, will you? The coffee's just perked and I'd like a fine Irish coffee."

Fiona shook her head as Keelin left the expansive kitchen that lay at the back of Flynn's large house. It was a far cry from cooking in her own small kitchen at her cottage, and Fiona loved visiting here and whipping up batches of scones while Keelin nursed. She'd missed out on the opportunity to help when Keelin was just a baby, so she was determined not to miss out on anything now.

Fiona sighed as she looked down at her hands. Her skin there was thin, but just showing the wrinkles of age. She'd be lying if she said she didn't add a little charm to her anti-wrinkle creams to help keep the signs of age away. But some days she felt it. Like today, when she looked at Keelin and her baby, so young and fresh. She remembered those days with Margaret. She'd been so young and innocent, at least for a brief moment in time. In that time of simplicity and love, Fiona had been so carefree, so in love with her husband and her life.

Sometimes she wished with all her heart she could have those days back.

And her John back in her arms.

Fiona shook her head at herself. She'd learned long ago that there was no use living in the past. No good could come of it.

She smiled brightly at Keelin as she came back in brandishing a bottle of whiskey.

"I think I'll join you for a cup. It sounds perfect on a day like today," Keelin said, as she placed the bottle on the counter and reached into a cupboard for her coffee glasses.

"There's nothing like an Irish coffee in front of the fire. Food's all set. Why don't we go in the other room and wait for Margaret?" Fiona asked as she measured sugar into the bottom of the glass and poured a liberal shot of whiskey into each.

"Sounds perfect," Keelin said, giving Fiona's arm a squeeze. "And, hey, thanks for the advice. I know it hasn't always been easy for you."

"Life isn't always easy."

CHAPTER 2

FIONA HAD ALWAYS liked Flynn's house, and this room was probably her favorite, she thought as she settled into the loveseat in front of a fire that sparked and crackled in a low stone fireplace. On either side of the fire were two long sets of windows, showcasing the reason Fiona had never moved from this area.

She sipped her coffee as she studied the ocean, grey and blustery today. Oh, but she loved the sea in all its moods. It was such an ephemeral and powerful entity. She always knew exactly what mood the sea was in. No subterfuge, no hiding. The sea proclaimed itself boldly.

Even more so in Grace's Cove.

But then, those waters were enchanted.

Fiona tore her eyes away from the point where the rolling hills dropped off into the sea, grey clouds hanging low on the horizon.

"When will Margaret be here?"

"They should be here soon. They had to haul themselves across the country to come to this. I feel kind of bad
for making them come all the way here," Keelin said,
sipping her coffee as she stared at the fire.

"Don't. You know Margaret is dying for a chance to
see Grace. A more besotted grandmother I've never seen.
Except for maybe myself," Fiona chuckled.

"She is, isn't she? I'm kind of surprised by that. She's
really changed since she's moved here... and, well, with
Sean. It's like there's this ease to her that was never there
before. Love looks good on her," Keelin decided.

"It does on most people," Fiona murmured, turning at
the sound of voices at the back door.

"Where is that baby?"

"And here she is," Keelin laughed, going down the
hallway to greet her mother. Fiona stayed where she was,
knowing that visitors always ended up in this room
anyway. She couldn't blame them. After Keelin and Flynn
had married, Keelin had put her touch on his house, and
the large open farmhouse had turned from a man cave to a
warm and welcoming home. Green plaid couches were set
off by leather armchairs, and dark wood shelves ranged the
room. A carpet in woven earth tones ranged in front of the
fire, just the spot to curl up with a good book in the colder
months. Or play with baby Grace on the floor, Fiona
thought as Margaret came into the room carrying Grace on
her hip.

"There's that little doll baby. Flynn was keeping her
out of the kitchen while we got the food ready," Fiona
said, tilting her head at the baby.

And a doll baby she was. She had the same sherry brown eyes as all the women in Fiona's family, but her deep auburn curls were her own. With a perky nose and rosebud lips, Baby Grace was a true beauty.

"I'm sorry I didn't get here sooner," Margaret said, sitting down on a plaid couch with Grace, fussing with her hair. Fiona felt a wave of guilt press against her from her daughter.

"Nonsense. You're running a thriving business. Don't worry about it," Fiona said, with a wave of her hand and a smile.

"Really? Because I feel like I should have been here to cook. We brought dessert," Margaret said, a guilty expression on her face.

"I sincerely hope you didn't cook it, and instead got it from that nice woman who runs the market down the street from you," Fiona said, raising an eyebrow at Margaret.

Margaret laughed and cuddled Grace closer to her.

"You got me. I didn't bake anything. Only because I love you all so much and don't want to poison you."

"Sure and that's kind of you, it is," Fiona said on a laugh, pushing herself from the chair with her empty cup in hand. "You keep Princess Grace entertained. I'm going to check on the food."

"Are you sure I can't help?" Margaret asked, a worried expression crossing her face.

Fiona dropped a kiss on her daughter's cheek as she walked by.

"Like you'd know what a done turkey looks like."

She bit back a laugh as Margaret muttered something

that sounded suspiciously like "you're a done turkey," and moved into the kitchen to check on the food.

It really was the perfect night for a Thanksgiving dinner.

CHAPTER 3

*H*OURS LATER, FIONA smiled from her seat at the head of the table. Flynn and Sean were at the kitchen sink, joking around as they cleaned the dishes. Keelin had disappeared upstairs to bathe Grace and put her to bed.

"This was perfect. Probably one of the best Thanksgivings I've been to," Margaret admitted, leaning back and patting her stomach under her red silk blouse.

"It's the only Thanksgiving dinner I've been to," Fiona said with a smile.

"And that's my fault," Margaret said. But where the sting would normally have been with her words, instead there was just a sense of remorse.

"It's nobody's fault. It just is," Fiona said. What was with all the melancholy tonight? People kept wanting to bring up the past.

"You're a very kind and forgiving mother," Margaret said with a smile.

Well, what was she supposed to say to that?

"Of course I am. I'm the best," Fiona joked, then excused herself from the table to use the restroom before she got teary-eyed. Saints, even *she* was getting a little maudlin tonight. It went with old age, she supposed. Family gatherings made her reminisce about times past.

Too bad not all of those times were good ones.

Fiona looked at herself in the bathroom mirror. Despite all her spells and potions, she hadn't been able to stop time. The effects of it were clear on her face, where lines creased her once-smooth forehead and eyebrows once full were now thin. Out of vanity she'd left her hair long, refusing to crop it short like most women her age did. Fiona was convinced that it benefited her appearance, and she smiled at herself in the mirror. She wouldn't be sorry for those lines; she'd worked hard for those. Even if vanity had led her to try to prevent them from coming, a lined face showed a life well-lived.

"We're in the living room," Keelin called as Fiona left the bathroom. She stopped in the kitchen to pour herself a whiskey, then walked down the hallway to meet the others.

Flynn and Sean stood by the door, cigars and beers in their hands.

"We're going to step out. You ladies enjoy yourself," Sean said, and Fiona smiled.

"Is this what the men do back in the States? Ditch the women after dinner?" Fiona asked.

"No, they go into the living room and watch football," Keelin said, fuzzy cottage socks on her feet as she curled into a corner of the couch. She'd changed into comfy pants when she'd been upstairs with Grace. The light of the fire danced across the wall behind the couch, adding warmth to the room.

Flynn snorted. "American football. Like that's a sport."

The men left before Keelin could debate with them.

"I like football," she complained.

"You'll not find a man likely to talk about any sport other than hurling or rugby here, you know," Fiona pointed out as she curled herself into an arm chair, pulling a blanket from the back of the chair – a blanket that her own mother had woven years ago.

"Did Dad play rugby?"

Fiona stiffened at the question from Margaret. They didn't often talk about John. If ever, really. Sometimes it just hurt too damn much to remember.

"Yeah, I want to hear about him. You never talk about him," Keelin complained.

Fiona felt her heart clench for a moment as she thought about the love of her life.

"You did promise that one day you would tell me the whole story. The choice you had to make? Now is as good a time as any," Margaret pointed out.

"If you want to," Keelin said immediately, her gaze bouncing between mother and daughter. "I don't want to upset you either, Fiona."

Fiona took a deep breath. She'd known that someday she'd have to tell Margaret and Keelin the story. They deserved to know this piece of their history. It just wasn't something she was fond of revisiting.

Fiona stared into the fire, its flames dancing as they consumed the wood, much like the emotions burning within her as she thought about her past.

"Settle in, ladies. This is going to take a while," Fiona said, taking a long pull of her whiskey.

"Hold on," Margaret said. She jumped up and all but ran from the room, returning quickly with Fiona's bottle of whiskey and two extra glasses. She topped off Fiona's glass, then poured herself and Keelin each a glass.

Leaning over, Margaret tapped her glass against Fiona's.

"Sláinte."

CHAPTER 4

"YOU KNOW, THE village was different back then," Fiona began, closing her eyes as she thought back to being nineteen. "It was much smaller. And I don't just mean in size. Small-minded, too, you understand? Televisions were a novelty here. The church really ran the town, all the social events. It was just a different time."

"What did your parents do for a living?" Keelin asked.

"My parents? Well, my father was a fisherman, as most people in this area are. My mother took care of me and wove beautiful tapestries that she sold to bring in extra money. She had a deal with a farm up the road. They would supply the wool and she would weave the goods. She was a bright woman, far more business-minded than my father, and her textiles were sought from all over Ireland. In fact, many people credited her with increasing tourism to the village."

"How old were you when you met Dad?" Margaret asked, taking a sip from her whiskey glass.

"Oh, I'd known John off and on for years. But I think the first time I really saw him for who he was…well, he was trying to help a lamb that had broken its leg."

Fiona shook her head as the picture came to her mind, so perfect and clear, like it was yesterday.

FIONA NEVER LIKED to see animals hurting. The waves of their pain seemed to tear through her. She was walking back from another trip into the hills to collect moss and roots when she saw John crouched on the side of the road. She could just barely make out the white coat of a young lamb under his hands. The animal was bleating hysterically as John held it down against the pavement.

"What's happened to it? What are you doing?" Fiona called out, tucking her basket under her arm and hurrying down the lane to where John crouched.

Fiona knew John O'Brien from school and around the village. Two years older than her, he was a quiet sort who always managed to be a leader in whatever group he was in. Whether it was his height or his startling blue eyes, John radiated authority and drew attention to himself wherever he went. Fiona had often caught her eyes following him across the schoolyard. She didn't see him as much now that they'd both finished school, but here and there they might run into each other.

"I'm not doing anything. This little guy's leg is broken. I'm trying to hold it still while I tie a brace, but I'm afraid there isn't much we can do. Mum will cook him up for dinner if I bring him back like this."

Fiona grimaced at the thought. It wasn't that she didn't

eat meat. It was hard to live in a village of farmers and fisherman and not understand where food came from. But it was another thing to look a baby animal in the eyes and consider it an option for dinner.

She crouched next to John and laid her hands on the bleating lamb. She could feel its terror pulse through her, and immediately sent a bolt of calming energy through its fuzzy little body.

"Is he yours?" Fiona asked, stroking the lamb as it calmed at her touch. She glanced at John to see his blue eyes surveying her openly.

"I suppose. Little guy's taken a liking to me. Follows me all over the yard. Which is how he broke his leg. Tried to follow me past the gate and fell off that little cliff there." John pointed behind them, his cheeks reddening a bit as he talked about the animal. Fiona could feel his concern press at her.

Fiona bit her lip as she considered what to do. She hadn't been healing all that long, and the recent discovery and development of her powers was something she was slowly exploring. If she healed the lamb in front of John – would he tell the whole village about her?

Fiona met his eyes again.

Throwing caution to the wind, she held his gaze. "I'd like to try something out here. But you have to promise not to say anything."

John nodded his head once, but didn't say anything.

Fiona shook her head at him. "You need to promise."

"I promise," John said, his mouth quirking up at the corner briefly. Then his eyes went back to the struggling lamb.

Fiona reached out and probed John's mind with her own, trying to see if he was being honest in his answer. Finding what she needed, she turned back to the lamb.

Reaching out, she ran her hand lightly over the broken limb, the animal jerking at her touch.

"Shh, it's okay," Fiona said and closed her eyes, finding the break in the bone with her mind. Focusing, she began to mentally knit the bone back together, whispering a Celtic prayer under her breath. The lamb stopped bleating, its eyes fixed solemnly on her as she healed its broken leg. When she was convinced that everything was fixed, Fiona pulled her hands back and brushed them against her skirt. Sitting back on her heels, she looked down at the lamb.

"I think he's okay now," Fiona said softly, afraid to meet John's eyes.

"Sure and you can't have me believing that, now, can you?" John's voice grated against Fiona's nerves, and she felt her back go up.

"It's not my job to make you believe anything," Fiona said hotly.

John stared at her for a moment before dropping his eyes and removing his hands from the lamb, who now struggled to stand up. His mouth dropped open when the lamb rolled and stood up, bumping its little head against his knee. John's mouth worked, but no sound came out.

"So, there's that," Fiona said awkwardly as she stood. This was the first time she had shown her power to anyone, and regret washed through her. There was no way John was going to keep something like this a secret.

"I... I..." John said, standing and stepping back a bit.

Fiona could read the fear that washed through him from where she stood.

"It's a gift. I'm a healer," Fiona said, straightening her shoulders as she met his eyes.

"A healer? But, but that's the stuff of lore." John shook his head at her in disbelief.

"Aye, and it's the stuff of life. *My* life. This is who I am. I can't change it," Fiona said softly.

"Is this the devil's work?" John asked, his chin coming up as he met her eyes.

"Oh, sure and you don't think the devil's work would be saving a little lamb now, do you?" Fiona sputtered, torn between anger and laughter.

"No, I suppose not," John said, taking his cap from his head and twisting it in his hands. The lamb darted in circles around John's feet, bleating its happiness.

"Listen, I know I'm different. But I'm still me. Just a girl from the village. Please don't say anything. You know how the village will get – they'll throw me out and I'll have no place to go," Fiona asked, desperately trying to keep the pleading note out of her voice. "I just wanted to help."

"And you did, at that. You didn't have to help at all, you could've kept walking," John said, running his hand through his hair as he thought about it.

"I don't like seeing animals in pain. And you seemed really upset. So, well, I thought I'd give it a try and see if I could help. Just…please don't say anything," Fiona said, stepping past him and reaching down to pat the little lamb on its knobby head.

The lamb looked up at her and bleated what Fiona took

to be a thank-you. She straightened and, with one last look over her shoulder, left John standing in the middle of the road staring after her, a healthy little lamb hopping around his feet.

She desperately hoped she hadn't made a tragic mistake.

CHAPTER 5

IONA HURRIED THE rest of the way home, dread lacing her stomach as she rounded the curve of the road that led into downtown Grace's Cove. Situated on the western peninsula of Ireland, Grace's Cove was tucked away in between a small mountain range and the ocean. Its staggering cliffs and sandy beaches provided dramatic contrast, and summers here often brought a slew of people taking holiday. That was when Fiona's mother, Bridget, really made her money from her cottage business selling woven goods.

Cresting the hill, Fiona paused – as she always did – to take in the beauty of her small village. Houses were scattered across the hills, connected by narrow winding roads, all flowing to meet at the entrance to the harbor. The sun was just peeking out from the clouds, its light beaming onto the water where boats were coming in with the catch of the day. Children raced along the beach, grateful for the sun after a particularly dreary winter.

This was her favorite place in the world, and Fiona prayed John wouldn't ruin it for her.

Though she couldn't entirely fault him if he did say something, Fiona thought as she made her way through town. It wasn't as if there weren't already whispers about her family throughout the village. Bridget had tried her best to raise Fiona as a normal child, even though she was far from it. Even with all of Bridget's care – rumors still drifted through the village.

Fiona sighed as she pushed open the gate to the back courtyard of her parents' small cottage on top of the hill. She was the only child of a weaver and a fisherman; their family was small and their needs were simple, as demonstrated by the three-room cottage her father had built for them to live in. Fiona's childhood had consisted of roaming the hills with her mother, and learning to fish at her father's knee. There had always been food on the table, though Fiona knew her mother was more to thank for that than her father.

Fiona pushed the back door open, stopping to pet one of the yard cats before stepping into the main room of the cottage. Light filtered through the paned windows, showing a room divided into three areas: a small kitchenette, a table for eating, and a few soft armchairs pulled close by a small peat fireplace. Bridget's weavings hung from the walls, energizing the room with their shocks of color, and a threadbare carpet kept the chill from the stone floor. Two doors led from the room to each of the bedrooms, and a small bathroom nestled in the space between the two rooms.

Fiona looked up when she heard a thump from the loft above her head. "Mum?"

"Up here, darling," Bridget called from her weaving room, and Fiona heard another thump as Bridget crashed through another row of thread on the loom. Fiona pulled herself up the ladder to the loft and moved towards a small wooden chair that sat near her mother's loom. The large loom took up most of the space, the threads woven intricately, her mother focused on the tapestry beginning to unfold in front of her.

Fiona loved it up here. It was like all of her mother's creativeness and warmth had exploded everywhere. Spools of thread in every color imaginable were stacked in baskets and on shelves, crowding each other for space in this small loft area below the eaves. Fiona had to duck a little as she walked to the chair, but the smallness of the space added to the charm of the loft. In the winters, with the peat moss fire going below and a lantern lit above, Fiona's mother would work for hours, creating beautiful tapestries and blankets that she sold from her shop and at the market in the summer.

"I've gathered the dock leaf you asked for," Fiona said, moving around to examine the tapestry. Bridget Morrigan was a sturdy woman with sherry brown eyes and honey-blonde hair shot through with grey and tucked into a braid, and she smiled up at Fiona, crinkles radiating from the corners of her eyes.

"That's lovely, thank you," Bridget said, her eyes trained once again on the loom.

"This is a pretty one," Fiona murmured, appreciating the mossy green textile woven amidst a golden hue.

"Thank you. Fiona, is something wrong?" Bridget stopped, tearing her eyes away from the loom and turning to take her daughter's hand.

Leave it to her mother to read her emotions loud and clear. Fiona shrugged and debated how to answer.

"Is Father here?"

"You know where he is," Bridget said.

At the pub. As usual. Cian Morrigan was at the pub more often than not these days. Grace's Cove only had two pubs and, aside from church, they were the social centre of the town. Her father was bringing in less and less of a catch these days, and spending more time telling stories with his cronies down at the pub. Which left Bridget to bring in the money.

"I'm sorry, Mum. I know how much you miss him," Fiona whispered.

Bridget shrugged.

"He's a good man. He's got a good heart. But the drink will be the death of him. There's not much we can do to change that. Only he can change his path in life." Her words came out clipped, and Fiona felt a tug of sympathy for her mother.

"We'll have a good selling season this summer. I've got plenty of new balms and tinctures that I've been working on. We'll be fine," Fiona said, moving to sit in the chair while her mother picked up the wool again.

"It will be fine. It always is, dear," Bridget said, getting back into her rhythm. "Now, tell me what you were all in a tizzy about when you came in."

Had she been in a tizzy? Fiona supposed she had been in a quiet tizzy of sorts, but her mother could read her energy, so there was no use trying to hide anything from her.

"I saw John O'Brien on the way home from the hills," Fiona began. Bridget smiled slightly.

"A nice-looking lad, isn't he?"

"Sure and I wasn't thinking about that when he was all but bawling over a lamb with a broken leg at his feet," Fiona said, dodging her mother's question.

"Really? I find that surprising," Bridget mused.

Wham! The loom crashed and shook as Bridget started another row.

"I did as well, seeing as they live on a farm. But he said the little fellow had taken a liking to him and followed him all over the place," Fiona shrugged.

"You healed the wee thing, didn't you?" Bridget asked, pausing to meet Fiona's eyes.

"I did. And he looked at me like I was a monster," Fiona said, crossing her arms over her chest angrily.

"Did he now? I find that surprising as well," Bridget mused, pushing her braid back over her shoulder.

"Well, I suppose he didn't call me a monster. Though he asked me if it was the work of the devil," Fiona admitted.

Bridget offered her a small smile and a raised eyebrow.

"Do you expect anything less? You know how this town is."

"I made him promise to keep quiet and then I just ran away. There wasn't anything else to say and I didn't feel like standing there being judged by him," Fiona said, combing a hand through her hair.

"Well, Fiona, you have had quite a lot of time to get

used to your gift. You can't expect people to understand or accept what you are overnight. Give it time," Bridget said.

Fiona huffed. "I wouldn't call three years 'quite a lot of time.'" On Fiona's sixteenth birthday, Bridget had given her a leather-bound book and taken her to the cove.

The cove that would forever change her life.

"He'll come around. He's a nice boy," Bridget said.

"I don't know if I would call him a boy."

"I suppose he's not any more, at that, is he?" Bridget shrugged. "We'll just have to see what happens from this."

"That's easy for you to say. Everyone here has already accepted you. They still haven't accepted me. Which isn't fair," Fiona said crossly. She'd been the quiet one in school, often overlooked and not included in tea parties or games, as though the children had sensed an otherness about her. She'd known she was different; it would have helped if Bridget had bothered to enlighten her sooner.

"Life's not fair," Bridget said.

It was one of her mother's favorite sayings, drilled into Fiona's head from early on. The Brogan's farm burned down? Life's not fair. The bucket of eggs toppled over? Life's not fair. Fiona was never courted for a date? Life's not fair.

"What happens if he tells the village? I'll be pushed out," Fiona said softly, running her hands up and down her arms.

"Fiona Morrigan, it will take a lot more than some village gossip to push us out of this town. Don't you worry about gossip. They've long known that I've a touch of something extra. It shouldn't surprise them that you do as well. I will handle this if it comes to light," Bridget said, stopping to tug a new ball of wool from the basket at her side.

"This is the first time I've ever showed anyone what I can do," Fiona said, shrugging one shoulder. "I don't know how you're supposed to become comfortable with it."

"Why, who says you have to become comfortable with it? I think that anytime you use the gift that has been bestowed upon you, you should be amazed. And if the people around you aren't honored by the fact that you've chosen to help them, that is their problem. Not yours. Sure and you have to be understanding the difference now?" Bridget was honestly confused by Fiona's angst.

"But, mum, your gift is different than mine. Healing is... well, people are going to think I'm a witch," Fiona looked around as she whispered the word.

"Well, and you are, in a loose definition, I suppose." Bridget leaned back and met Fiona's eyes.

A pulse of shame washed through Fiona at Bridget's admission. Fiona knew she wasn't a witch; well, at least not in the bad sense – but she couldn't shake years of Catholic church schooling. For the religious folk in town, the word 'witch' might as well equate to 'the devil.' And Fiona knew just what would come with that.

"I'll get dinner started," Fiona said softly as she rose from her chair, but her mother was already lost back in the world of her making, the loom shaking and banging as threads were woven together forever.

Just like her life, Fiona thought as she descended the ladder to the room below. One thread weaving into another, the pattern and depth still unknown to her.

CHAPTER 6

$\mathcal{T}$HE NEXT MORNING, Fiona packed her satchel in her small bedroom. Sleep had been difficult the night before – between her father coming home late from the pub and his resulting argument with Bridget, and her fears of John telling her secret, Fiona had tossed and turned much of the night.

In the early hours of the morning, she had finally admitted defeat. She rolled over on her small threadbare mattress, reaching beneath to pull her leather book out.

She traced her fingers over the cover, feeling power radiate from inside of it, and wondered if other people could sense power like she did. In fact, she wondered how she ever managed to come across as slightly normal, even half the time. Everywhere she went, power and moods pulsed at Fiona. She could read someone's energy from across the village, and it was easy for her to know who was angry or when someone was contemplating doing something bad. This jumble of energy and emotion had been maddening for her, until Bridget had gifted her with the book. It had been handed down over generations, and each person who was touched with Grace O'Malley's power had added to it over the years.

The leather cover was old, creased with oils and cracked with age. The pages inside were vellum, and Fiona always took great care to turn them with the soft cloth the book was wrapped in, never letting her fingers touch the actual pages.

Inside, the book held a world of its own making. Spells, rituals, elixirs, tinctures, and even historical accounts of healing. There was a wealth of history pressed between those pages, and Fiona had read and re-read it until the words became familiar, absorbing the lessons within until she could all but recite the entire book word for word.

It had been the gift that had changed her life forever, setting her apart from the rest.

Fiona had been upset with her mother last night, when she'd told Fiona to just accept her lot in life. But now she realized that Bridget wasn't being cold. The truth of it was that Fiona had the opportunity to step out on a path of her own, helping others and changing lives with the gift she had been given. She could either own it or hide it. There was really no in-between.

Anxiety kicked low in her stomach as Fiona thought about openly declaring to the world that she was a healer. Most nineteen-year-olds were thinking about dating and getting married, and here she was thinking about how she could help others and change the world.

Every once in a while, Fiona desperately wished that she could be normal.

Taking a scone from the basket on the counter, Fiona wrapped it in a cloth and pulled a glass jug of water from the cooler. Putting both in her satchel, she quietly let herself out of the house. She was too keyed up to stay around and talk to her mother or her father. Instead, a good walk over the hills and to the cove might work off some of this nervous energy. Fiona quietly unclasped her bicycle from a hook in the back yard and rolled it out of the courtyard.

Light was just crowning the horizon of the hills behind the village. A thin strip of light blue illuminated their gentle peaks, the dark blue of the night sky being chased away by the sun. The morning was crisp, with dew clinging to the hills and the smell of spring drifting on the gentle morning breeze. Fiona walked her bike down the hill towards the harbor, the men loading their fishing boats and the baker the only other people awake this early.

Fiona's dad should have been up with the fishing crew, and Fiona felt a slice of sadness go through her as she looked at his worn boat, bobbing gently at its dock, waiting to be taken out. She wondered if the boat would even leave the harbor this week.

Fiona raised a hand to the fishermen; a few of them nodded at her, knowing her to be a fisherman's daughter. She wondered what they thought of her or her father. She knew it was useless to worry about what other people thought of her, but was still unable to let those thoughts go. Fiona shook her head at herself as she reached the beginning of the paved road that wound around the hills towards the cove.

Throwing a leg over her bike, Fiona began the ride to

the cove. Today she wore khaki pants in deference to riding her bike, a button-down blouse, and a soft grey sweater knitted by her mother. She'd pulled her long hair back in a single braid and wound a scarf around her neck. Even though it was technically spring, the morning was still chilly.

Fiona pumped the pedals harder as she approached a hill, determined to work up enough speed to zip past the house she knew to be at the top of the hill.

The O'Brien's farm.

If she was lucky, they wouldn't be up quite yet and she'd pass by without having to acknowledge the family.

The O'Brien's were one of the wealthier families in town. Between ample farm acreage and a family of fisherman, the O'Brien's had many streams of income, from wool to seafood. Fiona had always thought it was smart of them to diversify, considering the unstable economy of the village – there was always a way to make ends meet.

There wasn't much diversifying going on at home, though Fiona was determined to fix that with her newly-developed tinctures and elixirs.

"Shite," Fiona muttered to herself as she crested the hill and saw John carrying two buckets over to a pasture fence, the little lamb from yesterday happily following him around.

His back was towards her and Fiona was able to study him for a moment. With a close cropping of thick dark hair, strong shoulders from working on a farm, and a tall lean build, John certainly wasn't hard on the eyes. It wasn't the first time that she had admired him from afar, though she had often wondered why he didn't date more.

The lamb saw her and bleated a cry of acknowledgement. John turned immediately, stopping in his tracks as he
saw her on her bicycle.

Fiona paused for a moment, unsure of what to say, fear
curdling in her stomach. The moment hung suspended
between them before Fiona pushed the pedals down,
moving the bike forward. Just as she was about to head
down over the hill and out of sight, John lifted his hand to
his head, saluting her.

A smile split Fiona's face as she rode the hill down, her
braid streaming behind her on the wind, feeling joy
building up inside her to the point that she wanted to
scream.

And feeling a giddiness latch onto her heart.

CHAPTER 7

*F*IONA LAID HER bike against a crumbling stone wall at the top of the cove. There was only so far she could ride her bike before having to walk the rest of the way to the water.

She paused and looked around her, never surprised by the needy ache that filled her as she looked over the hills that flowed around her.

The land she desperately wanted to be hers someday.

Fiona knew it wasn't practical to live this far from town. But who cared about being practical, when the land rolled out its welcome mat for you?

Fiona smiled as she trailed her fingers along the stone wall, her gaze taking in the gently sloping green hills that rolled off into dramatic cliffs jutting out into the ocean. She could just picture it – a little cottage nestled at the base of the hills that rose behind her, the windows situated so they would catch the breeze and offer the best views of the water.

She felt at home here, more so than in the village, and

found herself constantly drawn to the hills that surrounded these cliffs. She supposed some of it was due to her tie to the cove.

Fiona stopped at the top of the cove, drinking in its beauty and taking stock of its mood today. It was always different, and she'd learned long ago to trust the moods of the water in the cove. Even though her magick and the cove's magick was the same, she'd been taught to give it respect.

The cove was a secret that hid along the dramatic cliffs of this coastline. It was what the town was named for, and its enchanter lay deep within its waters. Grace O'Malley had famously walked into the cove's waters, taking her own life instead of letting the sickness within do so, forever enchanting the waters of the cove and passing along a very real gift of magick to the women of her bloodline.

Which was why Fiona had the multitude of talents and gifts that she did, and why whenever she was near the cove, her blood began to hum.

The sharp half-circle of the cove lay beneath her, cutting into the impressive cliffs that sprang from the waters, almost touching at the entrance to the cove. A perfect sand beach, untouched but for the few birds that pecked at its shoreline, lay at the bottom of a trail that wound its way down the cliffs. When the sun set, a ray of light would shoot between the two cliffs, illuminating the back cliff walls and plunging the rest of the cove into darkness.

The cove lay in shadows this morning, the sun not quite high enough yet to touch its waters. Fiona reached out with her mind and tested the energy signature of the water and found it calm – nothing troubling it on this morning.

"Good. I want to try out some of that moss," Fiona said out loud, turning once more to glance at the expanse of green hills behind her, envisioning what it would be like to wake up every morning and walk here.

Fiona began the hike down to the cove, trailing one hand along the rock wall as she walked, stopping to pick up stones and a flower bud along the way. When she reached the bottom, she hesitated for a moment before stepping onto the beach.

She felt so much smaller here, the huge cliff walls enclosing her, making her feel like just another small pebble on the beach. Power pressed against her, the enchantment of the cove rising up to greet one of its own.

Fiona stepped forward and drew a circle in the sand with a stick. Stepping into it, she held her rocky offerings high into the air.

"I come to you with nothing but the utmost respect. I'm here to pull some healing moss from your waters, to help others with ailments. I present to you these gifts as a token of my respect," Fiona called, tossing the rocks into the water. She knew the rocks weren't really gifts as most people would think, but the cove didn't care what you offered.

So long as an offering was made.

Fiona smiled as she stepped from the circle and began to walk the beach. She never ceased to be amazed at the beauty found here – her own private paradise.

For years now, the villagers had warned people away

from the cove. It was understood that something was *off*
there. Though the official word was that a deathly
undertow meant people should stay away, that explanation
didn't really cover what happened on the beach if people
didn't make an offering. Fiona shuddered to think about it.

She didn't necessarily blame Grace, either. Fiona
would probably want her final resting place to remain
untouched too. It was about respect, above all else.

Lost in thought, Fiona approached a craggy outcropping of stones that formed several small tidal pools. She'd
been experimenting with some of the moss that slicked the
stones there, adding it to hand creams or putting a pinch
into a cough syrup. She'd found it to have some wonderful
healing properties and wanted to gather more so she could
expand the line of self-care products she was working on.
She'd yet to sell any, but word was building as she had
begun to give away small jars of this and that for free.
Fiona could already see the label in her mind: A pretty
white and green logo, wrapped around small white jars she
had bought in bulk. If all went well, she'd be able to sell
her wares next to her mother's this summer.

And provide another source of income that they
desperately needed.

Fiona crouched over a rock, pulling a knife and a jar
from her satchel, and began to scrape pieces of the spongy
moss from the rock, gently depositing them in the jar. It
was only when the waves began to kick up, knocking into
the tidal pools, that she looked up and realized she had
been working for hours. The sun now hung in the middle
of the sky, a few wisps of white clouds covering it. As

Fiona shaded her eyes and looked across the beach, she realized the water was getting moody for a reason.

At the top of the cliffs stood John, the silly little lamb at his side, his hand up to shield his eyes. Fiona swore when he started to come down the path, the lamb clambering along behind him.

"Sure and that man has no sense of self-preservation? He knows not to come into the cove," Fiona grumbled as she raced along the beach, her feet digging into the sand, her heart pounding with fear and uncertainty. She didn't want to have to go through the protection ritual with John. She'd already shown him she was strange enough.

Fiona climbed steadily, her muscular legs gaining ground, years of climbing this path and the hills around her making her quick and light-footed. She reached John in a matter of moments. He had stopped where he was when he saw her ascent, and now she faced him on the narrow ledge of a path.

"What are you doing here?" Fiona asked, her chin up.

"It's a free country, isn't it?" John pointed out, putting his hands on his hips.

"You know it's not safe for you to go down there," Fiona hissed, looking down at the little lamb, who walked forward and looked up at her.

"I'm not sure I've ever really believed that rumor," John said.

"Oh? So you think the smart thing is to test it out alone? And here I thought you had a brain in your head," Fiona muttered.

"Well, I wouldn't be alone since you were on the

beach, now would I?" John asked, his eyebrow quirking up.

"Yeah, but…" Fiona trailed off. She couldn't say it was okay for her to be on the beach but not him. The last thing she needed to do was point out how different they were.

Again.

"If it's so bad in there, should *you* be going there alone? Maybe I was coming down to save you." John's easy smile slid across his handsome face, and Fiona's breath caught in her throat for a moment.

"I'm good, thanks. Doesn't look like I need saving, does it?" she asked lightly, stepping forward to encourage John to turn around and go back up the path. Instead, he stood where he was, forcing Fiona to stop, her face inches from his chest. She gulped, her mouth dry, as she turned her gaze up to his face.

"You can move now," Fiona said, as the seconds stretched between them.

"Ladies first," John said, a gleam in his eye.

"Fine, I'll go then," Fiona muttered, pushing past him, refusing to think about where her body tingled as it brushed past his on the narrow path. She rolled her eyes to the sky and forced herself to breathe normally as they hiked the rest of the way to the top of the cliffs, the only sound the crash of the waves below them and the little bleats of the lamb following up the path.

If time were to be counted in heartbeats, then it took them 111 heartbeats to reach the top, the significance of the repeating number not lost on Fiona. Forcing herself to focus, she stepped back from the top of the path and turned to face John.

And caught him looking at her bum.

Putting her hands on her hips, she raised an eyebrow at him.

A rush of pink colored John's face and he shrugged sheepishly, as the lamb wandered away to graze in the green grass.

"How come you can go down there, anyway?" John asked, distracting Fiona from the way his shoulders filled out his shirt.

"Because I can," Fiona said simply, refusing to explain more.

"Does it have to do with, you know, the stuff you did yesterday?" John asked, not meeting her eyes but instead looking over her head.

"It's really none of your business why I can or can't do anything in my life," Fiona pointed out hotly, and John held his hands up.

"Hey, easy, I was just curious."

"Well? I don't owe you an explanation, do I? I'm not hurting anyone. In fact, I was digging up special moss to put in healing elixirs, if you must know. All I want to do is help people. I don't care if you think I'm strange or weird – I'm not here to please you, am I? Sure and it'd be nice if you didn't give me third degree and follow me around like I'm some suspicious criminal," Fiona said, her heart picking up its pace as anger ratcheted through her. Tears threatened to fill her eyes, which made her even more furious and she turned away from John, kicking at the grass with her toe.

"I wasn't trying to scare you," John said from behind her. "I was just curious, 'tis all. I'll go now." Fiona didn't turn, instead keeping her eyes trained on the horizon. She heard the lamb's calls getting softer as they moved away and in moments, Fiona knew she was alone.

It was better that way. Alone, that is. Fewer questions. No expectations.

Suddenly Fiona gasped and tore her eyes away from the horizon just in time to see a brilliant blue flash of light, shining from the depths of the cove, like the waters were singing to her in joy. She stood frozen, her eyes riveted on the sight, as the wind picked up and kissed her cheeks, seeming to whisper a song of love and promises to her.

It was too bad Fiona had stopped believing in promises a long time ago.

She turned her back on the cove and walked away.

CHAPTER 8

*I*T HAD BEEN two weeks since that day at the cove, and Fiona felt like she saw John everywhere now. She did her best to avoid him, but it was just the way the universe worked sometimes. The law of attraction. The more she thought about him, the more often John showed up in her path.

It wasn't something she was used to, the way he looked at her. Like he had a question that only she could answer.

Her fear of him saying something about her healing abilities had died down as the days passed. The village was just too small. If he had said something, Fiona would have heard about it by now.

"Will this spot work for you?" Bridget asked, and Fiona snapped back to reality. They were setting up at the local market, for today was one of the first nice weekend days in ages and tourists would be making their way through.

The market was set up along the harbor walkway, with

a few trees canopying them for shade. Tables were scattered throughout with a feast of homemade goods to sell, but Fiona noticed nobody pulled their table close to Bridget's.

"Yes, this is lovely, mum. A great spot," Fiona said, catching the eyes of two women standing over jars of honey, their heads leaned close in order to whisper to each other. When they realized that Fiona was staring them down, they snapped their attention back to rearranging their jars. Fiona rolled her eyes.

"Will people ever just accept us?"

"Who? What happened?" Bridget asked, pushing her braid behind her shoulder as she glanced around.

"Nothing. Two women whispering about us, 'tis all," Fiona said, putting her basket on the table.

"That's their problem, not ours," Bridget pointed out as she pulled out tapestry after tapestry, separated with sheets of tissue paper, and began to lay them across the table in a colorful display.

"They're probably jealous. Just look at your work, would you? Mum, you've outdone yourself," Fiona gushed as she ran her hands over a particularly brilliant blue tapestry.

The same blue as the light from the cove.

Fiona had told no one about what she'd seen. Not that she had anyone to tell secrets to, anyway, really; her mother was pretty much her only confidant.

"You're woolgathering today, aren't you?" Bridget asked, and Fiona shook her head, realizing she had missed what her mother had said.

"I'm sorry. What was that?"

"I said, thank you – I designed it after the cove."

"I can tell, it's stunning," Fiona said, running her hands over the tapestry once more before turning to her basket and pulling the towel from the top. Nestled inside was her first run of creams and elixirs. She'd decided to keep her offerings simple and had stuck with four items today: A face cream, a hand cream, a cream to soothe sore joints, and a tonic for chest colds. If they sold well, she planned to expand into other areas. She'd learned from watching her mother, though, and knew it was best to start small and carefully build a reputation for herself.

Pulling the jars from the basket, she hummed softly to herself as she lined them up, biting her lip as she considered angles and the best presentation. Her pretty hand-drawn labels made her smile; she'd spent hours late at night perfecting the look until it was precisely what she was going for.

Fiona's Magick Face Cream.

At first, Fiona had been resistant to the idea of adding the word 'magick' to her labels. But Bridget had insisted upon it, pointing out that perhaps their reputation could work in their favor. Plus, who wouldn't want a face cream charmed by magick? Bridget's persistence had paid off, and the word had gone on the labels.

Fiona felt her stomach turn as she saw a few people draw near to take a look. What if putting 'magick' on the label had been the wrong idea? Fiona worried she would be ostracized. Unable to change the path she had set in motion now, she smiled brightly at the two women who approached the table.

"Sinead, Mrs. Brogan, how are you both?" Fiona

smiled, feeling her shoulders tense up as the most popular girl in her graduating class and her mother stopped in front of the table. Of course it had to be these two who would come to the table first. She could feel herself all but slumping in defeat.

"We're fine, thank you," Mrs. Brogan said automatically, her lips pressed in a tight line of disapproval as she picked up one of the face cream jars and read the label.

"Magick cream?" Sinead giggled and rolled her eyes at her mom. "Great, like we need a witch selling magick potions in town. It'll probably cause everyone to break out in a horrible rash."

Fiona felt her blood begin to boil at this stupid girl, so callously dismissing all her hours of hard work, setting the stage for her downfall. She opened her mouth to speak.

"Oh, thank goodness you're selling more of your magick cream," a voice cut in, and Fiona looked up in shock.

John stood before her, a smile on his handsome face.

"Oh, you need face cream, do you then, John?" Sinead laughed and preened, smiling flirtatiously up at John. "What do you want with a witch's brew anyway? It'll probably give you warts or something."

John shook his head as he looked down at Sinead. "It's not for me. It's for my aunt's shop in Dublin," he said, a bit louder than necessary. "She can't keep it in stock. All the finest ladies are buying it up; she's got a waiting list a mile long. I promised I'd see if Fiona had made any more."

Fiona could have hugged the man. In one moment, he'd saved her reputation with the gossips in the village and had given her budding remedy line a chance.

"Is that so?" Mrs. Brogan's eyes sharpened in a predatory manner, and she reached into her small purse. "I'll take one of each. Will you be making more? Maybe I should buy two." She bit her lip as she considered the jars and Fiona almost choked on a laugh when she saw anger cloud Sinead's face.

"John, send this along to your mum, will you?" Fiona asked, smiling up at him and mouthing 'thank you' as she handed him a jar of her face cream. A tingle shot up her arm as his hand brushed hers. "And I've already got a batch made up for your aunt, ready to go and waiting back at the cottage."

"I'm sure she'll be thanking you then," John said, winking at her and slipping the jar into his pocket. Turning, he smiled at the Brogan's. "Ladies, have a nice day."

"Fiona, you didn't answer my question – will you be making more? I'm not sure I should wait. Maybe I should buy two of each."

"Yes, that's probably best. I take extensive care when creating these creams. Only the freshest, hand-picked ingredients, all culled and made with love. It can take me quite some time to prepare a fresh batch, especially if I have trouble finding any of the ingredients." Fiona said, pulling out brown paper to wrap the jars in.

She could barely keep the smile off her face as more women lined up behind Mrs. Brogan, murmuring to each other as the word passed that this was *the* cream all the ladies in Dublin were using.

Fiona could've kissed John.

And maybe she just would.

CHAPTER 9

FIONA FELT LIKE she was walking on a cloud. She could hardly believe her day had turned out so well. She'd sold her entire stock out in less than an hour and had taken a list of preorders for her next batch. She clutched the paper with the names of her customers on it to her chest, excitement coursing through her. She could actually make a living doing this and help ease the burden from her mother's shoulders.

She curled up in her bed with the ancient book, running her hands lovingly over the cover with a soft cloth. So many generations of wise women had contributed to this path she was on. Fiona hoped she could live up to it.

She leaned back on the bed and crossed her arms over her head as she thought about the past. Was it enough, using her gift to sell face creams and cough syrup? Fiona wondered if she was really fulfilling her potential or if there was more she could be doing. She thought about her mother's gift. It lay in the realm of art, not healing, and Bridget focused on it wholeheartedly. She wasn't saving the world with her tapestries, but she was certainly bringing joy. Fiona wondered if that was enough. Was it possible for her to be happy just selling a few basic creams and charms?

There was a part of her that knew it wouldn't be – that knew she wouldn't be living up to the legacy of the generations of fierce women who had come before her. There would come a time when she would have to face who she was as a healer, and embrace it in a way that she wasn't quite comfortable with at the moment. For now, though, she'd revel in her success for the day.

"Fiona?" Bridget knocked lightly on her door.

"Come in," Fiona called, pushing herself upright to sit on her bed. Her room was small, just a single bed tucked under the eaves, a nightstand, and a wooden chair in the corner. But her mother had decorated it with vibrant tapestries on the wall and an earth-toned quilt on the bed. It was homey, and Fiona had never wanted for more.

Bridget bypassed the small chair and sat on the bed next to Fiona.

"Are you reading the book?" Bridget asked, nodding to where the book lay on the nightstand.

"I was just looking at it for a moment. I feel like there's more I could be doing…I mean, not that I'm not happy with what I sold today," Fiona hastened to add, not wanting her mother to think that selling her wares was beneath her.

Bridget smiled, lines creasing in her face, the soft light

picking up the sherry tone in her eyes. She reached out and ran a hand down Fiona's arm.

"You should be proud of what you sold today. You had smashing success on your first day," Bridget said, raising a finger to shush Fiona when she opened her mouth, "But, I also know you're destined for greater things. Still, you have to start somewhere, as it doesn't all come overnight. This is a journey to greatness you are on. Each step leads towards the next. Your first step was probably the hardest – and that was to publicly acknowledge your magick on your labels today. I'm really proud of you."

Fiona swallowed past a lump in her throat as her feelings all seemed to rush up inside of her at once.

"I'm just worried that I'm not doing enough. I..." Fiona gestured to the book. "I want to make these women proud. Our legacy proud. And you proud."

Bridget reached over and smoothed Fiona's hair away from her face before leaning over to place a gentle kiss on her forehead.

"You've already made me proud. Remember that. The only person you have to prove anything to is yourself. Never me."

With those words, Bridget got up and crossed the room. She stopped by the door and turned back to Fiona.

"That John O'Brien seems like a really nice man," Bridget said, a smile flitting across her face.

"He is. Though I don't think I've treated him all that well," Fiona said, looking down at her hands, clenched in her lap.

"Yet he still came over and was kind to you today.

That's something to take note of – kindness in a man. It was clear that Sinead girl was trying to flirt with him, but he only had eyes for you. I'd start paying attention to that," Bridget pointed out.

"Was that what it was like for you? With Father?" Fiona found herself asking. Her skin flushed with embarrassment at the question; her parent's relationship wasn't usually up for discussion.

Bridget smiled ruefully. "I met your father a long time ago. Things were different then, child. It wasn't like I had a lot of options. I'll always love him and he's a good man. But he's not the love of my life."

Fiona felt like a bucket of cold water had been dumped over her head.

"Really? You have a love of your life?"

A trace of sadness worked its way across Bridget's face before she nodded once.

"I did. At one time. Ages ago. I didn't have a lot of say in my path, you understand? Not like you do. I'll never pressure you into marriage, my child. Not like I was," Bridget shook her head once, then slipped from the room when she heard her husband come in the back room.

Fiona listened to them talk for a moment, Bridget's voice a quiet murmur while her father's laughter rang out loudly. It wasn't that they had a bad relationship – but now that Bridget had pointed it out, Fiona could see it for what it was: A quiet sort of love, born from the test of time and tolerance, a dependable marriage, but certainly not a passionate love affair.

And was that what she wanted, then? A passionate love

affair? Her mind flashed to John, smiling down at her as she sat at the table, filling her with warmth at his nearness.

There were too many questions there that Fiona couldn't answer.

CHAPTER 10

"FIONA, HONEY, WAKE up." Bridget nudged Fiona from a fitful sleep, the night still dark beyond Fiona's window.

"Mum, what's wrong?" Fiona blinked her eyes and focused blurrily on her mother's anxious face.

"You're needed. In the village," Bridget whispered, casting a look over her shoulder. Fiona wondered what she was worried about. Her father's snoring echoed through the small cottage.

Fiona pushed herself from her bed, sliding out from under the quilt and padding silently to her chest of drawers to pull out pants, a soft woolen sweater and thick cottage socks. Even though spring was in full bloom in Ireland, the mornings were still crisp. She tiptoed into the bathroom and splashed water on her face, quickly plaiting her hair into a long braid as her mind raced with questions. What had happened that she was needed so urgently? Was it possible she would need to perform a healing? Nervousness ground her stomach into knots.

Slipping from her room, Fiona made her way across the dimly lit cottage to where Bridget stood waiting, holding a scone she had wrapped in a small towel.

"Mrs. Brogan's waiting in the courtyard," Bridget whispered, throwing a shawl over her housedress and stepping through the door.

Fiona found herself unable to move forward. If Mrs. Brogan was behind that door, that meant something was most likely wrong with Sinead. And besides being the most popular girl in town, Sinead was also the biggest gossip. It was one thing to quietly heal a lamb for John, but another thing entirely to put herself on display for the village gossip. Fiona felt her resistance grow.

The moment stretched out while Fiona deliberated, clutching the scone tightly in her hands.

Bridget poked her head back in the door.

"Fiona, what are you doing? We must go," Bridget hissed, her eyes a little wild.

"I don't know if I can do it," Fiona hissed right back.

Bridget cast a look over her shoulder into the courtyard before marching into the house and standing nose to nose with Fiona. Fiona almost took a surprised step back, as her mother was not the confrontational sort.

"Sure and I didn't raise my daughter to be a selfish one now, did I? You can't be telling me you're worried what others will think of you when a mother is standing in the courtyard praying that her own child won't be dying on her? 'Tis a cold day in hell that the Morrigans don't help where help is needed," Bridget hissed, clamping her hand around Fiona's arm. "Now you tell me if you could live with yourself if Sinead dies tonight because you're too scared to show yourself to the world."

Fiona closed her eyes as Bridget's words washed over her. *Could* she live with herself if Sinead died this morning? Shaking her head at herself, she took a deep breath and opened her eyes.

"You're right. I'll help," Fiona whispered. Bridget reached up and smoothed her hand over her daughter's cheek.

"Trust yourself. The rest will fall into place."

Fiona kept those words close to her heart when she stepped into the courtyard to see Mrs. Brogan's pale face, her hair in disarray, blood streaking down the white skirt of her nightgown.

"Please, if you can do anything, anything at all," Mrs. Brogan begged. "They've already called for Father Patrick to issue last rites."

Doubt fled her mind as she took in the woman's distraught expression. Or maybe it was the shock of red blood smattered across the pristine white cotton nightgown. Either way, determination replaced the cold ball of anxiety that had settled into Fiona's gut.

"Take me to her."

CHAPTER 11

*I*T WAS WORSE than she'd expected.

Fiona had arrived at the Brogans' house out of breath, having raced through the pre-dawn streets of the village until they'd reached the prosperous looking brick house in the center of town. All the lights in the house were blazing, and had Fiona not known otherwise, she'd have thought it to be in welcome.

But bright lights in the early hours of morning rarely signal welcome. Death was at the doorstep here, and Fiona feared she was too late.

A thought flashed through her mind, so quickly that Fiona almost didn't have time to register it before she was being muscled inside and moved rapidly up the narrow wooden stairs.

How had Mrs. Brogan known to come to their house and ask for her?

A question for another time, Fiona thought as Mrs. Brogan all but pushed her into a small, brightly lit bedroom in the back of the house.

"Father Patrick, please wait," Mrs. Brogan panted.

Father Patrick turned, a Bible clutched in one hand, startled by Mrs. Brogan's words. A man, presumably Mr. Brogan as he was still in his nightclothes, and the local doctor stood next to the bed, anguish lanced across their faces. Fiona dimly registered sobbing coming from another room before she shoved herself past the priest.

"Wait one minute, young woman," Father Patrick said gruffly, clearly annoyed by Fiona's presumptuousness.

"I most certainly will not." Fiona turned and glared at him. "Prayers won't save her now."

Father Patrick's eyes widened, his lips thinning as he looked down his bulbous red nose at Fiona.

"What are you proposing to do here?" Father Patrick all but shouted.

"I'm going to try and help her. Something you're unable to do," Fiona hissed, before directing her attention to the doctor. "Tell me what's happened to her."

The doctor, in his early forties and one whom Fiona had found to be fairly amiable, held Sinead's wrist in his hand as he slid his gaze over to Fiona.

"I believe it to be an ectopic pregnancy. She's hemorrhaging. And won't last the trip to the hospital in the next town."

Mrs. Brogan let up a wail from behind them and Fiona winced at the noise. Shifting her gaze to Mr. Brogan, she straightened her shoulders.

"Everyone out. Take Mrs. Brogan out, take Father Patrick out, everyone out but my mum," Fiona ordered briskly.

"I will most certainly not leave," Father Patrick blustered, clutching the Bible to his chest.

Mr. Brogan measured Fiona with a look.

"Can you save her?"

"I can't promise anything. But I know I can't do anything with everyone in the room bothering me."

"Then we must try," Mr. Brogan said, grabbing the priest's arm and hauling him from the room over his protests. Mrs. Brogan followed, weeping into her handkerchief.

Now all Fiona had to do was convince the doctor to leave.

"I'd like to watch, if you don't mind," he asked quietly, respect permeating his words. Fiona paused and raised an eyebrow at him.

"And why should I be letting you watch? How do I know you won't be talking of this all over town?" Fiona demanded.

"You've my word. I've sworn an oath to heal. I'm someone who respects healing – in all its forms," the doctor said gently.

Fiona squinted at him. "It's Dr. Collins, isn't it?"

"Yes, miss, it is," Dr. Collins said, still respectful.

Fiona took a deep breath, reaching out with her mind to scan the doctor's, to see if there was any subterfuge she was missing. Finding genuine curiosity and nothing more, Fiona finally nodded.

"Mother, close the door," Fiona ordered over her shoulder before turning to look at Sinead.

The girl looked as different from when Fiona had seen her earlier as night and day. It was like someone had turned the light off. Instead of the vibrancy of youth and beauty, her skin was pale – grey, and the white sheets around her were soaked with blood. This was beyond bad, and Fiona wasn't sure there was even any life left in her body. Reaching out, she slid her arms underneath Sinead, moving so she could slip her hips onto the bed and cradle the girl against her chest. Closing her eyes, Fiona went within.

She found the problem immediately. Her mind's eye was able to find the deadly pregnancy quickly, and Fiona scanned the small group of cells, to see if there was any flicker of life. Her lips thinned in sadness as she realized there was no hope for the fetus, but would she be able to save the mother? Scanning back up Sinead's body, Fiona sought desperately to find a glimpse of her soul left attached to her body.

And almost doubled over in relief when she found the dimmest of lights, deep within Sinead, slowly fading to a small dot of blue, the color of the hottest part of the fire.

"She's still with us," Fiona whispered, and Dr. Collins straightened beside her.

"What can I do?"

Fiona met his eyes.

"Pray that whatever universal god or energy has bestowed me with this gift is on my side tonight," Fiona said, before closing her eyes again and wrapping her arms around Sinead's limp body.

She sought the flicker of blue light again, and in her mind she began to carefully fan the flame, blowing on it with a gentle love, infusing it with strength to grow. As the flame sparked higher, Fiona moved her power down to the pregnancy, sending energy into it. In a shock of light, Sinead's body jerked as Fiona healed her, a lamp in the corner shattering into pieces as Fiona directed the pain from Sinead's body.

"Holy mother of..." Dr. Collins breathed, crossing himself, as Sinead began to cough in Fiona's arms, turning her head back and forth as she mumbled something. Fiona breathed out a sigh of relief.

"She'll need water, and should stay restful for a while. Her body will need to recover. But she should be healed of the pregnancy now," Fiona said. Slipping from beneath Sinead, Fiona adjusted the pillow under the girl's head and ran a hand across her warm forehead.

Sinead's eyes opened a sliver.

"Fiona. You did something to me," Sinead whispered.

"You're safe now," Fiona said.

"Don't...don't tell anyone," Sinead whispered, her eyes glinting with tears as she turned to stare at the wall in shame.

"It's not my secret to tell," Fiona said softly, pushing herself up from the bed and coming to stand in front of Dr. Collins. Her body trembled, as though she had used up her own life force to heal another's. She would later learn this was the cost of healing, but in this moment Fiona just wanted to lie down and sleep for twelve hours.

"What did you do here?" Dr. Collins asked, confusion in his eyes.

"I blew on the light of her soul, fanning it back into a fire," Fiona answered frankly, too exhausted to lie and wondering what he would make of it.

"I... I... I don't know what to say to that," Dr. Collins answered. Fiona could at least appreciate his honesty.

"You and me both, doctor; you and me both," Fiona muttered as she crossed the room and met her mother by the door.

"You did good, baby. I'm so proud of you," Bridget whispered, pressing a soft kiss to Fiona's cheek and smoothing her hair back from her face.

"I need to lie down," Fiona said, leaning into her mother's shoulder for just a moment.

"Let's get you out of here. Sure and I'll fix you a nice cup of broth when we get home," Bridget said immediately, wrapping her arm around her daughter and leading her from the room. They stopped short at the line of people in the hallway.

"Is she... is she gone?" Mrs. Brogan asked, her handkerchief clenched in her hands at her lips. Her eyes were glassy with tears.

"No, she's not. She'll need to rest for a good while, though," Fiona said softly.

Mrs. Brogan squealed and hurtled past Fiona into the room, dropping to her knees at her daughter's bedside and launching into a prayer. Mr. Brogan stopped in front of Fiona.

"Our family thanks you. If you ever need anything... just say it. Sure and we're beholden to you," he said gruffly.

"You don't owe me anything," Fiona said softly. "I didn't help so you would owe us or have to work off a debt of sorts. I helped because that's who I am."

Mr. Brogan took in her words and then nodded, stepping back.

"Sure and we're grateful for it. We're lucky to have you."

Fiona nodded once more, but found that it was becoming more and more difficult to talk. Between the healing and the emotions in the house pressing at her, she just wanted her bed. Fiona trailed past Sinead's brothers and sisters without even bothering to look them in the face, not willing to try and interpret the expressions she would see there. She stumbled down the stairs, ready to leave, but was brought up short by the priest.

"Father Patrick, please move. I'd like to leave," Fiona said dully, the strength of her mother the only thing holding her up.

"Witch," Father Patrick hissed, crossing himself in front of her and brandishing a bottle of holy water in her face.

Fiona huffed out a laugh, too tired to even care what he was saying.

"Father Patrick, you should be ashamed of yourself," Bridget hissed, reprimanding the stout priest. "Fiona's a good girl and what she did tonight was done to help a dying girl. Not for money. Not for accolades. Not for anything but the goodness of her heart. You should be holding her in high esteem instead of judging her. How dare you!"

But Father Patrick was having none of it.

"Witch, be gone," he said again, crossing himself and holding his crucifix out in front of him.

Fiona wanted to rip it out of his hand and throw it

across the room – to tell him that symbols were meaning-less when life force and omnipotent power were universal. He'd never know that though – not until he passed on. It wasn't her job to educate him either. Deciding she'd had enough for the day, Fiona shuffled around him.

And prayed that coming here hadn't been a grave mistake.

CHAPTER 12

FIONA SLEPT THROUGH the entire day and late into the evening hours before her mother shook her awake.

"Fiona, luv, you must drink some water," Bridget whispered, worry creasing her face as she peered down at her daughter. Fiona blinked the fuzziness from her eyes and swallowed against a dry throat.

"How long have I slept?" Fiona croaked, as she eased herself up to lean against the wall, gratefully accepting the glass of water from her mother.

"Nigh on fourteen hours or so," Bridget said, pressing her lips together in a thin line.

"I feel like I've been flattened by a horse," Fiona said softly, gingerly moving her body, her muscles protesting.

"Aye, it's the healing. You can't bring someone back from the brink without nearly going over it yourself, then," Bridget said.

"Is that the truth of it, then?" Fiona asked, wondering how she'd missed that detail in the book. Perhaps it hadn't been written there and was something that was just known?

Too bad Fiona didn't have a teacher.

"I remember now – I was once told..." Bridget shook her head in disgust.

"By whom? What were you told?" Fiona said, placing the empty cup on her bed stand and focusing on her mother.

"A woman I knew long ago. She was touched with something too. She always warned me about life or death healing situations. You must be careful, Fiona. Sometimes if you go too far in trying to save someone – you'll pay the ultimate sacrifice. You must learn to recognize where that line lies."

"I'm not quite sure I'll know how to do that," Fiona admitted, running her hand over a wrinkle in the sheet.

"You'll have to figure it out. There are too many lives for you to touch, to lose you to a careless healing," Bridget said.

"But...what if I am put in that position? Where I must choose to give my life to save another? Would you still want me to pull back then?" Fiona asked, honestly wondering if she would be able to choose or not.

"Oh, my dear darling child, yes, I would want you to choose your own life. You must, in fact. You're destined for much more during your time on earth."

"I don't understand how I'm going to know that line," Fiona said, biting her lip.

Bridget sat on the corner of the bed and reached over to smooth a wisp of Fiona's hair back from her forehead.

"Fiona, you've been blessed with a great gift. One of

the greatest, not to mention your myriad other forms of intuitive gifts. God didn't put you on this earth to burn yourself out on one life. You're here to help many. Remember that, should you ever be on the edge."

Fiona felt like she'd grown up in just a day. Yesterday she'd been worried about what people would think of her skin cream with labels reading 'magick.' Tonight she was worried about the effects of her healing power and where the line between life and death lay. Suddenly the trivial stuff didn't seem to matter so much anymore.

"Mum, Father Patrick is going to talk. He hates me," Fiona said. "But I just can't bring myself to care after what I did today. It was such a rush of power…no, not even power. Just, it felt good to be able to *do* something."

"Even if he talks – so what? You did a good thing today, Fiona. You can hold your head up high, knowing that you saved a life. Don't fret about Father Patrick. He's not worth your energy."

Fiona wondered if that was what growing up was all about – not caring what others thought about you. If she had to admit it, she was proud of herself for handling the priest the way she had. It was nice to know she didn't fold under pressure.

"Have you heard from the Brogans? How is Sinead?"

"She's well, child, she's well. They sent over an entire meal for you, if you feel like you can eat."

Fiona's stomach rumbled in response and she realized that she was ravenous. Moving gingerly, she threw her arms around her mother.

"Yes, I'm famished. Thanks for pushing me in the right direction today, Mum."

"It's the best I can do," Bridget murmured as they got up from the bed.

CHAPTER 13

*D*ESPITE WHAT SHE'D said about being proud of her healing power, Fiona kept a low profile over the next week. It wasn't that she was embarrassed, but she was still dealing with her own feelings and responses from the healing. Dealing with an outsider's view on what she had done was just something that she wasn't ready for.

She caught herself thinking about John over the week – more than she'd like to. She wondered if his mother had liked the cream she had sent over. Or if he thought about her the way she was starting to think about him.

Fiona was far out into the hills on one of her walks to gather ingredients for her line when she heard bleating. Looking over her shoulder from where she knelt in the sunshine, she stiffened.

Sure and she didn't have the magick to make the man appear just when she was thinking of him, did she now?

Fiona felt her cheeks heat as she watched John walk confidently through the field, a walking stick in his hand,

and the silly little lamb – bigger now – happily trailing behind him. What a picture he made.

No wonder people were drawn to him. He walked easily, with a grace and confidence that came naturally. His strong shoulders were thrown back and his easy smile made Fiona's lips twitch in response.

Damn if that man wasn't handsome as all get-out.

Fiona rose from her crouch, leaving her bag on the ground.

"Nice day for a walk," Fiona said, smiling up at John. The lamb rambled over and bumped its head into Fiona's knee, bleating a short welcome. "Hello there, sweet thing." Fiona bent and nuzzled the lamb's head before it danced off to nibble at a flower.

"Damn thing follows me everywhere," John grumbled, but Fiona wasn't fooled. He was sweet on the little lamb. She thought it was adorable, though she wouldn't be telling him that and wounding his male pride.

"Probably because it trusts you," Fiona pointed out. John just shrugged. The sun caught the blue of his eyes, making them seem to sparkle – much like the blue light from the cove.

"What are you doing out here?" John asked, squinting down at her.

"Gathering this and that. Ingredients for my creams and tonics," Fiona said, feeling a little foolish to be caught digging in the mud.

"My mother sure does like the cream you sent along for her. Says her skin feels ages younger."

Fiona's smile widened at his words. She dropped her eyes and dug her toe into the ground, feeling a little shy.

"Thanks, that's kind of her to say."

"Is it really magick?" John asked bluntly.

"Are you asking me because you want to make fun of me, or are you asking me because you really want to know?" Fiona asked, putting her hands on her hips and angling her chin up at him. Damn if he wasn't always poking his nose where it didn't belong.

"I'm asking because I really want to know. I'd like to get to know you a little better. To understand..." John extended an arm to gesture down to the bags at her feet.

"Well, John, since you've gone and asked so nicely, I'll tell you," Fiona said, unsure why she was feeling so annoyed with his questions. "Yes, I suppose you could say there's a wee touch of magick in my creams and tonics. They are centuries-old recipes, passed down from generation to generation. I like to add a little extra dose of my healing touch to them, is all," Fiona said, shrugging.

"So your whole family is magick then? Passed down from generations?"

Fiona rolled her eyes. It could never just be one answer, could it? Once she gave a little, the questions would keep coming.

"I don't know, John, is that how you think it works?" Fiona parried, not sure how much information she wanted to give him.

"I'm not sure. I don't really know enough about magick. Just folklore and the like," John said softly.

Fiona sighed, feeling resignation wash through her. He really was a kind man. A man with too many questions, but a kind one nonetheless.

"Is that why you've come out here today, then? To find

out about my family's history?" Fiona said, smiling up at him to take the sting from her words.

"No, I've been walking out here every day, hoping to find you in the hills," John admitted, his blue eyes intent on her face.

A wash of heat rushed through Fiona. Sure and this man wasn't actually admitting that he liked her, was he? That was the last thing she'd expected him to say. Her words died on her lips as she stared into his eyes, a wave of lust dancing across her skin, the energy of his intent palpable against her skin.

"Well, here I am," Fiona said, her eyes never leaving his.

"Yes. I've found you, haven't I?" John smiled at her, his words holding a double meaning.

Fiona felt the punch of it in her gut – the dawning realization that *this was the one.* The faceless stranger in her dreams. The one who would someday hold her hand as she gave birth to their child. The one who would hold her heart. It was so simple to see now what the cove had been trying to tell her. This had certainly been a week of lessons for her.

Fiona pushed her thoughts away. Babies? She'd never even been kissed before. At least, not unless you counted that time Seamus McGowan had snuck a kiss from her in the schoolyard. It had been sloppy and sudden, and hadn't given Fiona a really good impression of why people even did this to begin with. But looking into John's eyes now made her reconsider. For the first time ever, she wanted to kiss someone.

Fiona jumped when John held out his hand.

"Walk with me?"

He wasn't going to kiss her, then. Just a walk. Fiona breathed and nodded, bending down to pick up her bag and mentally kicking herself for getting all hot and bothered.

Straightening, she slipped her hand into his and tried not to blush when the rush of emotions hit her. One of the many extra facets to her gift was that she could often read other people's emotions. And right now, John O'Brien was most definitely interested in kissing her.

The thought made her break into a smile, and she glanced up at him as they moved across the field.

"Tell me about yourself. Why haven't you gone off to uni then? Decided village life was more to your taste?"

John glanced down at her as they walked, approaching a small hill that Fiona knew to drop off into the water on the other side. The sun played across their shoulders and a gentle breeze kicked up her hair. It was one of those rare perfect days in Ireland, and Fiona found the simple pleasure of walking with a handsome man across the hills to be a perfect complement to the day.

"No uni for me. I'm done with school. I'm a simple man, really. I want to continue to work the farm, maybe branch out into a few more areas. I love it here. We live in one of the most beautiful parts of the country," John shrugged, his eyes going out to the water. "City life just isn't for me. What about you? You don't want to leave either?"

Fiona thought about it as they crested the hill. For years she had wanted to leave, the angst of youth pushing her to discover something new over the horizon. But once she'd discovered her gift, she realized that being away from the familiar would only make her unhappy. And exploring her gift had given her all the excitement she had craved.

Fiona turned and pointed across the rolling fields.

"See that spot? Just at the base of the larger ridgeline behind it?"

"Aye," John nodded.

"That's my spot."

"Is it now? And what happens on that spot?" John asked, smiling down at her.

"That's where I want to build my house. A cottage with enough windows that I can catch the breeze from all angles, but built well enough that I'll stay warm in the winter."

John studied the spot, turning a bit to look at angles and nodded.

"I see it. 'Tis a lovely spot, really. You'd be quite happy there. But word is the landowner is very particular about who he'll sell it to. Luckily, I know how to get it from him," John said, pulling away from her, laughter on his face.

"John! Wait! I didn't know anyone owned the land. Tell me how to get it!" Fiona laughed, racing after him as he ran down the hill towards a small beach, the lamb bleating and racing after him. She caught up with him as he stopped at the beach and tugged on his arm.

"John! Tell me!" Fiona gasped, half laughing and half out of breath from racing down the hill. She gasped when John turned and put his arms around her waist, pulling her up to swing her around in circles.

"The price of ownership is a kiss," John said, laughing down at her.

Fiona's heart skipped a beat and tingles raced up her arms. She pushed against his chest, forcing herself to look up at his face as he continued to whirl her in a dizzying circle.

"Are you the owner?"

"Is that the only way I'll get you to kiss me?" John said, his lips quirking as he looked down at her. He stopped suddenly, causing Fiona's body to slam against his and slide down, until her feet just touched the sand.

"No, I would've kissed you either way," Fiona blurted, and then blushed.

"Good, because I'm not the owner. My father is," John laughed at her.

"John!" Fiona said, reaching out to push him away, embarrassment kicking in her stomach.

"But I'll accept the kiss on his behalf," John said, and then he made Fiona's world tilt when he slid his lips over hers in a kiss so gentle she found herself sighing into it. Her hands, once pushing him away, now gripped his arms to pull him closer. A wave of tenderness washed over Fiona, pulling her closer, enveloping her in his touch.

He felt like home.

Fiona was trembling when he pulled away – trembling from the kiss and from the thoughts that battered her mind. Would she be able to handle this rush of feelings that suddenly clouded her brain, making her feel almost sick to her stomach?

Gathering her wits, she smiled cheekily up at him.

"You tricked me, John O'Brien."

"It was worth it," John said, laughing as he pulled her along to walk the shoreline. A little wave of giddiness washed through her at the simple pleasure of walking with someone on the beach while holding hands. All these new experiences for her this week!

"So does your father really own the land, then?" Fiona said, detouring back to the topic at hand. She wasn't sure it was safe to talk about the kiss.

"He does. It's been in the family for positively ages, but we've done nothing with it because of the cove."

Fiona's shoulders braced a bit as she registered his words. She wondered if this was all a ploy to figure out more about the cove so that his family would feel comfortable using the land.

"So is that why you've gone and kissed me then? To find out the secrets of the cove?" Fiona asked, pulling her hand away from John in order to face him. A wave crashed against the shore, making her jump before she reminded herself that they weren't in the cove and these weren't enchanted waters. Sometimes a wave crashing was just that – a wave crashing.

And maybe sometimes a kiss was just a kiss, she reminded herself.

John's eyebrows drew together in confusion.

"I kissed you because I've been wanting to for a while now. Since long before you did your magick thing with the lamb. And even more so afterwards then," John said, raking his hand through his hair. "Don't you be making up reasons for why I wanted to kiss you."

Fiona dropped her eyes, immediately chagrined at having been so rude.

"I'm sorry," she said immediately. One thing Fiona was good at was apologizing when she was wrong.

"Prove it," John said, his eyebrow raised.

"Prove it? Prove it how?" Fiona demanded. What was with this man? One moment she was laughing and the next angry and the next chagrined. Was this what it was like to be in a relationship?

"Kiss me. Because you want to," John challenged.

Fiona immediately felt awkward. What was she supposed to do? Just walk up to him and lay one on him? The guy was supposed to do the kissing. As soon as the thought crossed her mind, Fiona threw back her shoulders. She was nothing if not stubborn. Marching over to him, she leaned in and placed her lips against his matter-of-factly. Pulling back, she nodded.

"There. Done."

John let out a peal of laughter that left Fiona almost stomping her foot in anger.

"So now my kiss isn't good enough for you?" Fiona asked hotly.

"Oh, it's good enough. Even for my grandmother," John hooted, slapping his knee as he laughed.

"Does your grandmother kiss like this then?" Fiona asking, stepping forward to grab John's shirt and jerked him forward.

She poured everything she had into the kiss, anger fueling her to prove him wrong.

But in the end, she didn't know who was wrong or right, as their lips melded together and she became lost in the pull of sensations that pounded her heart and raced through her body.

They broke apart, Fiona feeling dazed and John looking bowled over. What had, just moments ago, been a fun flirtation had now taken a serious turn.

They measured each other for a moment, neither saying a word, their chests heaving as they caught their breath.

John held out his hand.

CHAPTER 14

"**Y**OU SLEPT WITH him?" Keelin squealed, jarring Fiona from her memories.

"Keelin!" Margaret exclaimed. "That is not a polite question to ask."

The silence stretched out between them as they all studiously examined the fire.

"So did you sleep with him?" Margaret asked, and Keelin squealed with laughter.

"We need more whiskey," Keelin decided, getting up from the couch to pick up the bottle at her feet. Walking around the room, she refilled everyone's cup, then stopped at the fire to stoke it. The flames crackled and danced, the popping of the burning wood the only sound in the room.

"I didn't," Fiona finally said with a small smile. "I'd just healed a pregnancy a few days before, mind you, so I was well aware what a dalliance like that could do for me."

Fiona saw Margaret grimace.

"I didn't mean it like that," she rushed to assure

Margaret, realizing she had unintentionally hurt her daughter's feelings.

"It's fine. I know. I was young and stupid. Luckily, I got Keelin out of the deal. And perhaps, if I had listened to my heart like I think you're going to tell me you did with my father, I wouldn't have waited so long to be happy in love," Margaret said, taking a small sip from her whiskey.

Keelin reached out and squeezed her mom's arm.

"Okay, so go on, go on. What happened next? Did you start dating?"

Fiona sipped her whiskey and smiled.

"He courted me, if you can believe that…"

CHAPTER 15

IONA HUMMED AS she mixed up her newest batch of tonics for chest colds. She'd caught herself humming more often in the last few days, her mind on John and the way his kisses made her feel. It was her own little secret, something she was holding close for just a while longer.

Her mother had been right about John – he was incredibly kind. Just today she'd gone out back to find a little package with her name on it. When she'd unwrapped the crisp paper to find a book on Celtic healing, her heart had tripped up a bit. It was as though he knew just how to navigate his way straight into her mind and down into her heart. Fiona readily admitted she was already on the long slow slide into love.

"You've been full of smiles this week," Bridget called down from her loft.

Fiona's hand stilled on the ladle she was using to stir her tonic. Should she share with her mother this first taste of love? Or keep it secret just a little while longer? There was something nice about being sweet on someone in secret. No judgments could be made, no unwanted advice given. Just courtship in its purest form. Fiona hesitated.

"If you think I don't know you are sweet on that O'Brien boy, you've got another thing coming," Bridget called down and Fiona almost dropped the ladle.

Damn if the woman wasn't always too accurate, Fiona grumbled to herself.

"Yes, he's quite nice," Fiona called up, dodging the question.

A chuckle floated down from above, but no further questions were asked. Fiona blew out a breath and used the back of her hand to push her hair out of her face. She needed to concentrate on her incantation in order to put that extra touch of healing magick into the tonic.

Fiona closed her eyes and went within, pulling for the ball of light that she envisioned to be her magick. Humming softly, she began to incant the age-old healing rhyme. As the words left her lips, a small bolt of light zipped from her hands and infused the tonic, changing it from deep brown to warm honey color. Perfect, Fiona decided and pulled the bowl over to where her jars were lined up, their cork stoppers waiting nearby. Pulling out her funnel, she began to meticulously fill each bottle almost to the top. It was soothing work, repetitive and fulfilling, and as the line of bottles grew Fiona felt happy with her accomplishments.

She also felt happy about the note that had been tucked into the book she had found earlier in the day, telling her that John would call on her this evening for dinner and a pint. The fact that he wasn't shying away about his interest in her or trying to keep it a secret from the world filled Fiona with a warm sense of security. Maybe the cove had been right – this was the man for her.

Finishing up with her tonics, Fiona filled a crate with the bottles, knowing she would have time in the morning to label them. Right now, she needed to focus on what she was going to wear for her date tonight. With the loom still crashing overhead, Fiona moved into her room and flicked on the lamp next to her bed. Her wardrobe was limited, consisting mainly of economical and efficient clothing for the life that she lived. She did have a few nice church-going outfits, and she pulled out a dress with roses patterned all over it, as well as two different skirts. Laying the items on the bed, she bent to her drawer to rifle through the few blouses that she had.

"Dressing up this evening are you, then?" Bridget asked, causing Fiona to jump and whirl around.

"I...yes, I am," Fiona said. Bridget came in and eyed the clothes on the bed. She wore a simple housedress in lavender and had her hair pinned back from her face. No makeup marred her natural beauty.

"I think I might have some options for your date. Hold on," Bridget said, and Fiona raised an eyebrow at her mother's retreating back. Judging from her mother's everyday wear, she didn't think her choices would be all that interesting. Fiona pasted a polite smile on her face and waited.

"Here, I've packed these away years ago as I've no use for them. But we're the same size, and I think you'll like some of these," Bridget said, carrying a fairly large trunk into the room – an item Fiona had never seen before.

"What is this trunk? I've never seen it," Fiona asked, genuinely intrigued. It wasn't as if there was a lot of space in the cottage to store things.

"I've had it under my bed. Clothes from another life, I suppose," Bridget said with a small smile, unhooking the latch and throwing the lid open. Yellowed tissue paper lined the top. Bridget pulled it gently away to reveal folded stacks of clothing in a range of colors and fabrics.

"Mother, what are all these from?" Fiona asked, reaching out to pull a deep green silk blouse with mother-of-pearl buttons from the top of the pile.

"It was the year I was away at uni in Dublin. It was such fun to dress up and go out with the girls. Some of these styles may be out of fashion, but a few dresses and blouses could be mixed in with your current wardrobe, I think," Bridget said, pulling out a red blouse with white flowers splashed across it.

"That's lovely, I could wear it with my navy skirt," Fiona said immediately, pulling it from her hand and holding it against the skirt on the bed.

"Aye, that'd be fetching. There are some dresses in here that would be pretty, too."

"Thank you for this, mum. I was kind of worried about what to wear tonight. I've never really gone on a date before," Fiona said.

It felt odd to say that out loud as most girls her age had dated before.

"Well, it's far past time for ye to be out and about, having fun. You're young and John's a good man. Make yourself pretty for him," Bridget instructed. Fiona couldn't help but smile at her.

"I hope he thinks I'm pretty."

"You're stunning, Fiona. It's probably why you've had some trouble making close female friendships. They're most likely jealous," Bridget said, leaning against the door with her arms crossed. The soft light of the lamp highlighted the warm undertone of her pretty brown eyes.

"I thought it had more to do with that sense of otherness that clings to me," Fiona said, pulling a black and white dress with bright red buttons from the box and setting it aside.

"Perhaps there's a sense of that, too. But at the base of it, I'd say it's jealousy. Take a good long look in the mirror, Fiona. Any man would be lucky to have you. Don't you forget it," Bridget said, pushing away from the door to go get dinner started.

Was she pretty? Fiona never took too much care with her looks, more interested in getting out into the hills than she was in putting makeup on. But now, as she stood before the mirror and considered her face, she thought that – just maybe – her mother was right.

Then she immediately felt guilty for taking pride in her appearance. She'd watched plenty of girls get reprimanded by the nuns for wearing too much makeup at school. It hadn't been something that was ever a problem for her, but now she pulled out her secret stash of makeup.

It was embarrassingly little, now that she thought about it. Just a tube of red lipstick and canister of blush; nothing to highlight her eyes in the slightest. Laying her makeup on the bathroom sink, Fiona went back to examining the contents of the trunk. In the end, she settled on the pretty red floral blouse with the highwaisted navy skirt that hit just at mid-calf. She slipped on her low-heeled mary-janes, and went to the bathroom to pin her hair back in soft curls that fell behind her shoulders.

Fiona examined her makeup and then shrugged – there wasn't much else she could do. She brushed a soft hint of color across her cheeks and slicked her lips with the red lipstick. Looking at herself, she smiled. At least the lipstick matched her blouse – that was something.

"Let me see," Bridget demanded from outside the bathroom and, with a swish of her skirt, Fiona stepped out.

Bridget put her hands on her hips and ran a critical eye over Fiona.

"It's missing something. Hold on," Bridget murmured and left the room. Immediately feeling awkward, Fiona smoothed her skirt and hoped she didn't look foolish.

Bridget came back into the room, her eyes lit up as she carried a double strand of chunky pearls in one hand and a tube in the other.

"Here you go then – mascara and a necklace. That should polish you up."

"Mascara? Mother, I had no idea you had such a thing," Fiona said in awe, pulling the tube from her mother.

"I've been known to dress up on occasion, you know," Bridget said, as Fiona dashed into the bathroom and swiped the mascara awkwardly across her lashes. It really did make a difference; her brown eyes suddenly seemed startlingly large in her face.

"I love it," Fiona gushed, refusing to feel bad about beautifying herself. The Catholic Church certainly knew how to instill a healthy dose of guilt in people, Fiona thought as she shook off the words of the nuns and their feelings on makeup.

"Here, let me put this necklace on you," Bridget said, reaching out to clasp it around her neck. The pearls slipped across her neck, cool against her skin, sliding nicely into the V of the blouse. Fiona could feel a hum of love coming from the strands.

She ducked into the bathroom and studied herself in the mirror. Bridget was right, the pearls and the mascara added a polish that hadn't been there before, changing her from an eager girl to a confident woman.

"They're perfect," Fiona said, turning to look at her mother. "Where did you get these?"

A flash of sadness flitted through Bridget's eyes before she smiled gently.

"In another life, Fiona."

A knock at the backdoor made Fiona's stomach flip over.

"He's here," Fiona hissed, immediately turning back to check her reflection in the mirror again.

Bridget smiled and reached into the trunk, pulling out a small leather pocketbook.

"Put your lipstick in here. There should be a small mirror in the side pocket as well."

"Thank you. For all of this, really," Fiona said, hugging her mother quickly.

"Have fun," Bridget said brightly, as Fiona moved across the cottage to the door.

"I'll do my best," Fiona said, before opening the door.

John stood at the door, his dark hair combed wetly

down, a clutch of flowers wrapped in wax paper in his hand.

Fiona looked around.

"No lamb today?"

"No, I penned him up, though he wasn't happy with me," John admitted with a laugh. He wore a brown jacket with a crisp white shirt, and Fiona felt a little flutter in her stomach when she looked at his lips.

"Are those for me?" Fiona finally said after they had just stared at each other in silence for a moment.

"Och, yes, I'm sorry," John said, a flush coming over his face as he jerked his hand forward with the bouquet. "I was too busy admiring how pretty you look tonight."

Now it was Fiona's turn to blush.

"Thank you, let me just put them in water," Fiona said, turning back into the cottage.

"I'll do that for you, love. Hello, John. You two have a nice evening," Bridget said, giving Fiona a little nudge forward and closing the door firmly behind her.

John laughed, throwing his head back a little, and Fiona caught her breath just looking at him. She was so lucky to have a date with such a handsome man.

"John, you look nice as well," Fiona said.

"Well, then we're quite the pair," John said, reaching out to pull her arm into the crook of his own as they exited the courtyard and began to stroll down the hill into the village. The sun was dropping low in the sky, bathing the village in a warm light, and turning the water a deep blue. The mild night saw the streets packed with people going about their way, and more than one eagle-eyed villager raised an eyebrow at them as they passed.

"I do believe we're drawing attention," Fiona finally pointed out, after the third villager stopped to whisper to her friend as they walked by.

"Do you care?" John asked.

Fiona tilted her head up and twinkled at him.

"Not in the slightest."

John let out a booming laugh, and a woman leaving the market glanced up at them. Fiona stilled.

"Mrs. Brogan. How are you this evening?"

Mrs. Brogan pulled her grocery sack closer to her body and offered Fiona a smile, though Fiona could read the wariness behind it.

"Hello, Fiona, John. How are you this evening?"

"Good, thank you. It's a lovely evening for a stroll, isn't it?" Fiona said gently, realizing that the woman was terrified she would say something about Sinead.

"How's Sinead doing? I haven't seen her around in a bit," John said affably, and both Fiona and Mrs. Brogan froze.

"That's right, Mrs. Brogan, I don't think I've seen Sinead since that day you bought my face cream at the market." The words rushed from Fiona's mouth, and she kept the smile fixed on her face.

"Aye, she's gone off to stay with a cousin in Dublin, actually. She might enter uni in the fall," Mrs. Brogan said, hiking the strap of her bag further up on her shoulder.

They had shipped her off out of the village then, Fiona thought. Probably to avoid any embarrassment. She wanted to ask if Sinead had healed up all right, but couldn't do so without betraying the Brogans' confidence.

"Please be sure to send her our hellos the next time you

speak, then," Fiona said easily, and she saw Mrs. Brogan let out a small breath.

"I will, at that. You two have a nice night; I'm off to get dinner on," Mrs. Brogan said, nodding at them both as she hurried on.

"Sinead doesn't strike me as the uni type," John observed as they continued on. "I'd put her more for the marrying and having babies type."

"Well, one doesn't have to be mutually exclusive of the other now," Fiona pointed out, as they came to a stop in front of a large house with big glass windows in the front, bordered by bright blue window boxes. Cheerful yellow flowers poked out of the boxes.

"Of course not. This is the place for dinner," John said, pointing at the house.

"Isn't this the O'Reilly's house?"

"Yes. They've opened up a small bed and breakfast, and are offering meals on the weekends now," John said, pushing the bright yellow door open.

"Is that so? I hadn't heard," Fiona said excitedly.

Any time a new restaurant, shop, or pub came to the village, it was cause for excitement. Sometimes the sameness of everyday life in a small village needed to be broken up with new things.

"Mrs. O'Reilly, lovely to see you then," John said, smiling at a plain round woman with twinkling blue eyes and close-cropped grey hair who came out of the kitchen wiping her hands on a towel.

"Just in time, John. I've just pulled the brown bread from the oven."

"Hi, Mrs. O'Reilly," Fiona said shyly. She'd known the

O'Reilly's for years. With no children, the couple had been sort of adopted by the village, and were often busy babysitting and watching over their neighbor's children. They'd always been kind to Fiona's family, so she was even more excited to give back to them a little bit.

"Fiona, don't you just look the picture? Come, sit, sit!" Mrs. O'Reilly ushered them into the small front room, which held four tables set for two. Fiona imagined they could be pushed together for larger groups if needed. Each table had a pristine white linen cloth, pretty lace place-mats, and bright green napkins. A small lantern sat in the middle of each, casting a warm glow on the table. Mrs. O'Reilly showed them to a table in front of the window so they could look out over the village.

"Tea? Coffee? Wine?" Mrs. O'Reilly asked, as she poured them each a glass of water.

"Wine?" John asked, raising an eyebrow at Fiona.

"Sure, that'd be lovely, thanks," Fiona smiled. She'd probably had wine only once or twice in her life – communion at church didn't count. But she wanted to appear sophisticated for John, so she went along.

"Lovely, I've got a bottle of red breathing in the back. Tonight's options are monkfish with potatoes or a shepherd's pie," Mrs. O'Reilly called back.

"This is nice," Fiona said shyly, looking around at the room. The walls were painted a robin's-egg blue, and gilt-framed paintings of the coast crowded the wall. It was homey and charming, and just perfect for Fiona's first date.

"Isn't it? They've just opened so I doubt we'll be

crowded in here," John said, smiling across the table at her.

Mrs. O'Reilly bustled back in with two wine glasses and a bottle in her arms.

"Bread should be up shortly; Mr. O'Reilly is just slicing it as we speak. Now, what can I get for you tonight?"

"Monkfish," they both said at the same time, then smiled at each other.

"Ah, perfect. We've a lovely catch this evening," Mrs. O'Reilly said, beaming as she swept from the room. Fiona sighed at her words, wondering when her father would get back to fishing again.

"Something wrong?" John asked, tilting his head at her in question.

"No, nothing," Fiona said, shaking it off. It would just cloud the evening if she brought up her father's inability to get out on the water.

"So, Mrs. Brogan seemed pretty tense tonight. I wonder what's going on there?" John said, picking up his wine glass and raising it to hers.

"Sláinte," they both said and clicked glasses. Fiona allowed the robust flavors of the wine to settle on her tongue before answering John.

"John, you know some people aren't comfortable around my family. That's something you might have to get used to if you spend more time with me," Fiona said delicately.

They paused as Mrs. O'Reilly swept back into the room with a basket holding the bread wrapped in a linen cloth, and a small jar of butter.

"I'll leave you two to chat now. Dinner should be ready shortly," Mrs. O'Reilly said brightly as she left the room.

"Maybe you can tell me more about your family then – so I can understand," John said.

Fiona thought about it as she unwrapped the bread from the cloth, offering a slice to John first. The bread was still warm, the butter melting almost instantly when it touched the bread, and Fiona moaned when she bit into it.

"This is delicious," Fiona said, carefully putting the half-eaten piece of bread back on her plate before she devoured the whole slice.

"It is," John said, his eyes on her as he waited patiently for her to speak.

"Why don't you tell me more about your family first?" Fiona asked, dodging the question. "How did you end up with the land?"

John raised an eyebrow at her, but, obviously deciding to let it drop, he took another sip of wine before answering.

"You know we've been in the area for a while – at least a hundred years. I think the O'Briens actually came from County Mayo though. Strong stock; we've bred well through the generations. We were once brave warriors, but now find our strength comes from working from the land and fishing the waters that surround it. We may be salt of the earth, but we're a proud bunch, and always willing to put in a hard day's work for what we get."

"You've an older sister, yes?"

"Yes, Patty. She's moved to Kinsale with her husband's

family. She's pregnant now, a little one on the way," John said, a smile sliding across his face.

They paused as Mrs. O'Reilly came in from the kitchen with two steaming plates in her hands. She placed the plates down carefully in front of Fiona, then John, and then stepped back, wringing her hands a bit.

"Oh, just taste it, please. I'm dying to know if you like it," Mrs. O'Reilly blurted, and Fiona laughed.

"Well, it certainly looks pretty as can be," she said. The fish was swimming in a butter and garlic sauce, with pretty green coriander sprinkled across. Small red potatoes accompanied it, with a dash of warm spinach on the side. Fiona quickly cut into the fish, speared a sliver with her fork, and tasted it.

"You've outdone yourself. This is wonderful," Fiona gushed, meaning every word. "It's light, but packed full of flavor. The coriander was the perfect touch."

"I agree," John said.

Mrs. O'Reilly clapped her hands together in front of her ample bosom, her eyes shining in delight.

"I'm so pleased. Save room for sticky toffee pudding, though; that will be up next." Bobbing her head once, she left them alone.

"She's such a nice woman," Fiona said, taking another bite of her dinner.

"She is at that," John agreed.

"You looked really happy about your sister's baby. Is that something you want then? A wife, children, a farm of your own?" Fiona asked, studiously examining her potato as she cut into it, a part of her desperately wanting to know where his head was at.

"Yes, I'd like to be a father someday. It'd be nice to come home to a wife, a family. To have someone to share experiences with," John shrugged.

"Yes, I could see that," Fiona said, as she thought about leaving her house and living elsewhere. Starting her own little family. It hadn't been much of a thought before, but now the idea seemed to take hold inside of her, warming her core.

They smiled across the table at each other, their heart and minds in unison.

"Fiona…I –" John began.

"And how's the dinner? Would you like more wine? The toffee pudding is almost ready," Mrs. O'Reilly interrupted.

Fiona could've kicked the poor woman. She immediately felt bad for the thought, as it was clear she was exuberant at serving her first customers.

"Dinner is excellent. We'll have more wine and the pudding," John said with a smile.

"I'll be right back. And Mr. O'Reilly wants to pop in for a chat too," Mrs. O'Reilly said as she breezed out.

So much for their alone time, Fiona thought, almost annoyed. But she found it impossible to be irritated when Mr. O'Reilly popped in, his suspenders straining over his shirt and his white mustache muffling his words. She couldn't begrudge the couple their happiness.

Someday maybe that would be her and her husband.

Maybe even her and John.

CHAPTER 16

"FANCY GOING TO the pub?" John asked eagerly after they'd finally left the O'Reillys' with effusive promises to share the word about their new restaurant. Her stomach was full, and a warm haze of contentment enveloped her from the two glasses of wine she had finished.

"Aye, that'd be nice. Though I probably shouldn't drink too much more," Fiona admitted, leaning on him a bit as they walked. He felt solid next to her, and Fiona realized it would be nice to have someone to rely on to hold her up.

The sun had set while they were at dinner, and now the stars were just beginning to peek out in the midnight blue sky. Soft lights shone from windows all over the village, dotting the hillside with their warmth. They walked in silence for a while, simply enjoying the nice evening and the beauty of the village at night.

The lilting sound of a pipe reached them as they drew close to the pub.

"Sounds like a session's on," John said.

"It'll be great fun," Fiona agreed.

Light spilled from the front windows of the pub and a merry tune caught her ears, making her want to dance. John held the door for her and they stepped inside the packed room. Fiona's eyes were immediately drawn to the snug at the front of the room where five musicians were crammed around a table, instruments in their hands. The light was warm, the crowd was clapping, and drinks were flowing.

"Here, let's go to the bar," John said, grabbing Fiona's hand and pulling her through the crush of people until they could weasel into a spot at the bar. Fiona shivered as her body pressed close to John's and they flagged the bartender down.

"Two whiskeys. Neat," John ordered over the noise and Fiona wondered if she would be able to handle the whiskey on top of the wine. Granted, she had been sipping on whiskey with her mother for years, but she wasn't one for drinking a lot.

Maybe because she was naturally suspicious of what too many drinks could do to a person, or maybe because she had learned to be.

The bartender slid them two glasses of amber-colored liquid, and John handed over some money. Turning so his back was to the bar, he casually slipped his arm around Fiona's shoulders. They both leaned back and took in the crowd.

"Sláinte," John said in her ear, and Fiona looked up at him with a smile, clinking her glass against his.

The crowd cheered as the music wound to a rousing

finish, two teens jumping into a step dance in the middle of the room. Fiona laughed at their agility as they tossed their hair and bounced to the beat, so vibrant and full of energy.

Calls for another song went up, but the band waved them away so they could take a short break. Probably to get another beer and catch a smoke, Fiona thought with a smile as she turned back to look at John.

"Should we try to find a seat during the break?"

"I'd like that," Fiona said.

"I'll have you take your grubby hands off my daughter!"

A shout went up from across the room and Fiona stilled, closing her eyes a moment before turning. She could've kicked herself. Of course her father would be at one of the pubs. He always was.

Cian stood across the room, his arms straight against his side, his shirt un-tucked and his hair unruly. His bulbous nose seemed to darken even redder as spittle flew from his mouth.

"I said, unhand my daughter!"

"Cian, leave her be," a man next to Cian said gently.

Cian stormed across the room, pushing people out of his way until he was face to face with John. Well, not quite face to face. More like face to chest, Fiona registered just before her dad cocked his arm back and took a swing at John.

"Father!" Fiona screeched, but John jumped deftly out of the way. Cian had overcommitted to the swing, and when his fist met air, the momentum pulled him around so fast that he fell, hitting his head against the corner of the bar. Fiona screeched again and knelt beside him.

"Father, stop this nonsense. Are you all right then?" Fiona asked, anger and embarrassment making her short with him. A thin line of blood began to trickle from above her father's hairline.

"Damn O'Brien, thinking he can touch my daughter," Cian mumbled as his eyes began to flutter closed.

"John, we've got to get him home," Fiona said, as John crouched beside her.

"I'll lift him up," John said easily, hooking one of Cian's arms over his shoulder and pulling him up to a standing position.

"I'll have another," Cian slurred, and Fiona just shook her head at him. She wound her arm through his and, cheeks burning, stumbled with her father from the pub.

What an end to a first date, she thought as they half-lifted, half-dragged Cian back to their cottage. Luckily it wasn't all that far. But by the time they had reached it, Fiona was working up a good head of mad and doing her best to hold back tears. John wasn't going to want to put up with a father-in-law like this. Assuming they would even progress that far in the relationship after this.

"Mum," Fiona called as they reached the courtyard, dropping her father's arm and racing ahead to open the cottage door. "Mum, Father's in the cups again. He's hit his head as well."

Bridget was at the sink, washing a plate. Concern creased her face, but it was for her daughter, not her husband.

"I'm so sorry, love. How did you find him?"

"He tried to hit John at the pub and missed, and smacked his head on the bar instead," Fiona said tightly.

"That man," Bridget muttered, ushering John in. "This way please," she said, pointing towards the bedroom.

Fiona stood where she was, unsure what to do, her stomach flipping over in knots.

John came back out of the bedroom, his face unreadable.

"Fiona dear, why don't you say good night to John. I'll need your help in here," Bridget said.

Fiona wanted to stomp her feet and throw a tantrum like a toddler. It was supposed to be her night out. Now her father had ruined it, putting on display for John just what he was going to be dealing with if he got involved with her and her family. She silently followed John back out into the courtyard.

The moon had peaked, casting a soft glow on the backyard and illuminating it enough so she could see John's face.

"I'm sorry about all this," Fiona whispered, feeling the threat of tears as she looked down at her feet.

"Don't be," John said softly, hooking a finger under her chin and forcing her to raise her eyes so they met his.

"This is my life, though. That's my father. He's more often in the pub than out on the boat. There's no way to hide it. It's just something we deal with," Fiona said, shrugging one shoulder. She wouldn't make excuses for her father, that was for sure.

"And now you have to go heal his head wound," John guessed correctly.

"And now I have to go heal him," Fiona agreed. "Not for the first time, either."

"You're a good daughter," John said, his lips quirking in a smile.

Fiona just shrugged again and looked away for a moment before looking back up at him.

"I really enjoyed being with you tonight. I hope we can do this again. That you'll still give me a chance despite the way things ended tonight."

John leaned down and brushed his lips against hers. Fiona leaned into the kiss, surprised to find that it comforted as much as it excited. When John wrapped his arms around her and pulled her tight against him, she felt safe.

And soothed.

It was a heady mix of emotions, and one Fiona wanted to savor. Instead, she drew away and met John's eyes.

"Try and keep me away," John said.

And sure enough, Fiona found herself smiling as she went back into the house.

CHAPTER 17

"GOOD MORNING. DID you sleep well?"

Bridget stood at the counter, kneading dough, her movements practiced and precise.

Fiona hadn't slept all that well – instead she'd been tortured with fitful dreams about her Father trying to hit John and what would have happened if he had connected. Not to mention that she was more than guaranteed to be the hot topic in town after church this morning.

"I didn't."

Bridget's face creased in worry as she flipped the dough.

"It was kind of you to heal him last night."

Fiona shrugged as she poured a cup of tea from the kettle, which was still warm. Taking a scone from the basket, she went and sat down at the table, curling her legs beneath her on the chair as she ate the scone straight from her hand.

"Well, what am I going to do? Let him bleed out?" Fiona asked around a mouthful of scone.

"No. That wouldn't be very kind of you, now would it?" *Thump.* Bridget punched her hand into the dough.

"And one must practice compassion at all times," Fiona parroted back to her, a saying the nuns had been fond of repeating but not following.

"You should go to church today. Light a candle for your father. Maybe your prayers will do something. Lord knows mine haven't," Bridget said, the first trace of anger seeping into her voice. Fiona looked up from her sulk and really registered the look on her face.

"You're right angry with him, aren't you?" Fiona asked.

"I am. I'm quite upset that he's gone and ruined your first date," Bridget said as she punched the dough again.

"It's all right. John seemed not to be too put off by it. He said he'd like to see me again," Fiona said.

"Well, isn't that lovely? I knew that I liked that boy," Bridget said, a smile finally creasing her face.

"You know what? You're right. I will go to church and light a candle for Father. It's the least I can do. I haven't been in ages, either. It's probably good for me to get a good dose of prayer in," Fiona admitted as she rose from the table and took her cup to the sink. She pressed a kiss to her mother's cheek as she passed.

Even after years of being taught at a Catholic school, Fiona didn't consider herself overly religious. She liked some of the pomp and circumstance of the traditions, thought weddings were lovely, and enjoyed taking some time to sit in the back pew and listen to the music. But she communicated with God on her own terms – not to be boxed in by the tenets of a religion. Her showing up at a church was just a formality.

Because if she really thought about where she found her religion, it was out in nature. Fiona pulled the black and white dress with the bright red buttons out of the trunk and changed into it as she thought about her own personal church. It was out in the open, where the sky met the water and the hills rolled out for acres. In her opinion, that's where God really was. Not stuck in a church.

"It's good that you're going. Good to show you aren't embarrassed after last night. Most of the town will have heard about it by now," Bridget said. She'd wrapped the dough in a towel and was pouring herself a cup of tea.

"Would you like to come with?"

"No, I've got to keep working. I'm running low on inventory, and we need it," Bridget said, already climbing the ladder to the loft.

And so it went, Fiona thought as she left the courtyard and wandered towards the church. Her mother was so stoic. Never once did she complain; instead she simply got to work, because that's what needed to be done. Fiona wondered what her mother would be like in a different life, whether she would drive herself as hard or perhaps dabble in another form of art. Instead, day after day, Bridget created the tapestries that she knew to be consistent sellers. It kept food on their table and heat in their home during the winter.

And never once a complaint.

Once Fiona saved up enough money she was going to do something nice for her mother. Something completely frivolous that would make her remember the woman who had been hidden away inside the trunk of clothes she'd given Fiona.

The bells in the steeple of the church rang across the dewy morning, and Fiona picked up her pace. She'd be a little late, but she would just slip into the back and light a candle for her father while the sermon began.

The church sat at the top of the hill, fat and squat, a grey stone building with a steeple jutting into the sky. Two large wooden doors formed an arch shape, and Fiona pulled hard on one of them, gliding the door silently open. She ducked into the foyer and looked around.

Pews were filled with families, children kicking their feet and looking bored, teenagers doodling on pads of paper. Fiona eased herself inside and made her way behind the back pew to where an offertory sat with a row of candles in small red jars. The organ struck up an opening song and Fiona tuned it out as the priest walked down the aisle carrying the Eucharistic gifts.

Fiona knelt in front of the candles, reaching for a wick to light and closed her eyes as the song swelled over her shoulders. She focused on her father, sending her prayers up for him as the sermon began.

"Witch! The devil is among us! How dare you!"

A shout startled her out of her prayers and Fiona looked around, not having registered the words at first. Who was the priest yelling at?

Father Patrick stormed down the aisle, his royal purple robes fluttering behind him until he stood over her. Fiona gaped up at him, dread filling her heart. She wanted to kick herself. How had she been so stupid as to forget what

Father Patrick had said to her the night she had healed Sinead?

Fiona stood quickly, not wanting to be at the disadvantage of kneeling. Even so, Father Patrick towered over her. A hush had fallen over the congregation as everyone watched to see what would happen.

"I wasn't doing anything wrong. I was simply saying a prayer for my loved ones," Fiona said, pointing to the candle she had lit. Her voice carried across the quiet church.

"You perform the work of the devil. I've seen it! Magick pouring out of your own two hands!" Father Patrick shrieked, a drop of spit flying from his mouth.

"I have no idea what you are talking about," Fiona said stiffly. She refused to tell Sinead's secret, and technically Father Patrick had seen nothing that night.

"The devil's work is not welcome in this church," Father Patrick boomed, holding a cross out as he dipped his hand in holy water and flung it at her face.

Fiona gasped as it hit her, not because it hurt but because it was a shock to have water thrown in her face. The congregation began to murmur when she gasped, though, and Father Patrick got a gleam in his eye.

"See? See how she gasps when the water hits her?" Father Patrick turned to address the congregation, warming to his topic.

"I gasped because it's a shock to have water thrown in my face," Fiona protested, furious with the priest but refusing to back down.

"Lies, nothing but lies from this witch," Father Patrick hissed.

"Well, now, I don't know about that." The voice rang out from across the room, and Fiona closed her eyes, praying it wasn't someone who was going to hurt her more.

Dr. Collins stepped forward from a pew. Fiona opened her eyes to see him standing in the main aisle, just steps away from where the Brogans sat, frozen in their pew.

"I'd argue that hers is the work of God himself, not the devil," Dr. Collins said, and Fiona could have cheered. She knew she'd been right to let him see her heal that evening.

"You dare to question me in my own church?" Father Patrick sputtered.

"I'm merely saying we don't know everything. And from what I've seen, nothing but goodness comes from Fiona."

Fiona could have kissed the good doctor. The way he'd phrased it danced delicately around her capabilities and still kept the Brogans' secret.

"I refuse to believe it. What I've seen is the work of the devil!" Father Patrick shouted, and he began to shower Fiona with holy water, "Get out, devil. Get thee out, Satan!"

"Stop it! I'm not the devil," Fiona shrieked, putting her arms up to shield herself from the rain of holy water.

"Witch! Be gone, witch!" Father Patrick thundered at her. Fiona pushed past him, darting from the front doors of the church, not caring how it looked to the congregation. She refused to stand there and be publicly abused by the priest anymore.

Trembles began to wrack her body and Fiona fought the tears that threatened to fall from her eyes. She stomped down the steps, staring straight ahead, refusing to look back at the church, trying to push what she'd seen on the way out of the church from her mind.

Because last night hadn't been fun enough – the O'Brien family had been sitting in the second to last pew. Fiona had caught their shocked expressions just as she raced from the church.

"Wait! Hey, wait for me," a voice called behind her.

Fiona stopped, her nails digging into her palms as she forced herself to breathe normally.

Blinking back tears, she turned to face John.

"So, I'm sure you'll not want to date me now. I saw your family's expressions. The whole town will hate me," Fiona bit out, cutting off whatever he was going to say.

"I don't care what my family thinks," John said softly, coming to stand close to her. He reached out to wipe a drop of water from her cheek. Tears or holy water – Fiona couldn't be sure.

Fiona crossed her arms over her chest and looked away.

"That was horrific. It's bound to be the talk of the village. I might even have to move. Everyone's going to hate me," Fiona burst out. Nothing was ever going to be the same again.

"Hey, look at me," John demanded, shaking her a bit until she did.

"I won't let that happen. I promise. Dr. Collins stood up for you, and a lot of people respect him, too."

Fiona wondered briefly why the Brogans hadn't stood up for her. She'd kept their secret; Mr. Brogan had even promised that he owed her. That would have been a pretty good time to pay her back.

"They're going to brand me as a witch now," Fiona said softly.

"Well, is that so bad? I mean, aren't you one, kind of?" John asked, clearly thinking he was being helpful.

"No, I am not a witch," Fiona hissed. "I am a healer. They are worlds apart!"

"Are they though?" John asked, genuinely interested.

"John, I can't do this. I'm sorry. I can't sit here and get questioned by the one person who is supposed to be on my side. Just leave me alone. Go back to your shocked family and your proper congregation, and just leave me be," Fiona blurted, trying to pull her arms from his grasp. She was sick of being questioned – of being different.

"Listen, I understand you're scared, and that what happened here today was awful. But don't walk away from me because of someone else. If you don't want to date me, that's fine. But don't do it because of some awful priest making accusations."

"John, your family is never going to allow you to date me. Not after what they just saw," Fiona whispered, pleading with him to understand.

"Good thing my family doesn't control me," John whispered, brushing a soft kiss across her lips before releasing her. "I'm off to do damage control. Don't shut me out, Fiona."

Fiona felt like she could cry for more than one reason as she watched John walk away, so confident in his belief that everything was going to work out.

Her shoulders hunched as she dragged herself home,

the inevitability of it all weighing upon her. She'd been silly to think she could have a normal future.

Her mother had always told Fiona she wasn't normal – she was blessed.

Fiona had a hard time seeing it that way, just at the moment.

CHAPTER 18

IONA FOUND SHE couldn't go inside the cottage. She didn't want to face her father after last night – and she wasn't so sure she wanted to talk to her mother right now either. Even though she knew it was unfair to be angry with her mother over a gift that was passed down through the blood, nobody had ever claimed that teenage girls were rational human beings.

Though Fiona felt far removed from her teenage self; from the person she had been at fifteen, before she had learned about her gift, to the person she was now at almost twenty years old – they seemed like different chapters in totally separate books.

Fiona paced the courtyard, trying to will herself to calm down. An accusation of being a witch was no laughing matter. She could be jailed, or put on trial – all manner of things. Father Patrick calling her that in front of the village was essentially dubbing her a criminal. Tears clouded her vision and dripped unbidden down her cheeks as the full weight of what the priest had done registered with her.

"Fiona! Whatever is the matter?"

Bridget rushed towards her, but Fiona took a step back, hands clenched at her sides.

"Take my power away," Fiona whispered, lifting her chin to stare at her mother, who had stopped a few feet from her when she'd backed away.

"Fiona, what's happened? You must tell me what is wrong."

"I want you to take my power away. You gave it to me. I don't want it. Make it go away," Fiona hissed.

Bridget wrung her hands as she watched Fiona. Wisps of hair fell from her bedraggled braid and a smudge of flour dusted her cheek. Her eyes looked ancient, and so very tired.

"Fiona, I didn't give you your gift. It's passed down through the bloodline. I can no sooner take it away than I can take mine away."

"But you gave it to me. If I had been a boy, it wouldn't have happened. So take it back," Fiona spit. She knew what she was saying was useless, but the anger just kept flowing through her.

"Fiona, please, tell me what's wrong."

"You want to know what's wrong? I've just been dubbed a witch in front of the entire town by Father Patrick. Including John and his family. He screamed at me in church – screamed! And doused me with holy water, repeatedly, until I ran from the church. It was awful, and I know nothing good can come of this. There have been hints about our otherness here and there in the past, but to

be openly called a witch? You know they'll come for me."
Fiona bit the words out, her eyes burning into Bridget's.

"Not if I have anything to say about it, they won't.
Sure and they don't think they can accuse us of being a
bad influence on this town when we've been nothing but
upstanding citizens," Bridget seethed, beginning to pace as
well.

"He doesn't need proof, Mother. Religious conjecture
is enough to seal my fate," Fiona whispered.

"We will get through this, Fiona. He is but one man.
We've done a lot of good for people in this village – I'll
start calling in favors," Bridget said, crossing to run her
hand down Fiona's arm.

"Fat lot of good that will do. The Brogans were sitting
right there and didn't say a damn word," Fiona said,
rolling her eyes.

"Saints preserve us, they didn't? You leave the
Brogans to me," Bridget said, fire sparking in her eyes.

"I'm so angry right now," Fiona admitted, the frustration and injustice of it all making her stomach turn.

"Why don't you go to the hills? It's your happy place.
I'll hold things down here, and if anyone comes, I'll run
them off."

Fiona thought about it for a moment. She couldn't
imagine going back into the cottage and facing her father
after what he'd done the night before. And she certainly
didn't want to be sitting here if the villagers should show
up. But would it seem like cowardice if she took off for the
hills to avoid another confrontation?

"I should stay. Face the music," Fiona shrugged.

"Nonsense. Go. Take a walk. Go to the cove and relax

by the water. You'll feel better for it after," Bridget said, her voice earnest.

Fiona did want to go to the hills. She wanted somewhere to run to – somewhere that she could scream her frustration and fear without being overheard. Sliding a glance at the village and then back to the cottage, she finally nodded.

"I'll go. Don't plan for me until late though," Fiona said.

"Just let me pack you some food first," Bridget said, already scurrying towards the cottage.

"I should change anyway," Fiona called, following her. No point in ruining a pretty dress by tromping through the muddy hills.

In a matter of moments, Fiona was on her bike with her lunch wrapped in wax paper and tucked in the basket. She'd thrown her hiking clothes on quickly, with barely a glance at the bedroom door, behind which her father still slumbered.

As she pedaled from town, the church bell began to toll, signaling the end of services.

It sounded ominous to Fiona, as if it were signaling the end of her way of life.

She picked up her pace.

Fiona found she couldn't even look at the O'Brien farm as she rode past, and instead she turned her face towards the breeze that blew from the ocean. On any other day, she'd be singing and smiling at the sun that sat so cheerfully in the sky above her.

Her heart pounded with exertion, even though Fiona knew it was foolish to try and outrun what had happened at the church. One way or another, she was going to have to face the ramifications of Father Patrick's words. She could only pray it wouldn't be as bad as she was making it out to be in her mind.

Fiona reached her field in record time. She laughed at herself. It wasn't her field – it was the O'Brien's field. But in her mind it would always be her spot. Leaning her bike against the low brick wall, she grabbed her lunch and hiked across the field to the top of the path to the cove. Pausing at the top, she took a deep breath as the pulse of the magick there pressed against her. Fiona always thought of it as stepping through a thin membrane into another world – a secret spot just for her to enjoy.

Even though Fiona knew others could come here if they know how to properly respect the cove, she'd yet to see anyone else ever come down here. Trailing her hand along the rock wall, Fiona deftly followed the path that zigzagged down the side of the cliff until she reached the bottom.

Standing at the beach, she drew a circle and stepped into it, then pulled her gift out of her pocket. She looked down at the shiny gold tube, something she'd treasured just last night, but now seemed so frivolous. Fiona wasn't a normal girl, and she never would be.

Lifting her hand, she held the lipstick up so that the sun glinted off it.

"I offer this gift to honor the cove."

She threw the lipstick and it landed with a soft plop in the blue water gently lapping at the beach. It tumbled in the sand for a moment, before another wave came along and swallowed it. Fiona breathed out with a sense of loss –

almost as if she was losing a part of herself. The silly girl who had dreamed of happy endings yesterday now knew those dreams to be the silly fabrications of someone who had once thought she could pass for normal.

She ate her lunch in the sun, staring out at the cove, and eventually the sun's warmth and the sound of the water soothed some of the anguish in her heart. Leaning back, she closed her eyes and allowed herself to doze a little in the sun, hiding from the world for just a moment longer.

The crash of the waves and a spray across her face jolted her eyes open. Fiona held still, her eyes flitting back and forth as she tried to figure out what was wrong. Puffy dark clouds had rolled in front of the sun, and the cove – once serene – now raged in anger. A shout from above made her whip her head to the left.

Father Patrick stood at the top of the path, his purple robes billowing behind him, a staff with a large cross in one hand. Four men flanked him, one of whom Fiona knew to be the local Garda. It was a striking image, the cross held high against the dark clouds of the sky, the priest's purple robes reminiscent of royalty. Even though she knew Father Patrick had a flare for the dramatic, Fiona couldn't argue with his presentation. She stood slowly and smoothed her hands on her pants before crossing the beach.

The waves crashed against the sand, angry and violent. She knew the cove was angry for her, but there was little an enchanted body of water could do for her now. Straightening her shoulders, she climbed the path, slowing only when she was a few feet from Father Patrick.

"Father Patrick," Fiona said, raising her chin so that she met his gaze dead on.

"Fiona Morrigan, it is with great pleasure that I will have you brought in for the crime of practicing witchcraft, which is illegal in this village."

"I've committed no such acts," Fiona said, throwing her shoulders back and standing proudly as the cove raged in anger behind her.

"And yet you sun yourself so easily in this cove – one which we know to be enchanted and deadly to all who come here. You walk so easily along its beach. Sure and that's evidence enough, isn't it now?" Father Patrick's eyes lit with a maniacal joy, a spider closing in on its prey.

Fiona looked past him to the Garda standing behind him, nervously running his hands along the hat he held in his hands.

"Garda Roarke, you must know this is an abomination."

"I'm sorry Fiona. The good father here has made an accusation that can only be refuted at trial. That's just how it works." The Garda shrugged helplessly as though to say there was nothing he could do.

"So you're saying I can go around and accuse anyone of witchcraft in this entire village and just like that, they'll be taken and put to trial? That's positively absurd," Fiona seethed.

"It's not just anyone. He's clergy, Fiona," the Garda said softly.

Fiona stared furiously at the men, weighing her options. If she tried to run, they'd surely catch her. There was no use invoking the power of the cove either as that would only back up their claims. Hatred for Father Patrick began to wind through her, and as it did, the waves began to kick up in anger far below her, and a gust of wind all but blew them over.

"See? She's a witch – she's trying to use the power of the cove against us," Father Patrick said, pointing.

"Now who is the nutter here?" Fiona asked, pasting a pleasant smile on her face. "He thinks I can control the weather? If that was the case, we'd have sunny skies every day."

The men around Father Patrick broke into smiles, easing some of the tension. That was when Fiona realized she would have to play the game from within.

"I'll come along with you gentlemen, but only to show you once and for all that I'm not a witch," Fiona said, stepping forward until she was shoulder to shoulder with Father Patrick. She glanced over her shoulder to meet his eyes as she passed him. "And to make sure you never abuse your power in this town again, Father."

The words were a promise, and it was clear Father Patrick realized it as he stumbled back a step.

"Bind her! She just threatened me!"

Fiona closed her eyes as the Garda apologetically wound a rope around her wrists. Unable to look at the beauty of her field, she kept her eyes at the path at her feet, promising herself that once she got out of this mess, she would never live in hiding again.

CHAPTER 19

ER MOTHER'S VOICE woke her.

Fiona had no idea how much time had passed since she had been unceremoniously dumped in the small room off the Garda's office. As a gaol went, it was fairly basic. A single cot sat along a smooth stone wall, with a small jug of water and a single cup on the floor next to it. Bars lined one side of the cell, leaving Fiona no privacy. It surprised her that she'd even managed to doze off. Funny how the body works sometimes, she thought, listening to her mother's tone become more strident as she berated Garda Roarke.

"Why, I know your mother, Garda Roarke. How dare you hold my daughter without any evidence? This is unallowable!"

"I'm sorry, that's the God's honest truth, I am. Father Patrick has formally filed a charge of practicing witchcraft. I have to follow procedure, which means a trial before her peers is to be scheduled for this week. I suggest you start gathering your character witnesses, as she'll need people to stand for her."

"A trial? Sure and you're fooling me then," Bridget's voice registered disbelief. Fiona sat, stunned by the turn of events. How had she gone from lighting a candle for her father to being held pending trial? She never should have gone to church. Part of her wanted to blame her father for her problems, but she knew that blame was useless.

"Father Patrick has insisted." The Garda's voice was weary, and Fiona detected a hint of sadness in his words. She wondered if her mother did as well.

"Why is he doing this?" Bridget asked softly, using a voice that Fiona had heard often over the years. It had convinced many people before to answer her mother's questions, and Fiona had no doubt it would work again.

"A successful trial will place him in high esteem – he wants out, to oversee a bigger church in Dublin. This town is too small for Father Patrick. He wants the riches and the prestige that go with a larger congregation."

"At the expense of my daughter's life? I'll fight with everything I have," Bridget declared.

"Bring your best. Witchcraft trials demand an audience of her peers and a town vote. You'll need to persuade the town to let her stay. Now would be the time to call in any favors you can."

Fiona stood and walked across the room to wrap her hands around the cool iron bars of her cell. She pressed her cheek to the bar, her hope plummeting as she realized the town would have to stand on her behalf in order to overthrow Father Patrick's charges.

"Can I see her?"

"You're not supposed to, but I'll allow it," Garda Roarke said.

In moments, Bridget's hands were wrapped around Fiona's, and for the first time since she'd been arrested, tears pricked her eyes. There was something about looking at her mother through the bars of a cell that made her feel completely defeated.

"There's going to be a trial," Bridget whispered, her eyes searching Fiona's. Bridget's fear pulsed at Fiona in waves that threatened to overtake her and spiral into despair. They both left the dire outcome unsaid.

A guilty judgment would result in death.

Even though Fiona knew that, in other parts of the world, witch hunts were now considered backwards and unacceptable, that way of thought hadn't quite reached their small village. In Grace's Cove, religion ruled, and Father Patrick was akin to a king. The fact that she was even being allowed an audience of her peers was remarkable.

"I'm surprised even that's being allowed," Fiona admitted, bitterness lacing her voice.

"I'm going to call in all my favors," Bridget promised.

"Please – anyone you can think of at all," Fiona whispered, pressing her forehead against the bars.

"I will. Are you all right in here?"

Fiona laughed and gestured to the small cot.

"I've been better, but Garda Roarke has been fair to me so far."

"And I would expect nothing less, or I'll be speaking with his mother." Bridget said firmly.

Fiona flashed her mother a small smile.

"I'm scared." Fiona blinked tears from her eyes.

"Father Patrick is but one man. Do not doubt my power to persuade this village," Bridget said fiercely. "They've known me longer than him. We'll be just fine. But, in the meantime, I had best get to the gossip mills before Father Patrick. We'll want to turn the wind of talk against him."

"He's not a good man," Fiona said, clenching her fist at her gut, "I can feel it, deep inside. His core is black, like the roots of evil have twisted around his heart."

Bridget pressed her lips into a thin line.

"Sure and I'll take that into account. We can fight fire with fire then," Bridget nodded.

"How long will I have to be in here?" Fiona said, her eyes searching Bridget's. She hoped it wasn't longer than a few days – the solitary aspect of this cell would be enough to drive her crazy.

"Not more than a few days, I'm sure of it. I'll cry foul on holding you here without any evidence. And I'll be reaching out to some contacts of mine at the Archdiocese in Dublin. Father Patrick isn't the only one with connections."

Fiona felt hope bloom in her chest. Trust her mother to always protect her.

"Bring me one of your outfits, please. I want to look nice and approachable for the trial," Fiona said. Though she hated to admit it, appearance mattered. And in the court of public opinion, she would need to appear an innocent and pretty young girl.

"I will. Now, I must be off. Go inside, my love; you'll find the strength you need," Bridget murmured as she clasped Fiona's hand once more before disappearing down the hallway. "You take care of my girl, Garda Roarke. If anything unwieldy should happen to her in here, I'll be holding you accountable."

A smile crossed Fiona's face briefly at her mother's brisk no-nonsense tone and Garda Roarke's quick acquiescence. She could only hope her mother's clout would prove enough to sway other members of the town. Easing herself down onto the cot, Fiona stared at the ceiling and did just as her mother suggested – she went within.

CHAPTER 20

"*A*H, I'VE BREAKFAST for you, then, Fiona." Garda Roarke cleared his throat outside her cell.

Fiona waited a moment more from where she had been staring at the ceiling, counting the lines in the stone.

"Everything all right then, Fiona?" Garda Roarke asked.

Pushing herself up to sitting, Fiona thought about the question. In theory, yes, she was all right, so to speak. She'd slept off and on through the night, and she wasn't any the worse for wear. But emotionally, she was a wreck.

"I'm fine as one could be, I suppose," Fiona said, crossing to where Garda Roarke fumbled with the key to the cell door. The hinges of the door creaked as he pulled it open, handing her a tray of food. Fiona knew immediately that Garda Roarke's mother had done the cooking, as the tray was loaded with scones, porridge, eggs, and sausage, with a small vase holding a flower. It wasn't likely that other prisoners received such nice fare, and Fiona took the tray with a smile and a small nod of acknowledgement.

"Thank your mother for the food," she said softly, crossing to set the tray on the bunk.

"I'll do that. She's worried about you in here," Garda Roarke said.

"I'm not sure what to say to that, other than you and I both know that I shouldn't be here," Fiona pointed out.

A flush of pink tinged Garda Roarke's cheeks and he reached up to tug on the corner of his mustache.

"Would you like some tea?"

Fiona supposed he couldn't really be discussing the merits of her imprisonment with her, so she simply nodded, reaching down to tear off a corner of a still-warm blueberry scone. Though nerves clawed at her stomach, Fiona forced herself to eat, knowing she would need to keep her energy up for what she knew would prove to be the most attended and scandalous event of the season in Grace's Cove.

Her trial.

Fiona wondered how the format would go. She couldn't even remember there ever being a public trial in Grace's Cove before. Being a small village composed of families and relatives, most spats were settled over a pint at the pub. Rarely did something escalate to the level of Garda intervention. Fiona groaned and shoved another piece of scone into her mouth.

"Garda Roarke?" Fiona called, and heard a shuffle from the other room before Garda Roarke appeared before her cell door, a cup of steaming tea in his hands.

"Yes?"

"Can you explain to me how the trial will work?"

"Of course, lass. Here's your tea," he said, putting the

cup on the floor before unlocking the door and pulling it open. This time, he stepped into the cell and crossed the small room to hand the tea to her before stepping back to lean against the wall and cross his arms over his chest.

"I can't recall there ever being a public trial before," Fiona blew on her tea.

"I can't say there's been one since you've been born, now that I think of it," Garda Roarke said, smoothing his fingers over his dark mustache as he squinted his eyes in thought.

"Wouldn't this be a matter that goes before the High Court Judge? Not a common law public trial?" Fiona asked. She'd honestly never heard of such a matter being handled like this before.

Garda Roarke sighed and shook his head.

"Yes, in theory, if this is a criminal matter it should go before the High Court."

"So... I'm not sure I'm understanding why I'm being held then." Fiona raised an eyebrow at him.

"It's Father Patrick. He's demanded a trial of a court of public opinion. It appears there's a small loophole in the law. When things switched over from the common law to the courts, there was a loophole left that allows clergy to bring someone forward on charges. A decision by their peers is held as law – both by the church and state. Most other areas have done away with the loophole. We haven't, as it has never been invoked before and as such – well, it had slipped from our thoughts. Father Patrick knew of this rule and has used it," Garda Roarke said, his eyes woeful.

"Can we call a tribunal to revoke the law?" Fiona asked.

Garda Roarke raised one eyebrow.

"I'd have to look into that. I think you need at least a few weeks for a tribunal and that would only prolong your stay here. You might want to take your chances with the public trial."

Even as he said the words, Fiona knew he was right. A tribunal would only allow Father Patrick to recruit more people to his side. It could end up even worse for her.

"Is there anything I can do to prepare?" Fiona asked, knowing she was taking a chance by asking for help from the Garda. He leaned forward, peeking out of her cell door and down the hallway, before turning back to look at her.

"I've always liked your mother, you know," Garda Roarke began, his eyes darting about. "She's been kind to my mother and helped her in ways that only a daughter could – one which she'd never had. In fact, she gave her one of your tonics not too long ago. It cleared up a nasty chest cold that I was quite certain would turn to pneumonia. For that alone, I'm indebted to you."

Fiona smiled at him. She knew it was just Garda Roarke and his mother at home. He'd lost his father to a boating accident years ago.

"She's a good woman. I'm happy to hear I was able to help her through an illness."

"Well, I don't know if it's witchcraft or not, but I'd say the only type of magick you've done is the healing kind. And there can't be something so wrong with that, now, can there?" Garda Roarke came over to collect her tray of food. When he was bent close to her, he paused.

"Rumor is that Father Patrick's been stealing the donations at church."

The words, just a breath of air by her ear, nearly didn't register. Fiona's heart skipped a beat as she realized what she'd been told. Her eyes wide, she watched as Garda Roarke busied himself with her tray of half-eaten food, letting himself from the cell without a backward glance. Had she not been certain of his words, she'd almost believe she'd imagined the entire thing.

Hope bloomed inside Fiona and she sat back on her cot and began to consider her options. If this was really the case, she might be able to call action against the priest.

Now all she needed was evidence.

CHAPTER 21

"*I*'D LIKE TO see Fiona, please," John's voice echoed down the hallway to where Fiona sat, slumped over her legs on the cot.

"John!" Fiona couldn't help but call out, knowing he could hear her. He'd come for her. A warm glow began to pulse through her just from knowing he was close.

"Fiona! Are you all right then?" John called down the hallway.

"John, I'm sorry, but you can't be fraternizing with our prisoner. It's against the rules," Garda Roarke hissed.

"I'm doing well, John. Garda Roarke has been quite kind." Fiona thought it wouldn't hurt to butter him up a bit.

"Fiona, please refrain from shouting from your cell," Garda Roarke called, and Fiona bit back a smile.

"Just a quick word, please, Garda Roarke? I really must see her," John pleaded. Fiona held her breath and waited as silence came from the front room.

She gasped when John appeared at the bars of her cell,

having quietly padded down the hallway. Garda Roarke must have given his silent approval for John to come visit her.

"John," Fiona breathed, immediately reaching up to smooth her hair back, conscious that she hadn't bathed in a day.

"Fiona, I had to see for myself that you weren't hurt," John said. Dark circles ringed his eyes and Fiona could feel the worry pulsing from him. Her heart tripped a little as she fell off that last little cliff into full-on love for him.

"I'm not hurt. Garda Roarke has been kind," Fiona said, stepping to the bars so that her hands wound around the cold metal. John immediately reached up to place his hands over hers, his presence instantly calming her.

"Fiona, I'm worried. Father Patrick is on a warpath. The village is already torn. It's the only thing people can talk about," John said, his eyes searching hers.

"I'm not a witch, John. At least not like that. I'm a healer. There are many kinds of magicks," Fiona whispered.

"I believe you. There is nothing evil about you," John said, his heart in his eyes.

"Come closer," Fiona breathed, moving until her lips pushed between two bars. In seconds, John's lips were upon hers, heating her with the intensity of his feelings for her.

"John, listen closely," Fiona breathed against his lips, and John froze, his lips but a hairsbreadth from hers. To anyone who came down the hallway, they'd look as though they were stealing a kiss.

John's eyes widened as Fiona detailed what she'd learned from Garda Roarke.

"We'll need evidence," Fiona pleaded.

John straightened, a new light of purpose shining in his eyes.

"Say no more. Consider it done. I'll arm the troops," John said, winking at her before he turned to go down the hallway, Garda Roarke already calling down the hallway to inform him that his time was up.

"John... I... I..." Fiona called after him, and he turned, putting his finger to his lips to shush her.

"Say it when you're out. I want to hear it the first time when we're free to be together...walking the beach again."

Fiona blinked back the tears that reached her eyes at his words, the hope that filled her chest, burning to the point that she couldn't decide whether to squeal in delight or sob with anxiety. Doing neither, she clenched her fists so tightly that her nails dug into her palms, and began to plan. If she was to be accused of witchcraft in front of the whole village, she would need to anticipate the arguments against her. Hoping against hope, she leaned against the bars of the cell again.

"Garda Roarke, I have a favor to ask."

"What's that now, Fiona?" Garda Roarke walked cautiously down the hallway, shooting glances over his shoulder towards the front room.

"Can you help me plan my counterargument? As in, lob at me any arguments you think Father Patrick will try to undermine me with?"

Garda Roarke considered his words. Fiona said nothing, biting her lip as she hoped against hope he would work with her.

"First off, you know the Maloneys will be backing Father Patrick. They'll throw the argument at you that Serena shouldn't have lived through that bout of flu she had last year..." Garda Roarke began and Fiona squeezed her eyes shut, so thankful for him that she almost began to cry in earnest.

"You're right. They will. Go on."

CHAPTER 22

FRIDAY ARRIVED MORE quickly than Fiona had anticipated. Even though Garda Roarke allowed Bridget to check on her once in a while, for the most part, Fiona was on her own. Garda Roarke had proved invaluable for bringing up potential arguments that would be thrown at her during her trial, and she worked obsessively to counteract each and every argument, fast-forwarding and rewinding all the potential scenes in her mind.

After that, there was nothing else she could do but wait and send her positive intentions out into the universe. Fiona had to believe she'd done nothing but provide help and healing to others – therefore, that positive energy should be returned to her.

Or at least that is how she hoped karma would work.

Fiona worried the crease in her pants, running her fingers over the edge obsessively, the thin fabric smooth beneath her palm. The trial was only hours away and for once in her life, she felt completely out of control. Being at the mercy of others was a new experience for her.

A voice from the front had Fiona turning her head before she recognized the lilting tone of her mother's charming voice. Hopefully Garda Roarke would allow Bridget to see her daughter before the trial.

"Love, I've got a change of clothes for you," Bridget said cheerfully as she made her way to the door of Fiona's cell. Fiona was already waiting by the door, anxiousness beginning to claw its way through her stomach.

"Ladies, I'll give you some alone time. No funny stuff, though, you hear me?" Garda Roarke said sternly, jingling the keys as he unlocked the door to Fiona's cell. Today he wore his dress uniform, and Fiona knew it was to prove a point. He was following the rules of this village, even if he didn't necessarily agree with them. The onus was on her now to prove her innocence.

Bridget shot Garda Roarke a quick smile and then bustled into the cell, her hands full of clothes. A brilliant green blouse, with gold and pearl buttons, was tucked into a lovely tweed skirt that fell to her ankles. Gold drops winked at her ears and her hair had been woven into two braids pinned into coils at the nape of her neck. She looked lovely, put together, and carried an air of confidence that Fiona prayed would carry over to her.

"You look nice," Fiona said into her mother's neck as Bridget embraced her. For a moment, the women stood together, holding each other for strength. For a second, Fiona could feel her mother's worry before it seemed like a veil was drawn over the emotion and it was replaced with hope and strength. Her mother had done that on purpose to protect her. Even though Fiona had glimpsed the worry beneath the strength, for now she would focus on the courage that radiated from her mother. She absorbed her strength ravenously, feeding on it. It was a gift to be used later in the day.

"There now, love. You'll be just fine. Let's get you cleaned up," Bridget said briskly, pulling back to dig through the bag of items that she had brought with her. "You've bathed then?"

"Aye, Garda Roarke allowed me a sponge bath earlier today," Fiona said. It had been a cold and awkward experience, but one she was grateful for nonetheless.

"Good, let's get your hair together then," Bridget said, gesturing for Fiona to sit on the edge of the bunk. She pulled a pearl handled brush from the bag and began to run it through Fiona's hair. There was something incredibly soothing about someone brushing her hair, and each stroke helped to calm Fiona's frayed nerves.

"I think I'll pull it half up and then wrap it into coils at the nape of your neck," Bridget decided, "No sense in looking less than your best."

"Yes, thank you. That's a lovely look on me," Fiona agreed. She waited as her mother combed and pinned, knowing her to be an expert at hairstyles. Much like the magick she used when weaving strands of wool together, Bridget took pride in creating sophisticated hairstyles. Fiona supposed it was just another type of weaving when it came down to it. Different material was all.

"You know, John has been coming around this week to speak with me and your father," Bridget said evenly and

Fiona's head shot up. Bridget nudged her to put her chin down again.

"What has he been saying?"

"We're working together on your case. As well as the tidbit of information you've passed on," Bridget said softly. Fiona drew in a deep breath, feeling a sense of calm work its way through the worst of her nerves.

"You've a plan then," Fiona said finally.

"We've worked out a plan of sorts. But since we can't dictate the proceedings, we'll have to just wait and see how it all unfolds. I'm here to tell you to have faith, though. Trust in us to have your back." Bridget patted her shoulder once.

"I do. I also trust that, because I've spent my time helping others, it will come back in a good way," Fiona said.

"Aye, 'tis true. It will. But we can't always control or rush how these things unfold. I like John, by the way. He's a good match for you. Steady, with a kind heart. You could do far worse for a partner in life."

Fiona felt her heart clench at the thought of being with John for life. It was such an absurd idea when only months ago she'd barely even considered marriage as an option. Funny the twists and turns life could take.

"Aye, I really do fancy him," Fiona admitted.

"Well, let's make you look your best then. I suspect you'll have one very happy gentleman caller after we get through this nonsense of a trial," Bridget said matter of factly, pulling back to study Fiona's hair. "There now, you look lovely. Just a touch of makeup and to pick your outfit now."

Bridget held up a simple white blouse and a navy skirt, but Fiona shook her head and pointed to the slash of red silk she saw jutting out from the bag.

"What's the red one?"

"Ah, yes, I picked it up by chance. It may be a little risky, but I always consider red to be a powerful color," Bridget said, drawing a red silk dress from the bag with long sleeves and a skirt that went to mid-calf. White cherry blossoms peppered the red print, the hint of green in their leaves a lovely juxtaposition against the red. It was a demure dress, yet it spoke of confidence and an air of womanhood that Fiona wasn't even certain she'd achieved yet.

"This is stunning," Fiona mused, running her hands over the silky fabric. "But I'm concerned it may be all wrong for the trial. I suppose it would make sense to go with the staid blouse and navy skirt – much more Catholic school uniform."

The women eyed each other for a moment, considering their options.

"Red," they both said at the same moment, causing Fiona to let out a small laugh.

"No sense in doing the expected," Fiona said and Bridget laughed.

"Plus, you'll look beautiful in front of the whole village and for once everyone will be able to see the real you," Bridget pointed out, and Fiona paused in the process of unbuttoning her blouse.

"What do you mean by that?"

"I mean you have a tendency to dress to hide yourself – in khaki pants and work blouses, always scurrying through the hills, not a stitch of makeup on. It was nice to see you dress up for John the other night. I think the village will be surprised by what a beauty you've turned into. They want a show? Let's give them a show," Bridget said, handing the dress to Fiona.

"I didn't realize I've been hiding myself," Fiona said softly. "I just thought I was wearing serviceable clothes for the work I do."

"Aye, and there's certainly a time and a place for that, sure there is. But there's also a time and place for celebrating the power that a pretty dress and a nice hairdo brings you. Today is not the time to be a shrinking violet."

No, today was the time for Fiona to blossom – claiming her power in front of the whole village.

She swallowed against a suddenly dry throat as she slipped the red silk dress over her head.

CHAPTER 23

"NO NEED TO bind me, Garda Roarke. I'm not going anywhere," Fiona said with a smile when Garda Roarke stopped by the front of her cell to collect her. Bridget had left at half ten, wanting to arrive early and get a front seat at the trial. Fiona wondered if John would walk with her or if he would be sitting at the front of the trial. A part of her was struggling with trying not to be embarrassed in front of John and his family. It wasn't exactly the impression she wanted to make on her boyfriend's parents.

Garda Roarke paused as he took in her dress.

"Too much?" Fiona asked, running her hands nervously over her skirt.

"Just right, I think," Garda Roarke said, a ghost of a smile on his face as he unlocked the door and ushered her out. Fiona squared her shoulders, feeling a new resolve sweep through her at Garda Roarke's approval, and lifted her chin.

"Where's the trial to be held?"

"In the church. Only place large enough to hold the whole town," Garda Roarke pointed out as they left the small constabulary building and stepped into the street. Momentarily blinded by the cheerful rays of sun peeking from behind a cloud, Fiona held a hand up to shield her eyes and steadied herself. So the trial was to be in enemy camp then.

The village was like a ghost town, Fiona observed as they began the walk towards the church. Where typically she would find people bustling about their day, stopping at the market or the baker's, the streets instead were silent. Which meant the entire town was already in the church. The only sound Fiona heard as they approached the church was the gravel crunching under her shoes and the occasional cry of a gull hovering over the water of the bay.

They paused for a moment at the doors of the church. Garda Roarke turned, his glance sliding over her once before he straightened his face into an impassable mask.

"Ms. Morrigan, follow me to the front please," he said, his hand on the handle of the door. "I'm rooting for you," he whispered, before his face slipped back into a stoic expression. Pulling the door open, he gestured her inside.

The waft of incense hit Fiona first, the smell so pungent that her eyes almost watered with it. Hundreds of candles lined the foyer, and Fiona couldn't help but give Father Patrick a point for his flair for drama. Silence greeted her as she stepped forward, stopping at the beginning of the aisle. The building was packed to the rafters and where people couldn't fit in the pews, they lined the walls of the church and the balcony housing the organ above. Every last inch of available space held a villager, and Fiona had to immediately throw her mental shields up or be taken under by the wave of emotions that rolled over her from the crowd.

At the front of the church, Father Patrick stood beneath the stained glass window, a cross in his hand. He nodded to Garda Roarke, assuming command of this show and Fiona could immediately tell that Garda Roarke was miffed. Even though this was being held in a church, Garda Roarke would still be the one overseeing the trial.

Fiona kept her chin up as they walked the aisle, her eyes on Father Patrick's. She'd taken in where her mother was sitting, surrounded by friends in the front row. John sat on the other side of the aisle, his shoulders thrown back and a mutinous look on his face.

His parents were not with him.

Fiona refused to look around, instead keeping her eyes only on Father Patrick, telegraphing her intent to take him down in any way she could. She saw him swallow deeply, just once, but it was enough of a tell that she knew her proud demeanor had gotten to him. He'd obviously expected her to be a broken shell of a woman after having spent a week in jail.

They reached the dais and Fiona smiled brightly at Father Patrick.

His face blanched and he crossed himself.

"Fiona Morrigan, you are here to answer the charges of practicing witchcraft. A trial before your peers will make the decision as to whether you shall meet your death," Father Patrick boomed, swinging his arm around dramatically.

"Excuse me," Garda Roarke said, and stepped in front

of Father Patrick, deliberately cutting him off to face the crowd. Fiona watched as rage boiled across Father Patrick's face, though she kept the smile off her face as she turned to face the crowd, aligning herself with Garda Roarke.

"Father Patrick has brought charges against Fiona Morrigan. The charges are of practicing witchcraft. The only reason Father Patrick was even able to do so is because of a loophole in the law that has never gotten fixed. I am introducing a bill to fix that loophole, which will also be voted on at today's meeting. Let me be clear in stating that Father Patrick is not, in fact, in charge of this trial – I am. Father Patrick is allowed to produce any evidence he would like, but I am in charge of today's proceedings. So, with that, I'll ask Father Patrick to take a seat on the other side of the dais and Ms. Morrigan to be seated on this side. I will allow both sides to present evidence and refute any arguments brought against them. If any new charges or information are brought to light during this time, we will adjust the proceedings accordingly," Garda Roarke said, stepping backwards until he pushed Father Patrick from the center of the dais, forcing him from the platform to the side.

Fiona turned and demurely took the hard wooden chair that had been set out for her to the left of Garda Roarke, delighted to see that Father Patrick was being forced into the same chair on the right. It dawned on her what Garda Roarke was doing; he was making her and Father Patrick equals – both of them on trial. The effect wasn't lost on Father Patrick as he angrily arranged his robes around him, a red flush creeping up his cheeks. Garda Roarke was smart in setting it up this way, and for allowing arguments to be brought against both parties. Fiona hoped that Bridget and John had been able to secure enough evidence against Father Patrick to ensure that the charges against her would be dropped. She straightened her shoulders, lifted her chin, and folded her hands over her knees.

And stared out into the faces that would determine her future.

CHAPTER 24

"WE WILL BEGIN with Father Patrick. Father Patrick – what say you?"

Father Patrick started to rise but with a single glance from Garda Roarke, he sat back in his seat and crossed his arms over his chest.

"I say that Fiona is a witch. I saw her practice witchcraft with my own two eyes. She practiced it upon Sinead Brogan, upon whom I'd been called to perform last rites. One moment the girl is on her deathbed, then after a visit from Fiona – poof, she's up and walking around with not a care in the world."

A gasp went up through the crowd at Father Patrick's declaration and Fiona saw more than a few shocked faces in the crowd. A murmur began to grow as people whispered to each other.

"Fiona, were you at the Brogans' house on the evening that Father Patrick is describing?"

Fiona met Garda Roarke's eyes.

"Yes, I was called there to help."

"And what was wrong with Ms. Brogan?"

That was a tough question to answer. Fiona searched the crowd until she found Mr. and Mrs. Brogan, their faces ashen with nerves.

"I can't say," Fiona said finally, refusing to give up Sinead's private health issues.

"You can't say? Or you won't?" Father Patrick shot back.

"I won't say," Fiona clarified. There had to be a way to win this without disclosing the Brogans' private business.

"And why won't you say it?" Garda Roarke asked her, his eyebrows raised in question.

"Because I'm not a doctor and am not qualified to diagnose medical conditions," Fiona said. Voices rose in the crowd as people began to argue back and forth, a few even calling out to disclose the Brogans' business.

"But you knew what was wrong? You were told?" Garda Roarke pressed on.

"Yes, I was told. But I was taught it's not neighborly to gossip about the private business of others. As far as I'm concerned, one's health issues are their own private business. That's all I will say about Sinead's health that evening," Fiona said stiffly. She caught a smile on her mother's face from the corner of her eye. A wave of approval at her words went through the crowd.

"So you'll lie then? You'll lie in the face of all of these kind people in order to protect the Brogans?" Father Patrick seethed. He could obviously sense that Fiona's last statement had endeared her to the crowd. Little did Father Patrick know that the Brogans were held in high esteem in the village.

"I'm not lying. I'm simply not divulging information that is not my own to tell," Fiona pointed out primly.

"Sinead was all but dead. And in walked Fiona and performed magick. She is a witch, which goes against the holy teachings of this church! I'm surprised God doesn't strike her down just for being in this holy building!" Father Patrick ranted, waving his arm about vigorously.

Fiona schooled her expression because a part of her wanted to laugh at his dramatics. There was no way people could be buying what he said. But she scanned the crowd and found to her surprise that quite a few people were nodding along with Father Patrick's words. Fiona wanted to roll her eyes. She should have known better than to question the devout Catholics who blindly followed Father Patrick's word. He had a small but vocal following in the village, and now she wondered if their voices would over-power hers.

"Father Patrick, did you witness Fiona performing this magick?"

"He did not," a voice from across the room interrupted just as Father Patrick was about to speak.

"Mr. Brogan, you may speak," Garda Roarke said, slicing a glance at Father Patrick to shut him up.

"Father Patrick was not in the room with Fiona and Sinead. Everything he has stated is hearsay," Mr. Brogan said, his eyes fixed firmly on Fiona. She could read the apology there as though he had said it out loud. A gasp went through the crowd at his statement, and voices began to rise in argument.

"Was there any witness to what happened in Sinead's room that evening?" Garda Roarke asked, cleverly side-stepping the question of what had been wrong with Sinead and focusing on the facts at hand.

Fiona froze. Dr. Collins had been in the room with her. She'd allowed him to be. If he detailed any of the events he had seen, she was doomed. Her eyes scanned the crowd searching for Dr. Collins.

Mr. Brogan began to speak but Father Patrick cut him off.

"Aye, Dr. Collins was in the room with her."

Fiona stilled as she found Dr. Collins, standing in the far corner of the church, leaning against the wall with his arms crossed.

"Dr. Collins, I'll ask that you step forward and tell us how Fiona healed Ms. Brogan," Garda Roarke said.

"Aye, that's easy enough," Dr. Collins began, a smile on his kind face. Fiona closed her eyes and waited for the judgment to rain down upon her.

"And how did this witch heal Sinead then?" Father Patrick thundered, earning another glare from Garda Roarke.

"Well now, I'm not so certain I'd be throwing out accusations of being a witch at this lovely girl," Dr. Collins began and Fiona opened her eyes to see him smiling gently at her.

"So how did Sinead go from being dead to being healed? What did Fiona do?" Father Patrick hissed.

"Why, Father Patrick, she prayed for Sinead, of course."

Fiona bit back a smile as the church erupted into shouts.

CHAPTER 25

"SILENCE! SILENCE! FATHER Patrick, sit down this instant!" Garda Roarke thundered at Father Patrick, who stood bellowing at Dr. Collins.

"Dr. Collins, please, if you will clarify your meaning?"

"Well, as you know, I'm a doctor. I was there seeing to Ms. Brogan's needs. I was working on her and Fiona simply stepped in to offer prayers and comfort while I provided medical care. They were friends in school, you know, and Sinead obviously responded to having a friend her own age comfort her."

The lie was so smooth, Fiona wouldn't have been able to detect it had she not been there herself. It seemed that she had grossly underestimated Dr. Collins' kindness.

"So, in your estimation, Fiona is not a witch?"

"Certainly not. If anything, I'd say she is an angel with a direct line to God."

Pandemonium broke out through the church, with one woman clutching her handkerchief to her face as she wept.

Fiona could have hugged Dr. Collins for the brilliance of his counterargument. Instead of trying to disprove that she was a witch, he'd instead offered another option as to what she could be. His approach was flawless.

Fiona slid a glance to where Father Patrick stood on the dais, his mouth working like a fish gulping for air. No sound came out.

"Mr. Brogan, would you agree with this statement?"

"Aye, we both would," Mrs. Brogan said, standing and giving Fiona a small nod. "It was nothing but an honor to have Fiona attend as an assistant for Dr. Collins."

Fiona smiled at her and nodded back, acknowledging the apology behind her words. She knew the woman felt bad for not standing up for her sooner.

"So, the facts of the situation are that Sinead Brogan was ill, Dr. Collins was called to attend to her, Fiona offered her prayers, and Father Patrick stood outside the room ready to offer last rites if they should be needed?" Garda Roarke asked patiently.

"Aye." Dr. Collins and Mr. and Mrs. Brogan all spoke at once.

"But... but... that is not what happened! Sinead was all but dead! Then suddenly she was alive!" Father Patrick shouted, spittle flying.

"Sure and don't you be believing in miracles yourself then, Father Patrick? Isn't that what the good book teaches us? To believe in miracles?" Bridget asked from her front row seat. The crowd all murmured their agreement.

"I'm telling you there was witchcraft used!" Father Patrick seethed.

Garda Roarke raised a hand to quiet him.

"Does anyone else in the crowd raise a charge of practicing witchcraft against Fiona?"

The crowd fell silent as villagers craned their necks, looking at their neighbors to see if anyone would speak.

"There must be! What about you, Seamus? Didn't you tell me she fixed your broken leg?"

An elderly man in the back row blanched as his name was called and all faces turned to observe him. Fiona saw her mother give a subtle shake of her head at Seamus.

"Sure and I can't be recollecting anything of that nature now, Father Patrick," Seamus said easily, and Fiona could've kissed the old man. She had fixed his leg, and he'd been so grateful he'd been bringing them fish every week for months now.

"And you? Mrs. McGuinness? Surely you mentioned Fiona miraculously healing your baby of pneumonia?"

A pretty woman sat in the front row, holding a baby close to her body as she rocked, automatically soothing her child. She smiled serenely at Father Patrick.

"Twas just a small cold when the weather was damp. Catherine's right as rain now," Mrs. McGuinness said easily. Fiona had healed her baby when she'd come to her in the middle of the night, her eyes desperate in fear, her baby's small body wracked with mucus-filled coughs.

It was all almost too much for Fiona. The villagers were saying thank you to her in the only way they could – by saving her life. It was humbling and empowering at the same time, to feel the love and support pouring from the people who sat before her. A jury of her peers – and ones who weren't about to let Fiona be persecuted for doing nothing but helping others.

"This is nonsense! You are all lying! It is a sin to lie in church," Father Patrick screeched, dancing back and forth from foot to foot, waving his arms in the air.

"May we vote? I have another issue I'd like to introduce before the town," John said, raising his hand and causing Father Patrick to whip around and glare at him.

"I say when this trial is over! Not you! You have no power to call an end to the trial!" Father Patrick seethed, his eyes wide in anger.

"Actually, I have the power to call an end to the trial. Is there anyone else who can introduce any evidence to support Father Patrick's allegations?" Garda Roarke took his time scanning the room, giving a fair amount of time for anyone to come forward. When nobody said anything, he nodded once and turned to Father Patrick.

"With no evidence to support your allegations, they are just that – allegations. As such, I declare Fiona to be free and clear of the charge of witchcraft. She is not guilty and is free to go."

A cheer went up through the crowd and Fiona blinked back tears as she clenched her hands together and smiled at everyone. They had saved her. Right then and there, she vowed to spend her life helping the villagers of Grace's Cove.

"John O'Brien, you may have the floor," Garda Roarke said, his hand sweeping out to silence Father Patrick where he ranted on the dais.

"Yes, I'd like to bring a charge against Father Patrick

for theft." John's declaration was like a phonograph needle skittering across a record, scratching the music silent. The entire village froze and, as one, turned to look at Father Patrick.

Things were about to get interesting.

CHAPTER 26

FIONA KEPT HER mouth shut as the room rioted around her. Calling a priest's behavior into question was sacrilegious and something even the more lenient villagers found appalling, to judge from the expressions on their faces. A giddy sense of inevitability washed through her and she sat back to watch the show.

"That's blasphemy! He can't accuse me of such a thing!" Father Patrick shouted. "The devil is at work here today."

A few members of the church crossed themselves and looked nervously around. The air was thick with tension as everyone waited to see what would happen.

"John, that's a serious allegation. Can you present evidence to support that?" Garda Roarke said easily, his expression calm as he studied John. Fiona bit her lip as she wondered just how John planned to prove the theft.

"Yes. I'd like to introduce a few witnesses. First, I'll bring in Sean Connor from the next town over. If you recall, there was a big fundraiser for Sean earlier this year because his house had burnt to the ground. Except not only has Sean never heard of this fundraiser, he also never received any money from it." A gasp went through the crowd as a man who had been leaning against the back wall stepped forward.

"Are you Sean Connor?"

"Aye, I am."

"Did your house burn down?"

"Unfortunately, it did. The chimney for our peat fire-place went up and the thatch caught quickly after that," Sean said, running a hand nervously through his red hair.

Murmurs laced the crowd. Everyone knew all too well the fears of living with a thatched roof on your cottage. Fire was always the biggest concern.

"Mr. Connor, were you aware that the parish had hosted a fundraiser for your home?"

"Ah, no, I wasn't." Sean looked around nervously and raised a hand in apology. "I'm sorry, I am, for I would've come over to thank ye all for the donations. It was quite kind of ye to think of us during our hard time."

Fiona glanced at Father Patrick to see how he was taking it all. His face had turned an odd shade of red and he was puffing out little breaths through his nose.

"Father Patrick, as I recall, the parish had raised a size-able donation – enough for at least a new roof. Isn't that right?" Garda Roarke looked around at the crowd and several people nodded in affirmation.

"I sent the money along to him. He's clearly lying," Father Patrick said, pointing at Sean. "Shame on you for lying in this holy house."

Fear raced across Sean's face and he turned to the left and the right to look at the villagers.

"I'm not lying, I swear it to you. I'm a good Catholic and me mum's raised me to not tell falsehoods."

"I've more evidence," John spoke up to interrupt Father Patrick's tirade. "The outreach program Father Patrick takes donations for? The one for orphan children in Dublin? Well, it seems that the nuns have never received any monies from Father Patrick," he continued, his eyes hard in his face as he glared at Father Patrick. If Fiona hadn't already fallen in love with John, seeing him as he was today – resolute and fearless as he faced Father Patrick – she would have done so in this moment.

"Now, that's just beyond wrong. To think that you would accuse me of not sending Our Sisters of Perpetual Faith their donation money – why, I just, I'm astounded that you're allowing these lies to be told here!" Father Patrick blustered. Fiona could feel the pull of his charismatic nature as people looked around, confused as to whom they should support.

"It's no lie." A woman's voice from the back of the room carried clear and strong across the air, cutting through the chatter to reach the front of the church. The entire crowd swiveled to see where it came from.

A nun in full habit stepped forward, her face set in stern lines, her blue eyes bright and assessing as she stepped forward.

"I'm Sister Mary Hope of Perpetual Faith, and we've never received any donations from Father Patrick. Had I known he was taking donations for our orphans and not bringing them to us, I would have reported him immediately."

A silence went through the church, as though the entire village held their breath at once.

"She's an imposter!" Father Patrick screeched, clearly grasping at straws. Even Garda Roarke had a small chuckle at that.

"I find it hard to believe Sister Hope would come all this way to lie on behalf of John O'Brien," Garda Roarke pointed out.

"I most certainly would not lie," Sister Hope said sternly, jutting her chin up as she stared down her nose to where Father Patrick was having a conniption fit on the dais.

"I'd like to know where the money is, Father Patrick," Sister Hope continued. "There's a great need for it."

"Yes, I would like to know where the money is too," John said, crossing his arms as he eyed Father Patrick.

"I've seen him locking stuff away in a drawer in his office." A young man, one of the choir boys, cleared his throat from the second row.

"Father Patrick, we'll need to see the inside of your drawer before we render judgment," Garda Roarke said carefully, as he nodded to two men at the back of the church. Fiona recognized the men as the muscle who had helped restrain her when Father Patrick had come for her at the cove. They walked down the aisle and to the left, past Father Patrick and into a small hallway which, Fiona assumed, led to Father Patrick's private office.

"Stop! This instant. If you do not stop what you are

doing – you'll be banished to hell forever! Your souls will burn! This is the devil's work – the witch is making this happen!" Father Patrick lunged from his chair, racing across the platform towards Fiona's chair.

Fiona jumped and froze when Garda Roarke simply stuck his foot out, tripping the priest as he lunged toward Fiona and causing him to tumble in a roll of robes and curses.

"It's all here," a voice called from the hallway. Fiona jerked her gaze up from where Father Patrick moaned on the floor to where the two muscle-men came back from the hallway, their arms filled with stacks of money.

"Please split the money there in thirds. A third for poor Sean Connor, a third for Sister Hope, and a third to be kept here until we determine if any other money was promised to others in need."

The men nodded and moved to a small table to begin divvying up the money. Garda Roarke looked down at Father Patrick in disgust.

"Village of Grace's Cove, in the matter of Father Patrick what say ye?"

Fiona laughed quietly at the resounding cry of "Guilty!" that filled the church. Blinking back tears from her eyes, her heart filled to the brim with love for her town and for the man who stood at the front of the church, his heart in his eyes.

"Please restrain Father Patrick and place him in the cell. We'll be contacting the Archdiocese immediately," Garda Roarke instructed, and one of the men came over to Father Patrick, who lay wailing on the floor. Lifting him easily with one arm, he wound the priest's arm behind his back and marched him from the church while the villagers gave him the evil eye.

"Fiona, you're free to go. And," Garda Roarke turned to address the congregation, "I would like you all to know I hold Fiona in the highest esteem. She's done nothing but help others, and she has a heart that is pure gold. Remember that, should any of you feel the need to cast judgment even after what you've seen here today."

A bolt of light shot through the single stained glass window in the church, illuminating the myriad colors in the glass and bathing Fiona in painted light. If anyone had doubted Fiona was touched with a gift, they no longer did so. Fiona smiled, feeling awash in the love of her village and of the universe. It was all going to be okay, she told herself.

"I've an announcement as well," John said, and turned to address the church with a smile before turning once more and walking over to where Fiona stood on the dais. "I want the entire village to know I love this woman – in all her beauty and her gentle heart. I'd be honored if she would be willing to join me on my path, wherever this life and the next may take me."

Fiona's heart quite simply skipped a beat for a moment as she drowned in the love that poured from John's heart straight into hers. Her future blurred around the edges, tipping for a moment, before righting itself on a new path, with John at her side. Though they'd not been dating for very long, Fiona had known almost instantly that the man who stood before her would forever change her life. Perhaps that's why she had pushed against him at first. It was scary to know someone could hold her heart in the palm of their hands – to break or to cherish.

"Aye, John O'Brien. I'd be honored to walk this path with you. Both now and forever," Fiona pledged to him in front of the whole village, meaning every word of it.

"Ah, my heart," John said, stepping up to wrap his arms around her, and sliding his lips over hers in the gentlest of kisses. Tears dripped from Fiona's eyes and she began to tremble in his arms, the strain of the week just past finally catching up with her.

"Shh now, my love, it's all right now," John soothed, running his hands up and down her arms to calm her. Pulling back, he turned to stand with his arm around Fiona's shoulders.

Just in time to see his parents storm from the room.

Bridget looked around, confusion crossing her face, before she marched from the pew to smile up at John and Fiona.

"Congratulations, and welcome to the family, John. I couldn't have asked for a better match for my daughter. I wish you both nothing but happiness and good fortune. Now, let's go to the pub. Time for some craic," Bridget said, her smile drowning out the odd note of John's parents storming from the room.

And though the crowd cheered as they began to flow from the church, Fiona couldn't shake the feeling that something was dreadfully wrong.

CHAPTER 27

HEY STAYED AT the pub much of the afternoon, Fiona drinking cider while John enjoyed a pint. She was a bit dazed by the number of people who had congratulated her and John on their engagement – as well as the number of those who claimed they were convinced that Father Patrick's allegations had been false.

Noticeably absent were John's parents.

"Are you all right then, love?" John said, his face flushed with happiness as he looked down at her. Fiona's heart swelled when she looked at him, so it took her a moment before she responded to his question.

"John, I think we should go talk to your parents. Something's wrong. The way they left like that? And they're not here to celebrate with us? I don't know, I don't feel right about this," Fiona said, tugging on his sleeve to pull him a little closer so people couldn't hear what she was saying.

A lively session sprung up from a few musicians cobbled into the front booth, and John ducked his head lower so Fiona would be able to hear him.

"I'm sure it's nothing. They probably had to tend to the animals on the farm." John shrugged but his eyes shifted to the left ever so slightly.

"John, I can tell you're lying. That's something you'll have to understand about me – about who I am," Fiona said softly, realizing suddenly just how little John knew about her. With a sinking heart, she understood that she would have to show him all of what she was. It wouldn't be fair to their relationship if she didn't.

"I… well, I don't think they are too keen on us marrying, is all," John said gently, worry crossing his face.

"I can't say I blame them after everything that's happened this week. We should go talk to them. I don't want to start off on the wrong foot," Fiona said. Besides, the O'Brien farm was on the way to the cove. She'd need to take John there if she wanted him to understand the person he was marrying – and the lineage he was marrying into.

John nodded and stuck two of his fingers between his lips, turning to emit a sharp whistle that cut through the noise and music in the pub.

"Thank you all for celebrating with us and for your support today! We're going to meet up with my parents now. Please – carry on."

Cheers met his words and the band struck up a very dramatic wedding march song, making Fiona laugh giddily as they exited the pub, with a quick detour to say goodbye to Bridget on the way out.

"I'm so happy for you," Bridget whispered in Fiona's ears as she pulled her tight in a hug. She swallowed against the tears that threatened to spill.

"We've yet to see how his parents will be," Fiona whispered back. Bridget pulled back and met Fiona's eyes.

"All you can do is be yourself, love. Nothing more and nothing less. Let your own truth shine and leave it up to everyone else to decide what they'll do about it."

Fiona nodded at her mother's words.

"I'm going to take him to the cove. Show him everything I am," she said.

"As you should. If that light shines bright for you again, being with him is your destiny," Bridget said.

"Ah, so that was the light's real meaning then!" Fiona nodded, comprehension dawning as she realized what the cove had been trying to tell her that day. It only stiffened her resolve to make nice with John's parents and show him just what she was about.

"Go. Show him your heart. The cove is telling you this is right. Trust yourself and don't let the O'Briens intimidate you."

"I love you," Fiona said fiercely, drawing her mother in for one more hug, smelling the scent of lavender in her hair, before releasing her to smile brightly at John.

"Let's be on with ourselves then."

CHAPTER 28

FIONA WAS GIDDY with excitement and nerves as they bumped up the curvy road that led to the O'Briens' farm. A warm glow from the cider made everything seem a little softer around the edges, and dulled her worry about talking to John's parents a bit.

"Why do you think your parents left instead of coming to celebrate with us?"

John shrugged, his concentration on the road ahead. She wanted to push him on this point, but perhaps the first lesson of being in a committed relationship was to know how to choose her battles wisely. She didn't press.

In moments, they crested the hill to the O'Brien farm. The sun hung lower in the sky, its rays dancing across the turquoise water, and a gull swooped lazily in a circle over the sea. Fiona couldn't help but think that the O'Briens had chosen a perfect spot for their farm. It was almost as good as the spot that she so desperately wanted to be hers. Idly, she wondered if there was some way the O'Briens would be willing to sell it to her and John to start their family home.

Their family home.

Just the thought made her squirm a bit in her seat with the giddiness that had been rushing through her all afternoon. It was such a sharp contrast to the worry and fear that had sat like a stone in her belly all week. It was nice to think about the simple pleasures of starting a new life with a man whom she was certain was meant for her.

The O'Brien farm consisted of a large whitewashed stucco house with pretty green shutters and window boxes holding cheerful red flowers. Several outbuildings were clustered behind the house, with long walls of stacked stone and wire fencing making up the pastures for their animals. As John put his truck into park and turned the engine off, his little lamb toddled around the corner of the house.

"He's getting bigger. I can't believe he knows the sound of your truck." Fiona couldn't help but laugh at its cheerful bleats as it danced outside of the truck, waiting on John.

"I've named him Lir. He's a cute one at that," John smiled as he got out of the truck. Fiona got out and crossed to pat Lir on the head.

"It's funny – he acts a bit like a dog, doesn't he?" Fiona said, cocking her head at the fuzzy little guy.

"I've never had a lamb act like this before. Hard not to like him though," John agreed, reaching out to slip Fiona's hand into his. They couldn't dawdle any longer. The O'Briens would have heard his truck by now. Straightening her shoulders, they walked silently up the walk, gravel crunching under their feet, until they reached the bright green front door.

"I feel bad that I didn't bring a gift or anything," Fiona whispered as she looked up under her lashes at John.

"You're family now. No need to bring a gift," John pointed out and pulled the iron lever that disengaged the latch and pushed the door open.

"Ma? Fiona and I are here," John called.

"Yes, well, I've eyes in my head now, don't I?"

Celeste O'Brien bustled down the hallway, an apron tied around her waist and flour on her hands.

"Mrs. O'Brien, lovely to see you again. Would you like me to take my shoes off?" Fiona asked politely.

"No, that's fine. Come on back to the kitchen now, I've got to keep kneading my dough," Mrs. O'Brien said, her lips in a tight line. She shot John a look that made Fiona raise her eyebrows behind the small woman's back as she hurried back towards the kitchen.

Fiona glanced quickly around as they moved down the hallway. Two front rooms lined either side of the hallway, one looking to be a small library and the other a formal sitting room with a small fireplace. Framed pictures covered the walls, and Fiona was itching to peruse some of the photographs of his family members. They turned to the left at the back of the hallway into the kitchen, which Fiona wished Bridget could see. Her mother would have swooned over the size of it. With two stoves, a peat fireplace, two sinks, and a place for a long table – it was the size of their entire cottage in one room.

A squat cobalt blue vase sat in the middle of the table, a few of the same red flowers from the front window boxes poking out. A lace doily – ironed perfectly – sat beneath the vase. Matching lace placemats lined the table and Fiona wondered if she was expecting company.

"Are you expecting company? I'm happy to help," Fiona said, gesturing to the lace placemats on the table.

A look of confusion crossed Celeste's face and she glanced quickly at Fiona before looking at the table.

"No, Fiona. We always eat off lace placemats in this household."

Might as well toss a glove at her feet, Fiona thought as she raised an eyebrow at the woman who was to become her mother-in-law. It appeared that the gauntlet had been thrown.

"That's quite lovely of you to provide so nicely for your family," Fiona said, syrupy sweet as could be.

Celeste looked at her suspiciously, and went back to kneading her dough. "Well, now, when you've a man who comes home every night instead of going straight to the pub, you should put on a nice table for him," Celeste said pointedly, flipping the dough on her table.

It was one thing for Celeste to put Fiona in her place. But to take a shot at her mother and father? Not happening, Fiona thought as her temper began to rise. Before she could speak, John cut her off with a wave of his hand.

"Stop it right now, Ma. This is the woman I've chosen to be in my life. She isn't going anywhere. There is nothing you can say or do that will make me change my mind. Either you accept that and make nice, or you'll be seeing less of me around here. And shame on you for being mean about Fiona's mother. You know Bridget has to be one of the kindest women in town. I'm right ashamed of you, I am," John said, his hands on his hips.

Fiona wanted to crow in delight at the flush that crept up his mother's cheeks.

Instead, she took the high road.

"John, I'm sure it's just a lot to take in all at once. This must come as a surprise to her as we haven't been very public about our dating. I'm quite sure that after a little time to absorb the news, she'll be much more amicable to our relationship. Isn't that right, Mrs. O'Brien?" Fiona said sweetly, throwing the woman an out.

Celeste let out a small sigh and then picked up her dough and put it in a pan, covering it with a dish towel. Reaching for a towel to wipe her hands, she turned and smiled at the both of them.

"Yes, it's just quite a shock, is all. Why don't we take tea outside? It's still a lovely day and I'm sure your father will want to come speak with you."

It wasn't an apology – but a small olive branch. Fiona would take it, for now.

"I'll just set the water to boil. Take this tin of biscuits out with you now," Celeste said, handing off a pretty blue and white tin of name-brand biscuits. Fiona was getting the message loud and clear: The O'Briens did well for themselves.

Unlike her family.

It was funny; she'd never really considered her family to be poor. Granted, she knew they needed to work hard to make money, but their needs were always met. Her mother had raised her to never compare herself to others – so she'd never thought twice about others with more money than they had. As far as she was concerned, the more you had, the more you had to take care of.

For the first time, though, she felt the sticky shame of *not being good enough* creep in. It was abundantly clear that Celeste had expected John to pick a different type of woman for his wife-to-be. Perhaps highly educated and from one of the finer families in town – maybe even from Dublin. Settling down with the local daughter of a drunk and a weaver had most likely not been in her plans for him. Fiona lifted her chin higher as Celeste came out with a pot of tea and several cups on a tray. She refused to be embarrassed by who she was and what she came from. Bridget had raised her to work hard and to be kind to others – something she had said would never do Fiona wrong. Time to put that into practice.

"Tea?" Celeste asked.

"Yes, please," Fiona said, smiling widely at Celeste, hoping to charm her.

Celeste just turned her eyes to the fields, and waved to where John's father was pouring feed into a trough.

"It's pretty out here," Fiona said as Celeste turned back and poured her a cup of tea. It *was* pretty outside. There was a wood table with another pot of flowers in the middle and several chairs pulled up to all face the ocean. With the sun shining and a gentle breeze, Fiona would have called it the perfect spot for tea.

Aside from the cold wind blowing from her soon-to-be in-laws, that is. Fiona pasted a smile on her face as Mr. O'Brien shed his rubber gloves and made his way across the yard. Lir bleated at him and bounced over to bump his head against John's leg.

"Ah, a cup of tea mid-day is always nice isn't it?" Mr. O'Brien said, with a twinkle in his eye as he smiled kindly at Fiona. So it was just Mrs. O'Brien that Fiona would have to contend with, then. She smiled up at him, admiring how handsome he was and imagining that John would age well, if his father was anything to judge by.

"You know Fiona, don't you, Henry?" Celeste said evenly and Henry's smile broadened.

"Sure and I do, at that. 'Twas right glad I was to see that silliness of a trial dispensed with today. Though that was some news about Father Patrick, wasn't it?"

Fiona positively beamed at the man. It was always nice to be in the company of people who refused to ignore the elephant in the room. Fiona saw Celeste press her lips together again from the corner of her eyes.

"It was a rough week for me, that's the honest truth of it," Fiona said, taking a small sip of her tea. "But I'm lucky to have a lot of people who support me."

"So what really happened with Sinead then? I'm dying to know what was really wrong with her," Celeste said, her eyes brightening at the prospect of gossip.

Fiona looked at her askance.

"Sure and you can't be serious? That's not my story to tell. I believe that people have a right to their own privacy. I'm quite certain that if you were ill, you wouldn't want the gory details dispatched all over town now, would you? Could you imagine?" Fiona said gently, but inside she was shocked. Was this really the woman she would have to deal with?

"You'll have to excuse my mother. She loves to read the glossies and her nose is always buried in a book.

Stories are exciting is all," John said with a small smile, and Fiona could read the adoration he had for his mother. She blew out her breath. Obviously she'd have to step carefully here.

"Sure and it's natural to be curious about things. Human nature after all. I just wouldn't feel comfortable breaking someone's trust."

"And that makes you an honorable woman, sure enough. Now, Fiona, dear, tell me a little bit about what it is you do? You have to know we're curious, what with the week you've had and the charges brought against you," Henry said, and Fiona quickly saw through his affable smile to the steel beneath his words. Perhaps her initial impression of him had been wrong.

"Well, you know she makes tonics and creams," John said, tension lacing his voice as he sat back and crossed a leg at his knee.

Fiona drew a breath. This wouldn't be the first time she was openly questioned, now that there had been a trial. She might as well decide just how much she was comfortable sharing with other people – including her potential in-laws.

But just what line would people find acceptable? A little bit of magick? Prayer? God's will?

"Well, John is certainly right. I do make tonics and crèmes," Fiona said, nodding at John before turning back to Celeste and Henry. "I wouldn't say that I'm magick though. I try to infuse each of my healing tonics with…" She saw Celeste's eyes narrow, and finished, "Prayer. I pray over each one and set my intention for their healing abilities. I think it just adds an extra touch of love, is all."

So. A small lie then. Or perhaps a big one, depending

on how you looked at it. But if what she was reading from this family was right, magick would not be an acceptable answer for them.

"Well, now, isn't that nice? So you just add your love and prayers to each tonic and send them on their way? You know, Fiona? I like that. I really do. That's a good heart right there," Henry said, and Fiona could read that his words were true and the earlier suspicion he had housed about her was gone.

"Your face cream is lovely," Celeste said begrudgingly, and Fiona smiled at her.

"I'm so glad you've enjoyed using it. I use all natural ingredients found right here in hills and from the waters of the cove. Some of the recipes I follow are old Celtic traditions handed down from generation to generation."

"See there, Celeste? We're descended from great Celtic warriors, you know? It's nice that you're using some of the old recipes. I always say natural is best," Henry boomed, smiling at his wife. Celeste smiled back at him and Fiona could easily read the love found between them.

"I certainly hope you'll share products from your line with me first," Celeste said finally and Fiona grinned at her.

"You'll have first access to anything I make," she promised, finally feeling some of the tension leave her shoulders.

"How is it that you can go into the cove? Legend says it's enchanted. None of us go there – not since Conan lost his life there." Celeste raised an eyebrow at Fiona in question.

Fiona cupped the small porcelain teacup in her hand as

she thought about how to answer without setting off the O'Briens' suspicions again.

"I'm not really sure," Fiona decided to give them the honest truth – or at least partial honesty. "I know one of my ancestors died there. And because of that, it seems as though I'm allowed in the cove. Perhaps because her blood was sacrificed there? I do know that I have a strong pull to the land above the cove. Every time I walk there, I dream of building a little cottage at the base of the hill, situated just so to catch all of the breezes and so that you can see the ocean from almost every angle." Fiona realized they were looking at her with their eyebrows raised. "I'm sorry, I am. Sure and it's just a small fantasy of mine, is all."

She hoped the change of topic to the land above the cove would spur Celeste to move on to other topics, but the eagle-eyed woman honed in.

"Your ancestor died in the cove. How fascinating. I suppose that might make sense – you've already given a sacrifice therefore you're allowed there. I have to admit, I've always been dreadfully terrified of the cove. I don't hold with enchantments and such nonsense, now, you know," Celeste said, and shook her head in disgust.

"I don't think you have to understand it in order to respect it," John pointed out.

"Of course not. I know better than to go there. The entire village does." Celeste narrowed her eyes at Fiona. "But if I can get special creams and tonics made from ingredients found there, I suppose I won't mind."

Fiona wanted to roll her eyes at the dichotomy of it. So going to the cove and anything associated with the magick of the cove was bad – but healing and beautifying creams and tonics made from the cove were good.

"You'll be the first in line for anything I make," Fiona promised, deciding to bypass the hypocritical nature of Celeste's comments.

"What do you suppose will happen to Father Patrick?" John asked, deftly steering the conversation in another direction.

"I, for one, am astounded that a man of the cloth would do such a thing," Celeste said, horror lacing her features, though Fiona could read in her a level of excitement about the new gossip as well.

"He's not a good person. Only focused on his gain and not caring who or what he hurts in the process," Fiona said fiercely, taking a biscuit from the tin to munch on. The buttery flakiness of the biscuit complemented the tea nicely.

"I'm sorry you were the target of his wrath," Henry said evenly. "Though I'm right proud of my boy for standing up for you. Now, it seems we have your future to be discussing."

Fiona's eyes widened and she coughed on the biscuit, suddenly dry in her throat.

John laughed and patted her lightly on the back, before turning to his parents.

"I know this comes as a bit of a surprise and that you haven't had a chance to get to know Fiona very well. But, I know she is the partner that I want in life. I've known for a long time but she's never quite noticed me before. The time is right. It feels right. Kind of like when you saw mum for the first time," John said and Fiona's heart clenched at his words, giddiness snaking through her as this man – who months before had just been someone she knew in passing – declared his love for her to his parents.

Surprisingly, Celeste's eyes softened as she looked at her husband.

"I do remember when you first caught my attention. Who was this big hulking man who was suddenly bringing me clutches of posies at the bakery?"

Henry's face reddened a bit, but he grinned at his wife.

"It was hard not to bring you flowers once I'd had a look at you. Plus, I had to beat back all the other suitors."

"Oh stop," Celeste laughed, dimpling up at her husband. Fiona was surprised to find herself beginning to like the woman. Maybe this would work out after all.

"We'll need to plan a wedding," John pointed out, and Fiona's eyes bugged open.

A wedding! She'd completely overlooked that huge detail in the midst of all the chaos of the day.

Henry chortled at her expression. "Seems as though Fiona needs a little time to warm up to the idea of a wedding. Let's give her a little breathing room, shall we?"

"I don't want to get married in the church," Fiona blurted, and then looked over at John to see what he would say.

"Sure and I can be understanding that after what happened this week. We don't even know if we'll have a new priest soon," John said easily, and Fiona's tension eased a bit.

"What were you thinking then, Fiona?" Celeste asked politely.

"I wasn't – not really. I think maybe a simple handfasting, outside, would be lovely."

"A handfasting?" Celeste raised an eyebrow but Fiona could see the wheels turning in her head. "You know, it would be fun to do something different. We'd be the talk of the town. We could have a lovely celebration instead of a stodgy wedding ceremony. It'd be great craic."

"You hear that, Fiona? Mum thinks a non-traditional wedding could be fun. Maybe she isn't such a prude after all," John said, smiling at his mother to soften his words.

"I'll have you know that I've been known to have some fun too, John O'Brien," Celeste said, her nose in the air.

"Sure and Celeste used to dance me off my feet," Henry said, laughing at her.

Fiona smiled at the lot of them, feeling a bit dazed by the turns her day had taken. Just this morning she'd been worried about being sentenced to death, and now here she was planning her wedding – having tea by the ocean with her in-laws.

It was amazing how a life could change in a matter of hours.

CHAPTER 29

*A*FTER JOHN'S FATHER had taken himself back to the fields and Celeste had begun to outline ideas for a menu for their wedding, Fiona pulled John aside. She still had something important to discuss with him.

"Will you come with me? To the cove? While it's still light? I'd like to show you something," Fiona whispered into his ear in the hallway of his house.

"I'll follow you anywhere, my love," John said adoringly, and Fiona felt warmth wash through her as she lost herself in his eyes for a second.

She hoped he would still feel the same way after they went to the cove. Fiona grimaced a little, but knew she needed to press through – to show him everything she was. She could hide the truth a little for her in-laws, but she'd never live with herself if she had to hide herself from her husband.

They said their goodbyes to Celeste, claiming they were leaving for a private dinner, and waved to Mr.

O'Brien as they climbed into John's truck. Lir watched them go from behind the fence, his heart in his eyes.

"That silly lamb. I love him," Fiona said, watching the animal race along the line of the fence after the truck as they pulled away and headed towards the cove.

"I think he should be invited to the wedding. Seeing as how he's the reason you finally started talking to me. Well, yelling at me, that is." John sliced a grin at her and Fiona laughed.

"I talked to you before then. We just didn't see all that much of each other."

"I waited for you to grow up a little and finally notice me."

"Is that so? You've really waited for me?" Fiona just could not bring herself to believe it.

"Aye, I've known it was you for a long time. I just didn't know when to make my move. Plus, I had some growing up to do myself."

Fiona tilted her head at him. John was an old soul at that. There was no way a normal man of his age would be this focused and understanding of himself – and of what he wanted in this world. The understanding and the patience he demonstrated in waiting on Fiona made her fall just a little more in love with him. She wondered if that would continue to happen – if, each day, she'd discover something else that would make her love him a little bit more.

Her heart felt full to bursting as they jolted along the lane in his old truck, nearing her favorite place in the world. Fiona fell into silence, smoothing her hands over the red dress, wondering if the light would shine from the cove today.

Would John run when he saw the true magick of what she was?

Wordlessly, they got out of the truck, but John immediately rounded the front and captured Fiona's hand with his own. They began to walk along the old stone wall that ran the length of the field in front of the cliffs, following their way to the cove.

Fiona looked over at her spot. Would it some day be hers?

John followed her gaze.

"You know, I think you may be right about a little cottage there," John said, smiling down at her.

"It's a lovely spot, it is," Fiona agreed, feeling her throat catch at the thought that her dream could actually become a reality.

"What do you say, Ms. Fiona? Maybe I can convince my father to let us build a little cottage there? One where we could look out at this view every day, and maybe grow a family of our own?"

Fiona couldn't control the tears that pricked her eyes. It was all so close – so shiny that she almost didn't believe it could be a reality.

"It would be a dream come true," Fiona said softly and gasped as John put his hands around her waist, picking her up to swing her in a circle before holding her close and letting her body slide down his. She looked up at him, delighted with him, delighted with how her world had changed so quickly.

"That's all I want in this life, and the next – to make your dreams come true," John said softly. Fiona considered his odd choice of words, but then thoughts left her mind as he slid his lips over hers in a kiss that both heated and soothed. Losing herself to his touch, Fiona forgot the world outside of them and slid into a space that felt like home.

"Now, take me into this infamous cove of yours," John said when they had pulled apart, gasping a little.

"I'd be honored to," Fiona said, tugging him forward to the top of the path. She slid her feet from her shoes, knowing that the small heels would be useless on the trail, and proceeded to walk barefoot down the path. She pulled John behind her, her hand trailing along the rock wall, as she looked for items to gather as her token gifts along the way. Finding a sparkly quartz rock, she pocketed it and scanned for some flowers.

"Gathering stuff for your tonics?" John asked from behind her.

Fiona paused mid-way down the cliff and looked back at him. She froze for a moment as his image seemed to blur out and fade, suddenly becoming translucent. It was as though he was there, then suddenly he was an ephemeral being – a wisp of a man. Her heart tightened in her throat as a certainty hit her, so strong it left her gasping for air as John stepped forward to wrap his arms around her.

"Hey now, what's wrong? Are you feeling faint then? You look as though you've seen a ghost," John said, running his hands down her arm and pressing his lips to her head.

Fiona stared blindly out at the cove, the trickles of rage beginning to work through her as she realized what the cove had been trying to tell her.

She'd get to have her happiness with John.

But much like anything in life, it would be fleeting. She would lose him to the veil one day.

Fiona couldn't decide if it was a gift or a curse – to have her happiness dulled by the prospect of knowing she would lose this man someday. She wanted to know when, how, what would happen. Her eyes blurred as John held her, the waves of the cove placid as she watched, desperately waiting for a sign – something, anything – that never came.

And wasn't that just a lesson in itself?

Perhaps it didn't matter when she would lose him. Maybe that was the gift that the cove was giving her – to cherish each moment she had with him like it would be their last. So many people took their lives and the people in them for granted. If she had to lose John – or love him from outside the veil – she would do so wholly and completely then, never taking a moment of his time for granted.

"Let's keep going. I think I just had a moment. An overwhelming day it was today," Fiona said softly.

"It has been a day, hasn't it? One for the record books, that's for sure," John said easily, nudging her a bit to continue following the path down the cove. Fiona plodded forward as they wound their way down the cliff, the dirt and sand of the path pressing into her bare feet, her mind numb as she absorbed what the cove had showed her.

Everything had an end. It was the circle of life, and the sooner she came to terms with it, the better a healer and woman she would be.

Fiona skidded to a stop at the bottom of the path, putting her arm out to stop John from walking any further.

"Wow, sure and I've died and gone to heaven," John said, and Fiona froze at his choice of words. Turning, she tilted her head at him in question.

"This cove? It's just...it's breathtaking. From above it's stunning, but when you are down here, you can really feel the impact of it. Those high cliff walls seem to sort of hug you – don't they? Cupping you in your own private world. And this beach – it's out of a fairytale, it is. I can feel it too – that press of power. I can see why you come here. And why others stay away," John said, his face alight in awe as he looked around at the cove.

"Tis magickal, at that," Fiona said, stepping forward and beginning to draw a circle in the sand with her toe.

"What's that you're doing now?" John asked, cocking his arms on his hips and looking at her in question.

"I'm drawing a circle. This is how I'm allowed down in the cove. I lied a bit to your parents. There is magick here. I'm magick too. And this circle and the ritual I'm about to perform are for your protection." Fiona watched his face carefully.

John looked at Fiona steadily, simply waiting for her to proceed.

"So, if you're okay with that then, I'll be performing the ritual," Fiona finished, feeling a bit awkward at his continued silence.

"Go on. I certainly would like you to protect me," John said easily and Fiona felt herself stiffen. Were his words a foreshadowing of what was to come? Was she supposed to protect him from something in the future?

Swallowing against the very real fear that seemed to clog her throat, Fiona nodded and ushered him to stand inside the circle.

"The purpose of this little ritual is to offer a protection of sorts when you enter the cove. You must sacrifice something or give a gift, to show you mean no harm here," Fiona said.

"Sacrifice?"

"Well, give something of yours or something you find beautiful. Either way, just an offering of sorts. Energy is all about a give and take. Your intent should be pure and if it is, then you may enter here."

John stiffened and a flush rose on his handsome face. He raked his hand through his thick hair and looked at her sheepishly.

"My thoughts aren't exactly pure when it comes to you," he admitted.

Now it was Fiona's turn to blush, and she licked her lips, lust suddenly clouding her thoughts.

"Pure as in you aren't here to try to take or abuse any of the magick found here. You won't defile or litter this space. That you respect it," Fiona said carefully.

"Ah, yes. Then in that particular case, my thoughts are pure."

Fiona laughed at him. She couldn't help it. Lust and laughter and light filled her and she turned to the water, holding John's hand in one of hers. Pulling the quartz from her pocket, she held it high so that the sun caught the facets of the stone, causing it to explode into light.

"I offer this gift to the waters of the cove where the blood of my blood lies. We come here to celebrate joy and to share truths. No harm will be brought to the cove, nor is any intended."

Fiona launched the quartz into the water and they watched it sparkle its way through the air before landing with a little *plop!* in the water.

"Now what?" John whispered from the side of his mouth.

"Now we're free to go," Fiona said playfully, and launched herself from the circle, running across the beach, the sand warm at her feet. The sun hung low – a glowing orange bulb, hovering above the misty spot where the sky and the ocean blended to one. Its rays pierced the opening of the cove, bathing the beach in its golden light, freeze-framing the moment for Fiona as she laughed her way across the sand, John racing after her.

He caught her in joy, picking her up once again to spin around in delight. As his lips settled upon hers, Fiona felt the press of magick against her skin, and then the low hum of enchantment ripple against their bodies. Pulling away from his lips, she stayed pressed close to him and simply turned her head so that her cheek rested against the chambray of his shirt, her face turned towards the water.

"John – look," Fiona said softly, keeping her arms wrapped around his waist. She felt the moment he saw it – his entire body stiffened and he instinctively tightened his arms around Fiona to protect her. The reaction charmed her. There was something incredibly soothing about being held by someone who loved you and wanted to protect you.

"What's happening? Did the ritual not work?" John breathed into her hair.

"Oh, it worked," Fiona said softly, marveling at the beauty of what lay before them.

Brilliant blue light shined from the depth of the cove, seeming to illuminate every dip of the sand beneath the surface – every craggy rock and coral outcropping. The blue light shot high into the sky mixing with the golden rays of the sun and creating a beautiful rainbow effect of light that bathed the rocky cliffs that clambered over their heads.

"I don't understand," John whispered.

"It's said that the cove shines like this in the presence of love," Fiona said softly, blinking back the tears that threatened. She'd never seen something as beautiful as this in her whole life. Whoever said magick was scary had never witnessed something as benevolent and loving as the spectacle before them.

Fiona stepped back, distancing herself from John, forcing him to look at her. She stood with her back to the cove, so that the light surrounded her, and met his eyes.

"This is me, John. I come from this bloodline. Grace O'Malley is buried here. I have her blood in me. Which means I am magick. Completely and totally magick. I can heal people with my hands. I can read people's feelings. Every once in a while I catch glimpses of people's thoughts. I can perform rituals, create healing tonics, and work my magick into creams and lotions to help people feel more beautiful. I don't know if it comes from God or not, but the intent and the essence of what I am is to always help – never harm."

Fiona drew in a deep breath, her entire body shuddered from the effort it took to tear down the wall hiding what she was – to show herself completely to John. It was as though she held her heart out in her hands to him and waited to see if he would accept it or not.

John took a deep breath and she watched him as he considered her words. Fiona had to admit that she admired a man who thought things through before reacting. She couldn't always say the same for herself.

"I'm honored that you would share this part of yourself with me. My words stand, Fiona. I love you – all of you. The magick part, the woman part, and the kind-hearted person who has pledged her life to help others. Not only am I honored that you would share this with me – I'd be honored to have you as a partner for so long as I am with you. At least in this world."

There were those words again. About being loved for so long as he would be with her in this world. What did he mean by them? She wanted to ask, but couldn't, as he was sweeping her into his arms and pressing his lips to hers.

In moments, the thought drifted from her mind as another, more urgent need filled her.

Fiona closed her eyes and allowed herself to be swept under.

CHAPTER 30

"I THINK THE cove must be an aphrodisiac," Keelin said, her voice cutting through Fiona's story.

Margaret barked out a laugh, and then immediately blushed.

"Don't I know what you and Sean were doing down there all those years back," Fiona said, leveling a look at Margaret.

"You too? Jeez, Mom," Keelin said, raising her eyebrows at her mother.

"I think we can all agree that as women, we have loved and been loved in our lives. Let's just leave it at that," Fiona said brightly.

"Yes, let's," Margaret said, hurriedly.

"Let's refresh our drinks. I need some water if I am going to nurse the princess here shortly. And we should have more pie. I don't think I'm going to like the next part of this story, which means I want comfort food," Keelin decided, getting up from the couch and stretching. She ambled across the room to pull the poker from the side of the fireplace, nudging the embers until sparks flew, and tossed a few more logs on. Crouching, she blew on the embers softly until flames licked up, surrounding the wood.

A cry pierced the silence.

"Ah, that's about right. The princess calls," Keelin said with a sigh, even though a smile was on her face.

"Bring her down, she'll like the fire," Fiona said, waving at Keelin.

"I'll get the water and pie," Margaret said, standing up to stretch.

"I can help," Fiona began and Margaret waved at her.

"Stay. I don't think I'm going to like the next part of the story either. It's going to take a toll on you to tell it. I'll bring refreshments." Even as she spoke, Margaret picked up the whiskey bottle and poured another splash into her mother's cup. Pausing, she leaned over to press her lips against Fiona's cheek.

"I love you."

Fiona held onto those words as Margaret left the room, staring at one of the flames that sparked higher than the others in the fire, its core a beautiful blue.

Much like the waters of the cove that day.

CHAPTER 31

IONA DIDN'T WANT to leave him that night.

They stood outside her cottage, stealing kisses in the moonlight, over the moon in love and lust with each other. He'd shown her the physical act of love that day on the beach and yet there was so much more to it than just his touch. It was as though his very essence seemed to power over her and through her, intermingling with hers, weaving his DNA with her DNA, forever knitted together.

Fiona knew that in this life she would never love another. The certainty was as simple as the next breath she took.

"Must we wait? To be married?" Fiona asked, pressing her hand to his cheek as they stood in the courtyard of her cottage.

"Since we aren't being married in the church, I see no reason to wait," John said with a smile.

"Though we should probably give our mothers a little time to plan," Fiona said sheepishly.

"One month. That way they can't get too carried away, but enough for you to find a pretty dress that you'll wear just for me," John said, his eyes alight with love.

"One month," Fiona said, giddiness racing through her. She smoothed back the hairstyle that she had unsuccessfully tried to recreate in the truck on the way back to her house. She was hoping to sneak in past her mother's eyes and fix herself before Bridget got a look at her disheveled appearance.

"One month. And you'll be an O'Brien. Try not to let my mother steamroll you in the planning process," John said against her lips before pulling away. Watching him walk away was like watching a part of her soul separate from her and she was surprised by how intimately attached to him she had grown already.

Fiona clutched her hands to her chest for a moment, savoring the ripe feeling of fresh love to herself, knowing their love would grow and change in time. But right now – in this moment? It was so fresh and wonderful that it was almost painful. She couldn't wipe the smile off her face as she quietly eased the door to the cottage open.

Bridget sat in the far corner in her rocking chair, a ball of yarn on her lap, her two knitting needles clicking away. The soft light from the peat fireplace played over her face, hiding her wrinkles and, for a moment, making her look like just a girl.

"Mother. You're still up. Is Father home?"

"He's at the pub as expected. Drinking many a congratulatory pint." Bridget shrugged and Fiona immediately felt bad for her, sitting alone in the near darkness. She hoped her mother would one day tell her of her own love story.

Fiona crossed the room and took the chair across from her mother, smoothing her hair back from her face and pasting what she hoped was a not-guilty look upon her face.

"You took John to the cove then," Bridget said, her eyes on Fiona.

"I did. The light shone again. You were right," Fiona said softly.

"Aye, I'm glad for you then. You should never settle for less than your heart's desire," Bridget said, almost bitterly.

"We're to be married. Within a month. We'd like to do a handfasting – we won't be married in the church," Fiona said.

"Aye, for that I can say thank you. You're more than the restrictions of the church. Your love should shine with the magick of nature – free and in the light of the sun. I think it's a perfect choice for you," Bridget said, her face brightening at her daughter's happiness.

"Do you? I was worried, but John's family seemed to take it in stride," Fiona said, leaning back in the chair and crossing her legs. She couldn't help but glance around at the small cottage interior, a far cry from the much grander front room of the O'Brien's house.

"Don't you let that Celeste try to run things with her ideas. This is your wedding." Bridget humphed as she started a new line in her knitting.

"I won't. She didn't seem very keen on us marrying. But by the end of our conversation it seemed like she had warmed up to the idea."

"O'Briens are known to be stubborn. Well, I suppose

all of us Irish are, aren't we? She probably knows John's made up his mind about you. Either she can fight it and lose her son or accept it and be a part of your family."

Fiona shivered at her words. It just seemed like the universe kept nudging her about losing John in the future.

"Something weird happened today," Fiona began.

Bridget kept her eyes on the needles as they clicked away.

"Was that before or after you gave yourself to this man?"

Fiona coughed, embarrassment racing through her as heat crept up her cheeks. She shifted uncomfortably in her seat, suddenly aware of all the now-sensitive spots John had touched earlier in the day.

"Um, that would be before," Fiona mumbled.

Bridget laughed and gestured for her to continue.

"Love is love. Go on."

"It was so strange... we were walking down the path and all of a sudden I looked at John and I could see through him. It was like he shimmered in the light and then became transparent. I can't help but feel that the cove was warning me of something in my future," Fiona blurted, desperate to have someone else's take on what she had seen that day.

The knitting needles dropped to Bridget's lap.

Fiona looked up from where she clenched her hands in her lap, meeting Bridget's now-worried eyes in the dim light of the room.

"He'll be taken from you," Bridget said succinctly.

A cavern seemed to open up beneath Fiona and she felt

as though she were falling – falling into the darkness of a despair that she didn't even know yet.

"How am I supposed to love him – marry him if I am to believe that to be true?" Fiona said, enunciating each word slowly and carefully, doing her best to hold onto her control.

"Because the cove is giving you a gift of knowing. You'll get to love – ferociously and wholeheartedly – more than most do in their entire lives. But not for always. So do you take a chance on loving from the depth of your being for however long you are given? Or do you turn your back on true love and take a safer option?"

Fiona knew her mother spoke of herself.

"What did you do?"

"I turned my back. I can't complain about my life – and I got you from the deal. But I've lived without true love. Your life seems to fade into shades of grey when you live like that. I would rather you loved to every inch and molecule of your being – for however long you are given – than to settle for the safe route," Bridget said, her expression both serious and sad at the same time.

Bridget's words were like little knives to Fiona's gut, slicing through her bubble of happiness.

"But how can I truly be happy? Truly love this person? If I know he is to be taken from me?" Fiona whispered.

"You hold on to every moment with your whole heart. Your life will be richer for it, as you won't take each other for granted. It will be the best kind of love – and perhaps it will be enough to sustain you for your whole life. But in the end, we will all experience loss at some point in our lives. If you live your life thinking you can control fate, well, you're fooling yourself."

"So that's it then? Go into this knowing I will lose him?"

Bridget looked at her, her eyes serious.

"Do you love him?"

"Yes, I do."

"Then give him the best of yourself so long as you are together. It's all you can do," Bridget shrugged.

"I swear it's like he knows. The way he phrases things…he keeps talking about loving each other in this life and the next," Fiona said, clenching her hands together in her lap.

"He might know. If he's an old soul – he may understand that his time here is limited. One day he'll step through the veil into the otherworld. We all will."

Fiona rose. She'd reached her limit of emotions for the day – from fear to love and back to fear again. It was almost too much to take.

"I'm exhausted. This day has been so emotionally packed I'm not sure what to do or where to put all these thoughts and feelings," Fiona admitted.

Bridget stood and put her needles to the side, coming forward to kiss her daughter's cheek.

"Sometimes the best days are like that. Sleep well, and know that you have a love most people will never get to experience. We'll go into the next town over tomorrow and find you a pretty dress. Take this one day at a time, my love."

Fiona tried to feel happiness at the thought of buying a dress tomorrow.

But all she could think about were her mother's words.
One day at a time.

CHAPTER 32

HE WEEKS THAT followed John's proposal were a blur.

Fiona didn't even have time to make it back to her beloved hills. Between planning for a wedding and her sudden notoriety as a healer, her time was no longer her own.

John had been busy as well, planning a surprise for her that he refused to talk about. He was careful to think of other things when she was around, so Fiona couldn't even pluck the thoughts from his brain.

She'd pushed her worry about John to the side, and instead focused on planning their big day. It hadn't started out as a big day, actually, but as word spread that there was to be a handfasting, the entire village seemed to want to go.

There wasn't a day that could go by when Fiona walked the village but that people wanted to know if they were invited to the wedding. Finally, Fiona had thrown her hands up and left the invitations to Celeste and her mother

– who seemed to be taking to each other just fine now that they had a shared goal of putting on a party.

Fiona sighed as she stopped by Dr. Collins' medical practice. They'd been working together on a few of the harder cases plaguing Grace's Cove, and Fiona found that she really enjoyed the work. Even though some people still crossed the street and made the sign of the cross when she walked past, there were many others who were willing to take her help.

There'd even been a night or two where Bridget had awakened her because of a knock at the door from a fearful mother or husband, and she had dressed and slipped into the night to assist in whatever way she could. She'd be lying if it didn't make her feel good – at least to be able to help and to be needed.

But Fiona was already worried she would get a bit of a God complex if she didn't keep herself in check. She needed to talk to her mother more about this, because she could see how easy it would be to get an ego or think she was omniscient.

And Fiona knew, deep down, that no matter what power she had to help, fate and destiny were the true masters. She was but a conduit – a tool, if anything.

Sighing, Fiona shook her head as she walked up the street, smiling at various people, and ignoring the ones who hurried across the street from her. She'd taken note of those who refused to speak to her and made sure Celeste and Bridget knew not to invite those families to her wedding. The last thing she needed was people judging her or wishing her ill-will at her own wedding.

Fiona shook her head. Here she was thinking glum

thoughts, when tomorrow she was to be married to her love. She couldn't wait to marry him and see what his surprise was for her. She had a small surprise of her own to give him, Fiona thought with a small smile as she stepped into the local goldsmith's shop.

"Hello there, David, how are things today?" Fiona called as she stepped into the small shop. With one glass window and a single counter that divided the shop from the workshop, it wasn't much by way of a shop. But Fiona knew David to be a master in his craft, so she had commissioned him to a make a small wedding band for John to wear.

She wondered how he would feel about wearing a band. Not all men in the village did. But she promised herself she wouldn't be offended if he chose not to wear one.

"Looking forward to a fun day tomorrow, that's for sure. I'm closing up the shop and everything," David beamed at her, coming forward to wipe his hands on a small cloth tucked in his waistband. A bristly auburn beard concealed much of his jovial face and kind eyes looked down at her.

"I'm sure it's going to be great fun. I'll be looking forward to the planning being done, that's for sure," Fiona said with a smile.

"I've the ring right here. It was great fun to design the warrior's shield onto a ring," David admitted, unfolding a small velvet cloth to reveal the ring.

"Oh, David. It's perfect," Fiona breathed, picking up the ring and examining the craftsmanship. "The O'Briens are descended from great warriors. This is stunning."

"Tis pleased I am to be making something of that nature for you." David bobbed his head and grinned at her.

"It's perfect. Truly. Thank you again," Fiona gushed, then looked at the small watch on her wrist. "I must be going. I'll see you tomorrow!"

"Best wishes," David called after her as Fiona hurried out, breezing past people on the street as she made her way to the seamstress' shop. She had her final fitting for the dress that she and Bridget had found at a little shop a few hours away in another town.

"Caren, I'm here," Fiona called, pushing her way into the shop to find Bridget and Caren already waiting for her.

"Sure and you're running late then," Bridget said, raising an eyebrow at her.

"I'm sorry. I was helping Dr. Collins with a tonic and then I had to stop and get John's ring and – oh. Oh my. Is that my dress?" Fiona breathed, standing in awe before the dress on the dress form.

"It is. It's turned out beautifully, don't you think? Highly unusual dress," Caren commented, crossing her arms as she studied it.

"Fiona's not your usual woman," Bridget pointed out.

"No she's not. This is going to just shine on her too," Caren agreed.

It was a lace and chiffon dress with short lace sleeves, a sweetheart neckline, and then beneath the bust it just fell away in loose waves of chiffon. It was airy, ethereal, and impossibly lovely. Beading under the bust and at the shoulders added a touch of sparkle.

And it was pink.

A beautifully dyed, blush pink, that was just this shade

of unusual without being scandalous. The tone would suit Fiona's coloring perfectly and she could already imagine the looks of surprise on her guest's faces when she walked outside in this dress.

"It's perfect," Fiona breathed.

"Well now, off with your clothes. We can't have the most talked about event of the season not have a bride wearing a perfectly fitted dress. At least not on my watch," Caren murmured around the pins in her mouth and Fiona smiled at her.

"It really is going to be the event of the season, isn't it?"

CHAPTER 33

"*Y*OU LOOK BEAUTIFUL," Bridget breathed.

They were standing in an upstairs bedroom at the O'Brien farm. After careful negotiation, they had all agreed to hold the ceremony on the small hill above the O'Brien's farm where the view of the ocean was unobstructed. Almost as good as getting married by the cove, but Fiona hadn't pushed for that spot. She was trying to follow through on the "choose your battles" mantra she had recited to herself when she had first met Celeste.

It didn't matter to her – not really. All that mattered was that she got to wear a pretty dress and marry the man she loved.

Tonight she would be Fiona O'Brien. She shivered at the thought, already anticipating some of her new wifely duties. No matter how long she had John for, she was determined to be the best wife she could be.

She hadn't forgotten about her talk with Bridget in the

soft light of the peat fire that night. But she'd pushed it
low in her mind, refusing to give the thought of losing
John too much credence. It would be easy to fall glum and
worry about something that had yet to happen. Instead, she
was choosing to celebrate the moment.

Fiona turned to the mirror and studied herself.

The blush pink dress fit like a glove – managing to
show her shape and yet still flow in soft waves around her.
Her mother had braided her hair back from the crown and
entwined blush pink roses in the braid. Her hair then fell in
loose curls over her shoulder and down her back. Small
pearl droplets hung at her ears and a tiny seed pearl necklace – given to her by her mother – was all the jewelry she
wore.

Her mother had shadowed her eyes and added mascara
so they looked deeper, larger and more knowing somehow.
No blush was needed as a healthy flush tinged her cheeks.
A swipe of lipstick, and Fiona was a beautiful, ethereal
bride.

"I feel like a goddess or something," Fiona whispered.

"You look like one too. Just wait until the villagers get
a sight of you. You're going to be the talk of the town.
Nobody is going to want a fussy wedding dress after they
see yours."

"Are you ready then, Fiona?" Celeste called up the
stairs.

"Aye, I am."

"Let's go, love," Bridget said, her eyes shining with
happiness. She looked smart in a pretty lavender dress with
mother-of-pearl buttons. Her hair was tightly coiled
against her head, and pearls ringed her throat as well.

Together, they descended the narrow stairs with Bridget behind Fiona, carrying the short train of her dress so it wouldn't trail on the floor. They stepped into the foyer where Celeste, Henry, and Fiona's father waited.

"Oh. Oh my. I wasn't expecting this," Celeste said, her eyes trailing over Fiona from her feet all the way up to her hair.

"My baby. So beautiful," Fiona's father stepped forward and brushed a kiss across her cheek. The smell of whiskey on his breath blasted her and she gritted her teeth.

"Thank you," Fiona said demurely and then looked past him to the O'Briens where Henry waited to see how Celeste would respond.

Celeste pursed her lips as she considered Fiona's choice of gown. The silence drew out between them as they waited and Fiona shifted uncomfortably.

"You're stunning. You're going to set a new trend for all the brides in town," Celeste finally decided, as though decreeing a judgment over the land, and Fiona blew out a sigh of relief.

"I said the same thing, Celeste," Bridget said.

"My son is a lucky man," Henry boomed out.

They all left the front room, leaving from the front of the house so Fiona could pile into the wedding carriage Henry had designed. Two horses draped in roses stood at attention at the front of a wagon that had similarly been draped in pink roses and crushed velvet. Fiona was helped up into the carriage and the rest of the family piled in, with Henry on the front seat driving the horses.

Fiona clutched Bridget's hand as the horses ambled off, the carriage rocking back and forth gently as they plodded up the hill behind the farm towards the spot where row upon row of hay had been stacked and covered with blankets to form a makeshift aisle. Fiona's heart clutched as John came into view, standing in his Sunday best at the front, smiling broadly at her in the carriage.

The villagers all began to murmur to each other, and Fiona knew they were commenting on the color of her dress. Just wait until they saw the whole thing, she thought with a smile.

A few of the town's favorite musicians struck up a jaunty song, as Fiona had instructed them she didn't want anything traditional. Henry pulled the carriage to a stop at the end of the aisle and got out, first holding his hand out to Celeste and then to Bridget. He turned and smiled at the crowd, escorting both women to their seats and Fiona waited for her father to help her down from the carriage.

The crowd gasped as he stumbled from the carriage, almost slipping and hitting his head on the step up. Fiona closed her eyes briefly and then opened them again, pasting a smile on her face.

"Sorry about that, love. I've got you now."

Fiona looked down at her father and saw the embarrassment and regret in his eyes and she let go of any anger she had towards him. What mattered was that he was a good man – with a huge heart. And he was here to walk her down the aisle.

Holding her head up high, she stepped down from the carriage, and wound her arm through her father's. They stopped at the end of the aisle and the guests all looked a little shell-shocked by her dress. She didn't think anyone had seen a pink wedding dress before.

But Fiona wasn't looking at the crowd. Not when her eyes landed on John. He looked handsome as could be, with his hair slicked back and his suit freshly pressed. A wide smile wreathed his face as he looked at her, and he nodded once at her as though to say, *That's my girl.*

"Ready to walk me down the aisle?" Fiona smiled up at her father, feeling happiness wash through her on this most perfect of days.

The band struck up a merry tune, one that mixed longing and happiness all in one breath, and Fiona stepped forward, ready to claim her new life.

It felt like it took forever and no time at all to get down the aisle and in moments, her hands were tied with John's as they recited vows of traditional Celtic blessings and promises. Fiona felt the current of love rush through John and into her, and she could feel the magical bond wrap them together for life – much like the rope bonds that hung around their wrists.

She hadn't known – not really – what it would be like to be bound to a man. But this was something far different and much greater than she had anticipated. As she spoke the ancient Celtic words of love and binding, she felt the pulse of magick move through her and entwine her to John.

Their eyes met, and she knew that John felt it too.

Once bound, can't be broken.

Fiona smiled softly at John as the officiant invoked the elements, following the traditional Celtic handfasting vows. As the blessings rained down upon them, she made a promise to herself.

That for however long she was gifted with the presence

of this man, she would love him in a way that few would ever know. Wholly, thoroughly, and without hesitation or reservation.

For in this life, and the one after, she was bound to him.

CHAPTER 34

THE PARTY LASTED late into the day, with the musicians taking turns and being joined by the villagers. Food and wine flowed easily, and Fiona laughed more than she ever had in her life. It was a day of magick and of blessings, and few were the moments that John's hand wasn't entwined with hers or his lips far from her own. They danced, drank, and gave mighty cheers and blessings to those who shared in their joy.

And as the sun sunk toward the horizon, John pulled her aside.

"It's time to go. My surprise is ready for you," John whispered into her ear, his words causing shivers to run through her. She smiled up at him, positively vibrating with her love for him.

"Should we say our goodbyes?" Fiona whispered, glancing over his shoulder at the party that raged behind them.

"Not in the slightest. You know a proper Irish goodbye is to slip from the party unnoticed," John pointed out, drawing her down the hill and around the side of the house. Fiona gasped out a laugh when she saw the ribbons and streamers flowing from his truck.

"Your carriage awaits, my lady," John said, brandishing his arm wide as he opened the door wide and helped her up.

"Have I told you how beautiful you look tonight? My beautiful bride in a pink dress that the whole town is talking about."

Fiona winked at him.

"I think we should probably get used to the town talking about us," Fiona teased.

"Yes, life is never going to be dull when I'm married to magick," John teased right back as he drove the truck along the road that wrapped the cliffs towards the cove.

"Are you taking me to the cove to see if the light shines again?" Fiona said, smirking at him. "I'm fairly certain it will. It's obvious we are meant for each other."

John laughed at her but said nothing. She smiled as they approached the turnoff for the cove, thinking it would be a lovely spot to watch the sun sink into the horizon on a day that dreams were made of. Instead, he veered right and followed the road up the hill.

"Where are you..." Fiona trailed off as all words simply left her.

Her cottage.

The one she had dreamed of. Where a month ago, the fields above the cove lay empty – now a beautiful stone cottage sat. With pretty window boxes that had fat cheerful red flowers, a bright red door, and shiny new glass sparkling in the windows. Fiona choked down a sob as the truck rolled to a stop in front of the cottage.

"How? How did this happen?" Fiona whispered.

"Magick?" John asked, raising an eyebrow at her before he jumped from the truck and raced around the front to open the door for her. Tears leaked from Fiona's eyes – ruining her makeup, she was sure – but she didn't care.

Her cottage. Plucked straight from her dreams and into reality. It was perfect. John was perfect.

"I love you," Fiona gushed, falling into his arms as he pulled her from the truck.

"I hope you like it. That's where I've been all this time. The land is a gift from my parents. The house is a gift from myself, and your parents. We've all been working nonstop to get this done in time for the wedding. I'm not even sure that the paint is dry on those window boxes yet," John chattered, his face flushed with excitement.

"I've been wanting to talk to you about where we would live. I was dreadfully afraid we were moving in with your parents," Fiona slapped a hand over her mouth and widened her eyes. "I'm so sorry. That's awfully rude of me. Especially after they've given us this land."

"Trust me, I understand. I wasn't about to live with my parents and my new wife either," John laughed at her and then stopped her as they neared the door. Grabbing her shoulders, he turned her so that they could look out over the green hills that rolled out in front of them, before dropping off into the ocean. The sun shot its warm rays across the water, little spikes of yellow and red slashing into the blue. It was stunning and exactly as Fiona had pictured it.

"I can't believe I get to wake up to this view every morning," Fiona gushed.

"And you'll be close to all your herbs and moss from the cove – just imagine – you can hike right out onto the land from here," John said.

"I can't believe this is really ours," Fiona whispered, so happy she felt like her heart could crack.

"Let me show you the inside," John said, pulling her toward the door.

Fiona laughed.

"I was so excited about the outside, I didn't even think about the inside!"

John threw the pretty red door open and stopped, pulling her into his arms and sweeping her feet off the ground. Stepping through the door, he carried her inside to their new home.

"I love it," Fiona exclaimed instantly and John laughed, his lips warm against her neck.

"You've barely seen it."

"It's perfect though," Fiona insisted, twisting to look around the room. The door opened directly into one large room. To her left was a long counter with a sink and a stove. A large window stretched the length of the wall and allowed for an unobstructed view of the water. The wall along the middle was lined floor to ceiling with shelves for storage and was only broken by two doors. A beautifully oiled wood farm table sat in the middle of the room, with long benches on either side. To the right was a lovely little nook that had a table and two chairs set next to a small fireplace. One of the chairs was a beautifully carved wood rocking chair with a bow on it.

"What is this chair? Who made this?" Fiona asked as John set her on her feet. She crossed over to run her hands over the smooth wood. "Is this teak? It's gorgeous."

It was at that. Smooth teak wood, polished until it shone, with wide armrests. Fiona moved the bow and sat in the chair, smiling up at John.

"It feels like it's hugging me," Fiona said, amazed that something made out of such a hard substance could feel so soft and enveloping.

"I made it. For you. I want you to know I'll always cradle you with my love," John said shyly and Fiona's mouth dropped open.

"But John, I didn't know you could do something like this," Fiona said, her heart in her eyes.

"Surprise," John said softly.

"And on top of building the house? Oh, John, it's too much," Fiona said, standing to be closer to him. She wanted to touch him – all of him – and hold him near and never let him go. This man was her every dream come true and she gasped just thinking about not having him in her life.

"Take me to our bedroom," Fiona whispered into his ear and again, John lifted her easily, moving through the door on the right.

A large bed with a wrought iron headboard sat in the middle of the room, with a simple white coverlet stretched across it. One wall of the room had a large window, with delicate white lace curtains pulled back and tied with ever-green bows. Fiona could see a small bathroom attached to the corner of the bedroom. Large wooden beams criss-crossed above her head and added charm to the room.

"I can't believe this is ours. It's perfect," Fiona beamed up at John as he lowered her to the bed.

"I want everything to be perfect for you. My kind-hearted, beautiful bride. I would give you the world if I could," John said, caging her on the mattress with his arms, his eyes alight with love.

"Thank you for my chair, for our home, for being you. You've made this the perfect day – I can't wait to start our life together," Fiona said, reaching up to run her hand down his cheek.

"How about our family? Think you'd like being a mother, Fiona?"

With her heart in her throat, Fiona nodded.

She would do anything to keep a piece of John with her. Forever.

CHAPTER 35

IONA STOOD AT the kitchen sink, whistling as she washed a bowl out, mindlessly daydreaming. It was a grey day, as was wont to happen during a winter in Ireland, but her mood was anything but.

Well, it was almost spring, and Fiona could feel it in the air. The subtle changes, the popping up of a few shoots of leaves, and the birth of new life.

John wrapped his arms around her from behind, and Fiona leaned back into him, enjoying his warmth and solid presence behind her.

It had been almost nine months since their wedding day, and true to his word, they had started a family on their wedding night. Fiona had known it, just as she now knew she carried a daughter. She'd dreamed about her – a little girl with strawberry blonde hair and sherry colored eyes, but she didn't yet know which magickal gift would be bestowed upon her bloodline.

Both sets of grandparents-to-be were over the moon about the impending arrival, and they'd filled up the second bedroom at the cottage with all sorts of gifts suited for babies all the way up to toddlers.

Her life with John was perfect. He continued to work with his father, but at Fiona's prodding, he'd also begun carving and selling his wood furniture. Fiona sat in the rocker he had made for her every night, rocking their baby in her womb, and listening to John tell stories by the fire.

Fiona's practice had picked up as well, and not only was she beginning to be paid for healings, but her skincare and tonic line was in high demand. They'd been able to put away a nice nest egg in case of any emergencies and Fiona found there wasn't much else they needed. She loved her cottage – was thrilled with the cottage. It wasn't too large, was easy to clean, and was a perfect little spot for her to nest in. She hiked the hills every day – no matter the weather – and had continued her walks even when John had begun to plead with her to stop as she neared the end of her pregnancy. Finally realizing she wasn't going to stop her walks into the hills, John had given up and started joining her.

Fiona felt good – strong and healthy – and she just wanted to finish cleaning up her kitchen before her labor started.

She'd dreamed it the night before. The morning had been spent finishing up some food preparation and now that her kitchen was tidy, she was ready. Closing her eyes and leaning back against John, she gave her body permission to let go.

As the first twinge of labor hit, she turned and smiled up at John.

"It's time."

"What? Right now? It's time?" John's eyebrows rose and he immediately began to dance around the room, not sure what to do.

"Call Dr. Collins to come out. I'll be giving birth here," Fiona said gently, watching as John raced in circles around the room.

"Here? But, but…"

"There won't be much time. Now, I've already covered the bed. Call my mother as well, please. I'm going to heat some water."

Fiona laughed to herself the entire time as John ran around in hysterics, and even later – through the pain – she continued to smile and laugh with John hovering over her. She was determined to laugh her way through her daughter's birth – and in doing so give both her daughter and her husband the gift of a laughing mother and wife.

And so she smiled her way through her delivery, even when she yelled in pain, she smiled anyway, finally laughing in relief when her daughter was pushed rapidly from her body and into Dr. Collins' waiting arms.

"It's a girl," Dr. Collins crowed.

"Do you hear that, Fiona? We've got ourselves a pretty baby girl," John said, clenching Fiona's hand as he kissed her.

"Aye, that we do. Baby Margaret."

"Welcome to the world, Margaret O'Brien," John whispered, looking down at the pinch-faced pink baby as she opened her mouth to let out her first wail.

CHAPTER 36

*T*HE WAILS DID not stop.

Fiona smiled down at her inquisitive child, now three years old, as they walked through the hills. Lir, a full-grown sheep now, followed them. Though John had tried to leave Lir at the farm, he'd insisted on following them. Now they owned a small yellow fluffy cat and a pet sheep.

Margaret squealed and babbled to the sheep before yelling for her mother.

She had yelled through most of the first year of her life, until Fiona had figured out that her young daughter was an empath. Which meant that whenever she picked up emotions she couldn't understand, she would communicate in the only way she had known how – by crying.

John had taken it all in stride, patiently rising to walk with Margaret cradled in his arms, his love always instantly soothing his fussy daughter. Now that Fiona understood her daughter better, she was able to shield her from many of the emotions that pressed at her and caused her such distress.

Even though they'd had a fairly turbulent first year with Margaret, Fiona was happy here. John continued to be the patient and loving man she'd married and she continued to love him with all her heart. Never a day went by that she didn't wake in the morning and thank God for one more day with this man who loved her and Margaret so.

Even Celeste had commented on how happy John was. She'd had one drink too many one night and admitted she hadn't thought Fiona was going to be a good fit for her son. Yet three years later, John positively hummed with happiness and nobody could deny that he was a dedicated father.

"You're going to see grandma and grandpa today," Fiona said down to Margaret as they hiked across the hill back towards the cottage. Bridget had requested a day with Margaret in the village, which would give Fiona a day on her own to work on one of her tonics that wasn't quite where she wanted it to be yet.

"Puppy?" Margaret asked, looking up at her with her two pigtails bouncing.

"Yes, Grandma will take you to see the puppy," Fiona agreed, smiling down at her daughter. There was a new litter of puppies at a farm down the road from her parents' house in the village. Bridget had been taking Margaret to see the puppies each week to watch them grow.

John stood by his truck, holding a little bag that Fiona knew carried some of Margaret's favorite toys. As soon as

Margaret saw John, she raced across the grass as fast as her little legs would take her and he bent down to swing her high into the air when she reached him. Her giggles were contagious and Fiona was laughing by the time she reached them.

"She wants to see the puppies. Tell mum she should take her," Fiona said.

"Aye, I'm sure she knows. That's all Margaret talks about is the puppies," John said. He held Margaret in the crook of his arm and bent down to slide his lips over Fiona's in a searing kiss. The years had not dampened their love as Fiona had initially feared. Instead, it seemed to grow stronger and hotter each day – all but consuming her. Margaret patted both of their cheeks as they kissed, causing Fiona to turn and laugh at her.

"A kiss for you too, my little queen," Fiona said, smooching her daughter before turning to give John one last kiss.

"I love you," Fiona breathed against his lips. Every time she kissed him, she felt like a thread of power wrapped around them, creating a small circle of love that pulsed with its own energy.

"I love you even more," John said as he brushed his hand across her cheek, his eyes warm with love.

She sent them on their way, her mind already on the tonic she couldn't figure out. Fiona was quite certain that if she added a little anise, it might just do the trick.

Hours later, Fiona was deep into mixing a fresh batch of tonic – having discarded what she had started working on that morning – when the phone rang.

A wave of foreboding hit Fiona so hard she gasped, the spoon she held clattering against the bowl as she dropped it. Turning, Fiona stared at the phone – still a novelty to them this far out in the country – as it jangled loudly from its small table in the kitchen.

Fiona wiped palms that were now sweaty on her pants and moved briskly to the phone, shaking her head at herself. It could very well be nothing. She always defaulted to the worst case scenario in her mind. She picked up the phone, cradling the smooth receiver by her ear, and took a deep breath.

"Hello?"

"Fiona, it's John. We've had a bit of an accident here. I think Margaret's broken her leg." Fiona could hear Margaret howling in the background and every motherly instinct she had kicked into gear.

"I'm coming."

"No, stay. We're on our way out. It will be easier to bring her to you and have you heal her in our home. We're leaving right now."

Fiona almost told him to stay – that she would come to them.

It was an ignored impulse she would regret for the rest of her life.

CHAPTER 37

*F*IONA PACED OUTSIDE the cottage, praying that Margaret would be okay and that it was just a simple break that could be easily fixed.

Clouds had rolled in, as they were wont to do in Ireland, and the broody grey day suited Fiona's anxious mood. Lir toddled around the cottage and out towards the field to investigate if there were any plants that he had missed grazing on. Fiona strained her ears, listening for the approach of the truck, as she paced, her nails digging into her palm.

The noise of an engine finally greeted her ears and Fiona blew out a breath in relief. There was nothing worse than waiting – feeling as though she was powerless to make a difference. Now that they were almost here, Fiona could take action instead of just sitting there worrying.

Fiona tensed as she saw John's truck race around the corner of the road that hugged the cliffs.

But what was happening? The truck was going impossibly fast and Fiona's heart quite simply stopped – just for an instant – when she saw her father's face behind the wheel. John sat in the passenger seat, cradling Margaret, a look of terror splashed across his face.

They say that things happen so quickly – in an instant, really. Yet for Fiona each hairs-breadth of a second hung suspended, dragging out over an eternity, as the truck careened into the low stone wall, its speed and trajectory causing it to launch into the air. It flew for a moment – while Fiona's life hung in the balance – before it crashed on its nose, toppling end over end, the cab crushing in on itself in an awful sound of crushing glass and bent metal.

It was as though she had flown. Fiona had no recollection of racing across the fields, her heart in her throat, tears streaming from her face, screams echoing across an empty field.

What greeted her was utter destruction. She took in every detail and yet couldn't bear to look.

Fiona crouched by the flattened cab, closing her eyes for a second before her mind tried to take in what she was forced to look at.

Her family – her heart – lay crumbled in a tangle of limbs and blood. It was hard to make out who was who, until Fiona could focus on where John had turned his body to shield Margaret, cupping her into his embrace. Margaret stared out at Fiona, her eyes dazed as shock began to set in.

Fiona almost choked on a sob when John let out a breath that rattled deep in his chest. It sounded like the death rattle heard on battlefields, and Fiona knew instantly that she was about to go into war.

Reaching out, she placed her hands on her daughter's

chest, and gasped when they were met with a sticky wetness. Pulling her hand back, horror roiled over her as she saw blood dripping from her fingers.

"No, no, no," Fiona began to keen, and closing her eyes, she reached back in and began to do a mental scan of Margaret's small body. Her eyes flashed open as she realized how close to death Margaret's tiny frame was. Gulping back tears, Fiona pulled her hands back and touched John next, doing a mental scan of his body.

It was worse than she expected, the blue light of his soul barely flickering, like a flame caught in a breeze.

"John, no," Fiona sobbed, so scared she didn't know what to do.

"Save. Her," John breathed, his eyes slitting open for a moment to focus on Fiona. "Love you. Now and forever."

His eyes closed and Fiona wailed, feeling – for the first time in ages – completely helpless.

Her hands trembled as she wrapped them around Margaret's mid-section and closed her eyes. Damned if she was going to listen to John, Fiona thought. She'd save them all – even if it meant she would die trying.

Her hands shook as her power poured from her, filling Margaret's body with light, as Fiona raced against time to heal the wounds that threatened to take her small daughter's soul into the next world.

"Stay with me, baby," Fiona whispered frantically as she raced through her daughter's body – knitting bones, healing torn arteries, and piecing together a skull fracture that made her dizzy just looking at it. As she neared the end of her healing, Fiona's entire body began to shake with exertion, her seemingly endless supply of healing power sapped.

"Momma, momma, momma," Margaret whispered, her eyes open, as she blinked up at Fiona.

"Oh, honey, oh I love you," Fiona sobbed, wiping blood from her daughter's cheek. Gently, she untangled John's arms from around Margaret and pulled her from the wreck, hugging her tightly once and then laying her down on the grass next to her.

"Baby, you must stay still. I have work to do," Fiona said to Margaret, biting out each word as she bent and stuck half of her body into the crushed cab of the truck to wrap her arms around John. Closing her eyes, she went deep within, racing through John's body with her mind's eye, trying desperately to find the flame of his soul.

When the smallest flicker of light greeted her, Fiona wept, pressing her face against John's chest, not caring that his blood ran over her cheeks.

"John, you can't leave me. Stay strong, my love," Fiona whispered, near exhaustion from her first healing, but determined not to let the light of John's soul slip into the next world. She closed her eyes, power flowing from her hands, as she began to work on the largest injury she could find, a tear of his carotid artery. Blackness crept over her vision as she dazedly tried to repair the torn artery.

"Fiona, you must stop." A gentle voice with a hint of steel behind it washed over her. Fiona ignored it, so focused was she on trying to save her husband – the man she would love for all time.

"Fiona, I am ordering you to stop this instant," the

voice said again, and this time, it came with a mental slap of energy that made Fiona pause in her healing. Being interrupted at something so serious infuriated her and she turned to scream at the voice.

Fiona froze.

The land behind her was gone, as was her daughter sitting next to her on the ground. Instead, Fiona seemed to be almost floating in a cylindrical tunnel of white and blue light, with warm rays of pure love caressing her skin.

"What is happening?" Fiona croaked, turning to look back at John's body, only to find that she could no longer see him either.

"You're killing yourself," Grace O'Malley said, stepping into the light. Fiona knew instantly who it was, as she'd seen a rendering of Grace in the leather-bound book that had been passed down from generation to generation. Her eyes burned fierce, waves of hair flowed from beneath a red scarf, and she wore a regal dress. Grace threw her chin up and tossed her hair back over her shoulder.

"I'm not killing myself. I'm saving John," Fiona said, desperate to get back to healing the love of her life.

"You can't heal them both. Your father either. You must choose," Grace said, her hands at her hips.

"I can't choose. You can't force me to make that decision. They all matter to me in different ways – different types of love," Fiona gasped, pain ratcheting through her chest as she thought about what she could lose.

"If you continue to try to heal John, you will die. You must choose to stay alive and be a mother to your daughter – while also healing hundreds upon thousands of people in your lifetime – or lose your life yet to save your husband. You can't have both."

It was like a thousand pounds of weight crushed against Fiona's chest and she gasped for breath, frozen. How could she make such a decision?

"I'll save John then," Fiona decided, immediately offering up her life.

Grace walked forward and stopped in front of Fiona, reaching out to smooth her hand down Fiona's cheek – much as Bridget did to offer comfort.

"Daughter of my daughters, you've been given a great gift. One of a lifetime, really. You're needed in this world. The lives you save in the future will one day shape the pillars of our society – our world as we know it. In order to become the healer who can change the world, you must know sacrifice. Until you come this close to the edge and come back, you'll never be a true healer. This is your line – this is where you decide if you live or die. Though the choice is yours, as I can't impinge on your free will, I will *strongly* suggest you stay and be a mother to your child as well as a healer to this world. Even if it means losing your husband and your father."

Tears raced down Fiona's face, clogging her vision, making it difficult both to breathe and to see. There was no way she could make this choice.

And yet, with a finality that ripped her heart in two, she knew that she must.

Her head hung low as she nodded once.

"I'll bring him to you in your sleep. John will walk your dreams with you. It's the best I can do, to alleviate such a loss. I'm sorry, *a ghra,* my love, blood of my blood.

It must be this way," Grace said softly, the light beginning to dim as she faded away.

Fiona was instantly thrust back into the cab with John, her arms wrapped around his chest, as his blood flowed over her face. Tilting her head up to look at his face, she wailed in anguish as she felt him slip from her, his soul shimmering above his body for but an instant, seeming almost to caress her with love, before it snapped out of sight.

She knew instantly when he was gone, his once bigger than life presence now but a stillness. Fiona closed her eyes as sobs racked her body. She pulled one hand out to reach across to feel for Cian's body. As soon as her hand connected with his warmth, she performed a mental scan to find him already gone.

Fiona was powerful, but even she couldn't bring back the dead.

"Momma?"

She pressed her face into John's chest for one more moment, breathing his scent in, his body still warm with life, before she pulled herself from the cab. Fiona brought her shirt up to wipe the blood from her face, before she turned to Margaret.

Her daughter stood, her thumb in her mouth, looking up at Fiona with eyes that were wide and scared. As an empath, Fiona could only imagine what small Margaret was feeling. Her chin began to wobble, and big fat tears coursed down her small face, trailing clean lines through the blood found there. Instantly, Fiona dropped to her knees and wrapped her arms around Margaret.

"I'm here, love. I'll always protect you. I'm here,

baby," Fiona crooned into Margaret's neck, rocking her back and forth as she picked her daughter up and walked away from the truck towards the cottage.

And tried to stem the flow of grief that would forever haunt her life.

CHAPTER 38

"THEY SAY IT was the brake line. That it had corroded from the sea salt," Fiona said carefully, smoothing her trembling hands over the blanket her mother had woven years before.

Both Keelin and Margaret looked like they'd been hit in the face with a frying pan, almost bowled over with what they had heard. Margaret's hands shook as she placed the cup of whiskey that she was holding onto the table next to the couch and stood, rushing across the room to drop onto her knees and bury her face in her mother's lap.

The sound of her sobs filled the room.

"Shh, now, Margaret, it's years past now," Fiona said, blinking back her own tears.

"You saved me, though. And I've been such an awful twit to you all these years. But you saved me, when you could've saved the man you loved. You could've had more babies and lived a happy life," Margaret said. "And here I turned my back on you and this world for so long."

"I think that, even though you remember parts of my

grief during that time, you largely blocked it out. But the accident that day is what fueled you to resist your gift and to leave Grace's Cove. You had an aversion to living here since the day you lost your father and your grandfather. It wasn't just you being a snotty stubborn teenager; there was more behind it," Fiona said, smoothing her daughter's hair.

"But I was so awful to you. And you could've let me die," Margaret's voice cracked.

"I think every daughter is awful to her mother at some point, my love. I would make the same decision all over again," Fiona said softly.

"You would?" Margaret looked up at Fiona, her heart shining in her eyes.

"Of course I would, it's what a mother does. You could say the choice was made for me the moment the car hit the stone wall. Or perhaps it was made for me when I became a mother." Fiona shrugged. "It just is."

Margaret sat back on her heels, turning to stare at the fire, her head resting against her mother's thigh.

"I remember that time. I was so young, but I remember your grief almost dragging me under. It was like a sopping wet blanket of emotions smothering me and I could barely breathe."

Fiona felt shame slip through her.

"I should have protected you from that. I'm sorry. I was so caught up in my grief, I had a hard time remembering just how much my empath of a daughter would absorb."

"What happened to Bridget?" Keelin asked.

"We lost her ten years later. In her sleep. I suppose

after what I had seen of death, it was a kind one," Fiona said softly.

"So what happened after that? How did they figure out it was the brake line?"

"Things changed after John died. The O'Briens were furious at me for at least a year after his death – blaming me for not using my 'witchy powers' to save him. Every time they crossed the street and refused to speak to me, it was like I was back in that truck staring at John's soul slipping from his body. The guilt was incredible," Fiona admitted, taking a sip of her whiskey and letting the burn of it on her tongue warm her.

"It wasn't your fault. You would have died if you had healed John. And who's to say if he would have even made it? You could've died halfway through healing him and then Margaret would have had no parents. I think Grace was right to stop you," Keelin said, rocking her baby in her arms. Baby Grace turned and leveled a look at her.

"I know Grace was right," Fiona murmured and Baby Grace smiled at her.

Christ, were Keelin and Flynn going to have their hands full, Fiona thought with a smile.

"But that doesn't make it any easier when you are grieving," Margaret pointed out.

"True, 'tis true. Grief is a tricky bastard at that. Just when you think you've conquered it or you're finally healing, the strangest things will happen to throw you right back to where you were. You'll smell a scent that reminds you of him, or think you catch a glimpse of him in the market or walking down by the bay. It took years for me to get over the shock of seeing a tall dark-haired man of similar build walking around and not immediately dissolve into tears at the thought it could be John. Even to this day, I still think of him."

"Does he visit you? In your dreams like Grace said he would?"

Baby Grace tilted her head at Fiona.

"Yes, he does at that. John dreamwalks with me. I tell him all about my day and my life. He knows about all of you and what's going on. It's a small comfort to have that – but it's a comfort nonetheless."

"Do you think it's really him?" Margaret asked, turning from her spot on the floor to look up at her mother.

"Aye. I do. I think if he was reborn, I would feel that loss in me. I don't really know how to explain. You know how I said that it was almost like our DNA knitted magickally together? Well, I could feel that. Deep inside of me. And even when he slipped to the other side, I never felt like that part of me became unraveled. There is something there that still tethers his soul to mine. So, he waits for me. And visits me in my dreams," Fiona shrugged.

"You don't think you are going to leave us, do you?" Keelin asked softly, cradling Baby Grace so that her cheek pressed to her daughter's.

"I'm fit as a fiddle, Keelin. The day I can't hike through my hills is the day you can expect me to leave this earth," Fiona laughed at her.

"Mother…I have to ask…did you, was it…did you think your father had been drinking?" Margaret asked, stumbling over the tough question.

Fiona sighed and took another sip of her whiskey, her eyes returning to the fireplace, winds raging outside.

"Aye, I did. I was so angry. Almost inconsolably angry. I couldn't fathom why John had let him drive – knowing Cian's love of the drink. It was only after my mother told me he hadn't yet been to the pub that day, after I found out it was the brake line, that I finally forgave my father. And then ended up feeling incredibly guilty for being so angry and accusing him of driving my husband and child into a wall. I can only hope he heard my apology from the other side." Fiona shrugged.

"It's not like it was so far-out of a conclusion to reach," Margaret said, stretching her legs out so that her feet were closer to the fire. Keelin put Baby Grace down on the carpet and the infant began to squirm her way across the rug to Margaret.

"No, it wasn't. And I had anger at him for other reasons – like not being a good husband to my mother or a present father to me. But eventually, I came to understand that he had a disease and, much as I wouldn't get angry at someone for having cancer, I couldn't be angry with him for his addiction. At some point, you can't live your life being angry with people. Forgiveness is a much better path. We're all just here doing our best to learn and grow, you know," Fiona said, fluttering her fingers down at Baby Grace as she wiggled her way to Margaret. Margaret reached out and hefted the baby into the air, making her squeal in delight, and held Grace over her head to coo up at the baby.

"I'm sorry. Seriously, Fiona," Keelin said, biting her lip as she looked over at Margaret hoisting Baby Grace in the air. "It's one of my greatest fears – losing Flynn or having something happen to Gracie. I think I might just die if that ever happened."

"You wouldn't die. You can't. But you have to learn how to put one foot in front of the other again," Fiona said softly.

"What happened afterwards? Were you able to heal again right away or did it take a long time?" Margaret asked, smooching the baby's cheek.

"I made it back to the cottage – literally dropping from exhaustion – and called Bridget. Then I called the O'Briens. And Dr. Collins. And the Brogans. By the time I had called everyone I could think of, I picked up Margaret, toddled to the bedroom and fell face first onto the bed. They found us there, both sleeping, but I hear tell they thought we had died as well because there was so much blood on us." Fiona looked out at the dark window. "I never did get those blood stains off of that pretty white coverlet."

Silence fell as the women thought about that. Fiona shook herself out of her sadness.

"And I slept, for almost a week after that. I woke in time for the funerals. For months after, I was almost terrified to heal anyone as I was afraid to leave Margaret alone for too long. It took me a while to trust being away from her – and to trust my own healing powers again. As for the loneliness, well, that's just part of the fabric of my life," Fiona shrugged.

"Are you still lonely? I thought things were better now," Keelin said, her face registering sadness in the firelight.

"No, not since you've been here and Margaret is home.

Plus, I'm still quite busy with the villagers. I've led a nice life – a full one even, at that. I remind myself that I am quite blessed. More so than many in this world," Fiona said with a soft smile as she looked around the room with love in her gaze.

"Thank you for sharing the story with us. It's nice to have a piece of my father back," Margaret said, pressing her head to Fiona's leg. Fiona reached out and smoothed her hand over her hair, the gesture all the women in her family used for soothing.

"I'm glad I could share him with you. It's nice to talk about him again."

CHAPTER 39

SHE DREAMT OF him again that night.

"Pretty Fiona with the dancing eyes and healing hands – how I wish to be by your side again," John said, laughing at her. Tonight they were back at the restaurant where they had enjoyed their first meal together. Fiona could all but smell the brown bread baking.

"Handsome John with the booming laugh," Fiona laughed back at him, refusing to allow sadness to seep into her dream.

That was one of her rules. If she was to be given the gift of dreaming of her love, she refused to allow sadness, grief, or anger into her dreams. She willed it, even. Because of that, she had these snapshots of happiness with John, and her nights with him were enough to fuel her days.

"Baby Grace has gotten bigger," Fiona told him, much as she would have told him over dinner had he been alive.

"I'm sure of it. She's going to be a corker," John laughed, and Fiona laughed back. In her dreams they were always young, so it didn't make sense to be talking of a granddaughter. But what was the point of dreams if you couldn't shave a few years off? Fiona trying to imagine John as an old man just didn't jibe with her memory of him.

"I wish I could bring you back. I've searched, you know, for years now. I haven't quite found a spell to do it," Fiona sighed.

John reached out and clasped her hand in his.

"Make a wish, Fiona. One of these nights, when the moon is low and the stars are bright. Wish harder than you've ever wished."

Fiona woke up after that. It was a weird request and an unusual turn from the dreams she usually had about John. Wondering if there was any merit to his request, she got up to start her day.

Keelin had cooked enough food to feed a family of twenty, Fiona thought as she examined the contents of her fridge that morning. To-go containers packed the shelves and there was no way she could begin to eat her way through it.

Fiona started her morning tea and got a dancing Ronan his breakfast.

"Maybe I'll even throw some turkey in there for you, love," Fiona said down to Ronan, and he barked once at her, seeming to understand what she said. Smiling, Fiona took out the turkey container and cut up a few small pieces to add to his bowl of kibble. Ronan bounced around his bowl in delight, causing Fiona to chuckle.

"Ah, I sure do love having you here," Fiona said to the dog.

Turning, she considered the contents of her fridge again. Maybe she would take them over to Aiden Doyle. She knew he'd been feeling under the weather as of late. As a widower, he lived a similar lifestyle to hers in that he had a little cottage that overlooked the water a ways out from the village.

"That's just what I'll do, then," Fiona decided, picking up the phone to give him a ring. Staring out at the moody grey sky from the windows above her sink, Fiona listened as it rang for quite a while before finally being answered.

"Hallo?" The voice on the other end was Aiden's, but it sounded less robust and healthy than it usually did.

"Aiden? It's Fiona. Are you all right then? Did I wake you?"

"Just a touch under the weather, Fiona. Nothing to bother yourself about."

Fiona rolled her eyes. Typical Irish man – stubborn as all get out and refusing to admit when he is ill.

"I'm ringing you up because I had a huge Thanksgiving feast with Keelin last night. I've more food than I'll be able to eat over here. I was thinking I'd drop by and bring you some of the leftovers," Fiona said, her eyes on the sky where the clouds had unleashed a sheet of rain.

There was a pause and Fiona could just hear a bit of wheeze through the phone before Aiden finally answered.

"Sure and I can't say no to a nice meal from a pretty woman, now can I?"

The usual charm that radiated through his teasing flirting seemed to be missing and Fiona began to wonder if something was seriously wrong.

"I'll just pack things up and be over around lunch then," Fiona said.

"Sure and I'll be looking forward to it," Aiden said, saying his goodbyes quickly.

Fiona stood for a moment, staring out at the rain, before she turned and bypassed her fridge, going instead to the long wall of shelves that housed many of her remedies. Tapping her finger against her mouth, she considered her options. Based on the energy she had read from Aiden through the phone, she was suspecting he had a bad cold or even pneumonia. She doubted it was the flu as he wouldn't have allowed her to come over if it was.

Later that morning, Fiona finished packing food and some of her tonics into a small basket. She and Ronan had taken a walk after her phone call with Aiden, which had resulted in a bath for the both of them. The weather conditions were beyond nasty, and even Ronan had seemed relieved to return to the cottage after just a short stint out in the rain. Now, he lay curled on his blanket, cheerfully working on the stubborn edge of a bone.

"I'll be home later this afternoon, lovie," Fiona called to him as she pulled the hood of her raincoat on and bustled from the cottage, latching the door behind her and racing to her car.

"Nasty day," Fiona breathed as she bumped the heat up and turned her lights on to pierce the dimness of the rainy day.

Aiden lived halfway between her cottage and Grace's Cove. He'd purchased a part of the O'Brien land and had built a small cottage there when his wife had died – easily fifteen years or so ago now, Fiona reminisced. He'd been a great booming happy man – the life of any party he went to. Once he'd lost his wife though, it was like the light had gone off and he'd begun to fade to grey.

Fiona couldn't blame him. Serena had been a quiet and gentle sort – comfortable with letting Aiden take the attention – and always his port in the storm. He talked of her quite often, and Fiona didn't mind. He was one of the few people she could talk openly about John with. Between their conversations, it was like these two people who had stepped into the otherworld still lived and breathed with them.

Maybe it was a bit selfish of her, talking about John with another man, but since Aiden seemed so anxious to talk about Serena, both of them allowed the other to wind long tales of days past.

It was a blessing, really, for the both of them, Fiona thought as she slowly drove along the cliff path, taking caution on the high turns. Until Keelin and Margaret had asked her about John, she'd rarely had a chance to talk about him. People always get awkward when someone has passed on. They never knew what to say, so oftentimes they just didn't say anything at all. If she brought up his name, the room would fall silent before people would awkwardly move onto the next subject. Sometimes Fiona wanted to scream at people that she wanted to talk about John. He had lived – he still mattered! But she would just keep her mouth shut and move onto the next topic of conversation.

Taking a sharp left on a small gravel road that wound up a hill, Fiona pushed thoughts of John from her mind to focus on what she suspected was wrong with Aiden. If this damp weather was any indication, he's most likely picked up a bit of a cold. Fiona honked the horn to warn Aiden that she had arrived before hurrying from the car with the basket tucked under her arm.

She didn't bother to wait at the bright green door of the small stone cottage, as the rain was coming sideways now. Pressing the latch down, she burst into the cottage in a swirl of wind and rain, laughing a bit as she slammed the door closed tightly behind her.

"That's quite a gale we've got going today," Fiona remarked, pushing her hood back and looking up to where she expected to see Aiden sitting in his armchair by the fireplace in the small sitting room to the right of the door.

And yet the room was dark and no fire was lit. Concern laced through her.

"Aiden? Are you all right then?" Fiona called, knowing his room was down the back hallway to the left. It wouldn't be proper of her to just pop back and check on him because he very well could be changing or in the toilet. Fiona pulled her dripping coat off and hung it on a hook by the door before placing the basket under her arm on the small table in the eating nook.

"Aiden?" Fiona called again, her worry increasing.

"I'm here, I…well, I'm sorry. I don't think I can actually visit with you today," Aiden called from the bedroom. Fiona walked down the hallway to find the door shut tightly. Leaning against the wall, she knocked softly.

"Is it all right for me to come in?" Fiona asked.

"I'm fine, really, it's nothing," Aiden said through the door.

"Aiden, you know I'm a healer. I've pretty much seen

it all at this point. Why don't you let me come in and see what is going on with you?" Fiona asked, using her stern voice.

Silence greeted her words and Fiona waited.

"All right then, but none of this fussing about," Aiden grumbled and a grin crossed Fiona's face. Pushing the door open, she entered his bedroom for the first time. Fiona was surprised to see that it was quite large, with the ceiling going high up with beams crossing the rafters. A green and white plaid blanket lay across a large bed that was cradled by rough hewn log planks. The only light in the room came from a small lamp on the bedside table.

Aiden lay in bed, a white nightshirt on, his eyes lively and his expression cranky. His short white hair stuck out in every direction, making Fiona want to smooth it. Instead, she crossed her hands in front of her chest and cocked her head at him.

"Receiving your visitors in bed these days?" Fiona asked lightly.

"No, I just got this damn…" A cough interrupted Aiden's words and Fiona hurried across the room as Aiden began to hack, his body shaking with the exertion of coughing. She laid her hand on his shoulder, automatically sending a wave of healing light through him, before beginning a mental scan of Aiden's body.

"Thank you," Aiden said, wiping his mouth with a handkerchief.

"How long have you been feeling this way?" Fiona asked, and Aiden shrugged her hand from his shoulder.

"Off and on for a bit. Touch of pneumonia maybe.

Nothing I can't shake off," Aiden said, grumpiness crossing his features.

"Aiden...I..." Fiona began but Aiden raised his hand to stop her.

"What's this I hear about leftovers?" Aiden said, raising an eyebrow at her. His handsome face was animated but also brooked no further questioning. Fiona smiled at him as she considered how she would want to approach the subject of healing him.

"I'll be heating it up then and just bringing it back to you in a short while," Fiona said brightly.

"I can take it in the front room – start a fire," Aiden said, but his words came out weakly.

"This here's just fine. I see you've got a little fireplace over in the corner here as well. I'll just get some tinder started so we can have a nice warmth to chase away that damp," Fiona said, moving across the room to the small fireplace tucked in the corner, windows buffeting either side. She made quick work of the fire as she tried to tamp down her emotions.

"There we are now, much better," Fiona said as a cheerful flame took light.

"Thank you," Aiden said gravely.

"Now, I've got roast turkey, stuffing, rolls, corn, and something else, oh yes! Cranberry sauce too," Fiona said, "I'll just heat everything up and bring a plate back?"

"Are you sure? I could come out front to eat," Aiden said, but there wasn't much strength in his words.

"No, no. Stay. Rest when you need rest, you old coot," Fiona laughed at him as she left the room, but the smile immediately left her face once she was in the hallway. She could cure him, she knew that much. The question was whether he wanted to be cured or not. The last thing Fiona would ever do is force a healing on someone who didn't wish to be healed.

This was a first for her though. Almost everyone she had encountered in all the years of her being a healer wanted to be fixed – saved. Yet she didn't get that sense from Aiden. Fiona bit her lip as she piled food onto two sensible white earthenware plates and slid them in to warm.

She leaned back on the counter and stared out into the stormy sky as she considered what another loss would mean to her.

CHAPTER 40

*L*ATER SHE SAT by Aiden's bed, having cleared away their meal, and met his eyes.

"You and me – we've been pretty good for each other, haven't we?" Fiona began and Aiden smiled at her.

"You're a good friend to me, Fiona. The only one who would let me talk about my pretty Serena. You're pretty too, of course. But she's prettier."

"I've no doubt about that, Aiden. She was a lovely woman. And sure she was lucky to have a handsome man like you. Almost as handsome as my sweet John was," Fiona teased, eliciting a laugh from him that turned into a hollow cough. Fiona immediately reached out her hand and eased his cough with her power.

Aiden slanted a look at her.

"I don't suppose you know how not to help people, do you?" Aiden asked softly.

"It's part of who I am. I'll respect your wishes. The... the trouble I'm having right now is whether to be telling you just what it is you have," Fiona swallowed deeply.

Aiden moved his hand down until it slid over hers on the sheet.

"Aye, I know what I have. I've asked for it," Aiden said, squeezing her hand tightly and Fiona jerked away at his words.

"You've asked for it? To die? Why don't you just go out front and jump off the cliff then?" Fiona asked angrily and Aiden chuckled, this time reaching out to pat her – sending his own brand of soothing energy to her.

"Because everything in its own time, Fiona. You know that as well as anyone else. I just sensed that my time was closing in...and, well, I asked to be back with Serena. On the winter solstice, it will be exactly fifteen years since she left me. I think that would be a nice time to join her," Aiden said softly and Fiona closed her eyes.

"You did manifest this then," Fiona whispered.

"I suppose. In my own way. Though I'm not sure I would have chosen lung cancer as the way out," Aiden said, another cough ratcheting through his body. Fiona was surprised she had missed it over all the times she had visited him. But now that she looked closer, she could see he had lost weight and his skin was much more pale.

"I can't believe I missed reading this," Fiona admitted, feeling guilt wash over her. This was her friend and she should have taken care of him before it got too late. Even if that wasn't what he wanted.

"I hid it from you. When I knew you were coming over – I dressed and acted super healthy. But when you left, I would sleep for hours. I also purposely didn't think of it when you were with me – instead choosing to talk of happier times."

"You diverted me," Fiona murmured, clenching her hand around his knobby knuckles.

"I did at that, lass; it wasn't for you to worry about," Aiden said.

"You're my friend. It's my job to worry. And, good lord, Aiden, I have to tell you – I can heal you. At least I'm fairly certain I could. Or prolong your life and give you a healthy few more years. You must know that – that I want that for you," Fiona's voice cracked.

"Ah, my sweet Fiona, the best of friends to me. I do know that. I've known since the specialist told me six months ago that you would be able to help me. Please understand that this isn't about you though. This is my choice – I'm going to be with my pretty Serena."

Fiona's head felt leaden as she looked at the plaid comforter, her gaze tracing the stitching where the threads wove together. She reminded herself that each person's journey on this earth was their own tapestry, intermingling with other threads, some leading to completion and some fraying and falling short.

"Is this what you truly want? From the bottom of your soul and in the depths of your heart? Because saying it and going through it are two different things," Fiona asked, meeting his eyes once again.

"Yes. I've had many a lonely night to consider this. This is what I want. I know Serena would want it too. She misses me as much as I miss her," Aiden said softly, his eyes growing soft around the edges as he said it.

Her breath caught in her throat.

"Does she visit you? Do you see her?" Fiona whispered.

"Only in my dreams," Aiden said.

"Och, yes, that's what I meant. Does she dreamwalk with you?"

"You weren't asking if she sits down and has dinner with me every night? Her ghost sipping whiskey with me by the fire?" Aiden chuckled – a chuckle which devolved into another coughing fit.

"Aye, I suppose that I did mean that. But John dreamwalks with me as well. Some days it's the best part," Fiona sighed.

"Mine too," Aiden said, smiling gently at her.

"What can I do for you?" Fiona whispered.

"Come, sit with me, help me pass the time. I've most of my affairs in order, but maybe you could help donate a few things of mine. Also, I've told nobody in the village, but I wouldn't mind having one last feast – a spot of music to listen to with friends – before I go," Aiden said, raising his eyebrows in question at her.

"I'll stay here, in the second bedroom with Ronan to keep you company as well," Fiona decided. "And you'll have the best going away party ever."

Aiden laughed, his eyes lighting in delight.

"I like that. A going away party. Yes, let's have it."

Fiona tilted her head at him.

"You're certain it will be the winter solstice?"

"Near's I can tell. At least that's what Serena keeps telling me."

"Do you be believing her then? What she tells you in your dreams? I've always wondered what's my subconscious and what's really John." Fiona raised an eyebrow at

Aiden as she leaned over to pull the cover up a little further.

"Aye, I do at that. I suppose if you held my feet to a fire and demanded why, I would only be able to say 'tis a feeling. A strong one. My lass wouldn't be lying to me," Aiden said.

"No, I suppose John wouldn't lie to me either." Fiona's thoughts darted back to her dream the night before and John imploring her to make a wish. It seemed she would need to have a talk with him in her sleep this evening – maybe she could pull some more information out of him.

"I'm going to head home, Aiden. I'll bring over some sheets and towels, as well as pack up some clothes for myself. The solstice isn't all that far off, you know. I'll help you in your last days – and – I don't want to hear any argument about this," Fiona raised a warning finger at him, "I will ease some of your pain. I promise not to heal you. But I can make your last days more comfortable. Can we call that a compromise?"

Aiden closed his eyes for a moment and then took a deep breath, turning to smile at her from the pillow.

"Yes, I'll agree to that. I am in pain, though I don't like to admit it and I've refused treatments from the doctors."

"You let me take care of that. I have a few tricks up my sleeve, you know," Fiona winked at him as she stood up. "Now, you get some sleep. I'll be back in a short bit and you'll have Ronan to jump up here and keep you company. You'll like that – he's always taken to you."

"Fine dog," Aiden agreed, but his eyes were already slipping closed.

How had she missed how sick he was? Fiona marveled

at the fact that one of her good friends was near death and she'd never once glimpsed it.

Maybe Aiden was right – she hadn't been meant to. Even if she didn't agree with his path, it wasn't her place to change it.

CHAPTER 41

*T*HE DAYS LEADING up to the winter solstice flew by and yet seemed to slow down – each moment frozen – as she helped Aiden to celebrate the last of his time on this earth.

True to her word, she'd moved in that afternoon and there had been a steady stream of villagers arriving to visit since. Fiona quickly learned how tiring this was for Aiden so she began limiting visits to just one hour in the morning and one hour in the afternoon.

It was nice to have someone to cook for again, though he wasn't eating much. Fiona gave away most of his belongings as he'd asked and had deeded his cottage to the local tourism office. She heard tell they were discussing making it a tourist center with information on all the stone circles found in the surrounding hills. She supposed the building could have a far worse use.

Ronan was his comforting self as usual – hopping up to keep Aiden warm and provide comfort in his pain. Fiona had borrowed her old leather book back from Keelin and they'd conferred over which rituals to use that would ease pain but not heal. It wasn't as easy as she had thought it was going to be, as the very act of easing pain often went hand-in-hand with healing the root cause of the pain.

Keelin was here now, helping with the party preparations for the afternoon. Fiona had wondered if she should host the party on the winter solstice, but Aiden had asked for privacy on that night.

One must always respect a dying man's wishes.

And so Keelin came, and Cait would be arriving shortly with drinks from the pub. The rest of her girls would be following suit. They'd agreed upon a rotating party of sorts – so that the house was always full of music and voices but never getting so packed that it would overwhelm Aiden. It was more of an open house really.

"He told me to leave baby Grace with him. Isn't that the darnedest thing? I hope she doesn't run him ragged," Keelin said, coming from the bedroom where she had stopped to say hello to Aiden, Baby Grace on her hip all decked out in a pretty green velvet party dress.

"Somehow that doesn't surprise me," Fiona muttered, stirring the pot of beef stew she had set to simmering.

"What's that supposed to mean?" Keelin asked.

Fiona wondered when she should tell Keelin that Baby Grace was actually the soul of Grace O'Malley – the infamous one who had birthed their bloodline. She figured they had a little more time yet before she needed to reveal that information. Keelin needed to settle into motherhood and learn herself and her baby first before Fiona dropped a huge proclamation on her head. All in good time, she reminded herself.

"He loves babies, that's all. And Gracie's quite the charmer," Fiona pointed out. She secretly wondered what sort of magickal conversations the two were having back there.

"She is, isn't she?" Keelin said, her heart in her eyes as she spoke of her baby girl.

"Aye, I suspect she's going to be unforgettable," Fiona laughed and focused again on her cooking, "Now, get plates set out on that table. I'm thinking we should stack everything in one long row and people can serve themselves as they come and go."

"Sounds like a plan," Keelin said, moving across the room to place the plates on the table. "Fiona, are you all right? I'm worried that Aiden's death is going to be another great loss for you."

Fiona tapped the spoon against the side of the pot and then placed it in the rest beside the soup pot. Turning, she wiped her hands on the towel and studied Keelin.

"Aiden's but a good friend to me," Fiona said gently.

"I know. I guess I had kind of hoped for more – at least for a while when you were stopping over here so much," Keelin shrugged and folded napkins in neat little squares.

"We are good company for each other, but much of our time is spent in the past – remembering our loved ones."

"So you're okay with him passing on?"

"I wouldn't say I'm happy about it as I'll certainly miss him. But Aiden wants to be with Serena. And I can't begrudge a friend his happiness now, can I?" Fiona asked. The front door swung open and they both turned as Cait, nimble as ever, breezed in with her arms full of wine bottles.

"I've more in the truck," Cait said, her slim body strong.

"You didn't leave that baby in the truck on its own, did you?"

"Of course not. I left the baby to pull pints at the pub." Cait rolled her eyes and set the bottles on the table before breezing back outside into the windy grey day – a pint-sized bundle of energy.

"She's a mouth on her, that one," Fiona observed and Keelin chuckled.

"And motherhood has certainly not dimmed it," Keelin said and then tilted her head at the back room. "I think I've heard a cry from Grace. I'll just go check."

The wine glass Fiona was wiping a smudge from almost fell out of her hand when Aiden walked out from the back room – fully dressed and color blossoming in his cheeks – following Keelin, who cradled Baby Grace. Fiona gaped, looking between Baby Grace – who had a decidedly mischievous expression on her face – and Aiden. His hair was combed back neatly, and he wore a nice red plaid shirt tucked into pleated corduroy pants. The greyness had vanished from his skin tone and his eyes seemed to twinkle even more.

"Aiden, I can't believe you are up," Fiona said, putting the wine glass down and crossing to stand by him. She tried not to hover, but a part of her wanted to pat him down and do a mental scan. Had Baby Grace done something when they were alone in his room?

"I'm not about to miss my going-away party," Aiden said pointedly, brushing a kiss across Fiona's cheek before moving to the front room where he bent stiffly and stoked the fire. "Tomorrow we'll have to get a Yule log burning for the solstice."

Fiona narrowed her eyes at his back. He still wanted this to be his going away party and yet he wanted to burn Yule log that was typically burned for twelve days? She opened her mouth to speak but the door blew open again – and this time half the villagers followed Cait, their arms full of food and instruments.

"Hallo all! I made it out of bed just for some good craic," Aiden boomed, settling into the armchair by the fire, and in moments, he was surrounded by friends. Fiona just shook her head and moved to pour him a glass of Middleton Very Rare, his favorite Irish whiskey. She stopped at the tall highchair where Keelin had placed Baby Grace with a few pieces of mashed up banana in front of her. Crouching, Fiona met her eyes.

"I'm on to you," Fiona whispered.

Baby Grace chortled and threw a piece of banana from her chair.

"Nice try at distraction, but I'm sure as the sun does shine that you pulled a little trick back in that bedroom."

Baby Grace slapped her palm on the tray, mashing a banana between her fingers gleefully.

Fiona reached out and ran her hand over the soft curls on Grace's head.

"And I'll be thanking you for it too. This is a fine gift," Fiona whispered, kissing her head. Baby Grace stilled as she pulled away and sure enough, the baby winked at her. Fiona found herself chuckling as she moved into the kitchen to stir the soup again.

"Soup's almost done and we've plenty more food to go

around," Fiona called to the room as the first lilting note of a tin whistle floated across the room. In moments, a fiddle joined it.

Late into the night, the small cottage rang with laughter and music – the notes carrying high on the stormy wind that battered the cottage – light spilling from every window. From afar, it looked like the cottage was aflame, a beacon of life and love in the dark December night.

CHAPTER 42

"$\mathcal{M}$AKE A WISH, pretty Fiona. Make a wish," John whispered to her in her dreams that night. He'd been repeating the same thing in her dreams every night for weeks now. Maybe it was the whiskey she'd drunk at the party that night, but Fiona broke her rule about being angry in her dreams and swung on him.

"You keep saying that! But you don't tell me what you mean!" She seethed, walking in circles around him. In this dream they were on the cliff overlooking Grace's Cove, the sun's warmth gentle on her shoulders – much like the love that radiated from John.

"When the moon is low and the stars are bright – wish you may, wish you might," John sang to her. Even though his voice was teasing, she caught a hint of seriousness behind his words.

"John, nursery rhymes aren't helpful right now," Fiona said, surprised to find herself near tears. She never cried in her dreams with John – ever. The moments spent with him were far too precious to be wasted in tears or anger. And yet, here she was – angry and in tears.

"Wish you may, wish you might," John sang, brushing his hand across her cheek before he faded from sight and she was left blinking up at the beams that crisscrossed the ceiling of the guest bedroom in Aiden's cottage. Her eyes watered and Fiona couldn't help but feel anger roil around in her stomach. It wasn't fair. It wasn't fair that she'd lost John and now she was losing her friend Aiden.

Life's not fair.

Her mother's favorite phrase breezed through her mind and Fiona closed her eyes for a second. Her mother hadn't taught her to weep into her pillow when something bad happened. She knew well enough that tears didn't make the bad go away.

Fiona blinked again as she looked around at the room. Daylight peeked in her windows. Mid-day light at that. Fiona sat up as silence greeted her.

"Oh shite, shite, shite," Fiona breathed, swinging her legs from the bed and slipping her feet into her house shoes. She hadn't meant to sleep so late, but the party had raged late into the night – Aiden staying strong through the thick of it. More than one person had pulled her aside to comment on his good health. Fiona had just shrugged her shoulders helplessly, unable to explain it.

"Aiden?" Fiona called, stuffing her arms into her robe and tying the belt around her waist as she opened her door and called for him once again.

"I'm here," Aiden called and Fiona turned towards the bedroom before stopping. The voice had come from the front room. Her head tilted in confusion, she marched out into the front room.

"And what is it you think you're doing?" Fiona asked him sternly, as he stood by the stove – a rasher of bacon in the frying pan.

"Cooking me last breakfast, that's what," Aiden said cheerfully.

Fiona eyed him. His color still looked good and he certainly didn't look like he was on his deathbed. She moved across the room and nudged him out of the way of the stove.

"Sure and you won't be cooking your own last breakfast now," Fiona said, nodding at him to go have a seat by the table. "Get yourself some juice and I'll have tea popping in a bit."

"Actually, I wouldn't mind a fine Irish coffee," Aiden decided.

Fiona turned and leveled a look at him.

"I suppose since you aren't operating any heavy machinery today, you can have your drink with breakfast," Fiona decided and Aiden chuckled. She set the bacon on low and moved to the fridge, finding a bottle of heavy cream. As she whisked it in an aluminum bowl, she looked over her shoulder at Aiden. "Great craic last night."

"'Twas at that. A fine going away party – fit for a king." Aiden smiled at her and she just could not get over the change in him. It was the happiest and healthiest she had seen him in weeks. Finally, she tapped the whisk on the bowl and turned, her hands on her hips.

"That's it. You'd better tell me what went on with you and Baby Grace. I swear that child put a spell on you because this is the healthiest I've yet to see you. And you're just so happy," Fiona exclaimed.

"Ah, yes, fine baby that Grace is. I suspect she's going to do great things in this world," Aiden nodded, taking a sip of his orange juice.

Fiona waited. This wasn't the first time someone had avoided her questions. Finally, Aiden sighed.

"How's that bacon coming along?" he asked hopefully in a last ditch effort to avoid her question. Fiona just raised an eyebrow at him.

"Listen Fiona, I'm happy because I get to see Serena tonight. I've waited a long time for it. Gracie gave me the gift of peace, 'tis all," Aiden said, shrugging his shoulder as he looked at Fiona sheepishly.

Fiona thought about it for a moment. She supposed all he had talked about was seeing Serena again. Perhaps his own happiness was the cause for his burst of health.

"I suppose that makes sense. People sure were questioning me about you last night," Fiona said, turning back to pour a cup of coffee for him with a healthy dash of the Irish in it. She scooped some cream – now thick from her whisking – onto the top of the coffee and set it in front of Aiden.

"That's a fine cup of coffee right there," Aiden said, his eyes shining – the picture of health.

Fiona dropped it. This was the man's last day on earth. If he wanted to talk about easy things, that was his choice. She wasn't about to badger him with questions all day.

"So, Aiden, why don't you tell me how you'd like to spend the day?"

"I'd like to go to the cove."

Fiona turned. "Sure and you won't be fooling me into thinking you're healthy enough to hike down into the cove now?" Maybe the man had taken complete leave of his senses.

Aiden chuckled, saluting her with his coffee.

"I just want to see it. Prettiest part of all of Ireland. I'd like to fill my last day with pretty things."

"Well, I should probably go then," Fiona teased.

"You're a beautiful woman, Fiona," Aiden said seriously. Fiona turned and eyed him.

"You're not so bad yourself," she smiled back at him. He really wasn't either. He reminded her a lot of John with his tall build and broad shoulders. Nobody would replace her John, but that didn't mean she couldn't admire a handsome man when she saw one.

"John was a lucky man," Aiden observed as Fiona brought him a plate of a full Irish breakfast, complete with a sliced roasted tomato on the edge of the plate.

"I was a lucky woman," Fiona sighed and made herself an Irish coffee before sitting across from Aiden and taking a small sip. "I think I'm a little jealous of you."

"Fiona O'Brien, I'm shocked," Aiden said, his fork stopping halfway to his mouth.

"Not that you are thinking you're dying today – but that you'll get to be with Serena again. Good lord, but that will be quite the reunion," Fiona held up her coffee cup to him.

"It'll be divine, I'm sure."

"Tell John I love him," Fiona whispered, turning to look out at the water for a moment so that the tears that spiked her eyes wouldn't fall.

"Tell him that yourself," Aiden said, and Fiona whipped her head around.

"What's that supposed to mean?"

"Just that, you know, they're with us. He can hear you," Aiden said quickly, shoving a forkful of eggs in his mouth.

"Right, of course," Fiona said immediately.

"What say you, pretty Fiona? Care to drive me to the cove after breakfast?"

Fiona scanned the horizon again. Though grey clouds hung low in the sky where the water met the air, no rain fell.

"It looks like you'll be having yourself a clear winter solstice. I'm happy to drive you over to the cove," Fiona said, automatically reaching out to stroke Ronan's ears when he pressed his snout onto her knee. "And Ronan would probably like a good run."

"It will be a lovely last day," Aiden all but sang and Fiona marveled at him. She wondered if she would be able to greet her own death with such grace and joy as the man who sat before her.

If John was waiting for her she certainly could.

CHAPTER 43

OR LAST SIGHTS, you couldn't go wrong with the cove, Fiona thought as she and Aiden walked slowly along the path that would lead them to the top of the cliffs that hugged the enchanted waters. Their pace was slow, as though they didn't have a care in the world, and their thoughts were their own. Small talk had no place in a moment like this.

Fiona smiled as Ronan raced across the field, his ears streaming behind him, chasing after some imaginary fierce beast. She could just make out a wisp of smoke from over the ridgeline – and it comforted her to know that her family was safe and warm on this solstice day.

They finally reached the beginning of the path and Fiona pulled a worn tartan blanket from the tote bag she carried and held it up to Aiden.

"Shall we sit?"

Relief passed across Aiden's face. Even though he'd been showing good health over the last day, Fiona reminded herself that he was still very, very sick. She fluffed the blanket out in the grass by the side of the cliff and then offered her arm to Aiden. He lowered himself awkwardly to the ground, his weight slightly difficult for Fiona to support. A sigh escaped him as he settled himself and Fiona sat next to him, pulling a second blanket from her tote.

"And one to keep us warm," Fiona said, unfolding it and draping it over Aiden's shoulders, and then pulling it around herself until they were cocooned in the soft wool. Ronan ran back and nuzzled between them, panting with exertion, his furry body radiating heat between the two of them.

The cove lay at their feet – picture perfect on this grey day, its waters serene. The mood was calm, the waters unfazed by the enormity of the weight carried on the shoulders of the man sitting above them. Fiona took that as a good sign – that things would transition well for Aiden. A gentle sort of mood began to fill her as she watched the hypnotic rhythm of the waves rolling onto the beach and returning back into the cove.

Finally, Fiona embraced the calm. She found her own sort of peace with Aiden's happiness at leaving this world.

Relax, the water seemed to say, it's all a circle. He'll know nothing but happiness, the cove whispered to her on the wind. Fiona almost wondered if the trip to the cove had been for her or for Aiden. Leaning over a little, she bumped shoulders with him.

"I'm going to miss you my friend. But, the cove, well, it seems to be telling me that you'll enjoy an easy transition. You'll be at peace and you'll be so happy to be back in Serena's arms."

Aiden looked at her and his face positively glowed with happiness.

"This was a good choice. Just look at it here – it's really everything, isn't it? The cliffs jutting so proudly into the sky – the waters so stunning that wash onto these shores. They've seen thousands of years of change, sadness, love, life, and death. I'm going to leave this world and be planted in another. I'm as much a part of the fabric of this world as I am of the next."

Threads, Fiona thought. They were all threads woven together in the fabric of the universe.

"Would you like me to scatter your ashes here?" Fiona asked. They had discussed a few different funeral arrangements for him, but had yet to settle on one. Aiden had said it was too morbid and that he would leave it in instructions in a packet by his bed.

"No need to get all maudlin on me, Fiona," Aiden said gravely, and Fiona chuckled, bumping him again with her shoulder.

"I'm not the one choosing to die, you know," Fiona pointed out.

"Aye, you aren't at that. I think after the cove, I'd like to sit by the fire for a bit, with the Yule log lit. I have a few more things I wish to write. When the evening comes, I'm going to retire to my bedroom. I'll ask that you leave me be, until you know for sure I'm gone. I'd like to greet death on my own," Aiden said softly.

Fiona considered his words as she stared out at the

water of the cove, the low winter light turning the water almost slate blue.

"Aye, I'll be honoring a dying man's wishes, won't I?" Fiona said lightly.

"You're a fine woman, Fiona. I'll be sure to stop by in your dreams and say hello one of these days," Aiden teased, and Fiona found she could smile – even in her sadness.

"Shall we?" Aiden asked.

"We shall," Fiona rose, pulling the blanket with her and reaching out a hand to Aiden to pull him up. He turned and began to walk slowly towards the car, while Fiona bent to lift the blanket they had been sitting on and shake it out.

Ronan's soft bark made her head shoot up.

A brilliant blue light, ethereal and stunning in its display, shone deep from the slate blue waters of the cove. Fiona's mouth dropped open as she spun around to look at Aiden and then back to the cove.

"But... but..." Fiona whispered, as tears sprang immediately to her eyes. If the cove was telling her that Aiden was meant to be her true love, well, it had really crappy timing. It didn't even make sense, Fiona seethed in her head, as she shook her fist at the waters. She didn't even have romantic feelings for Aiden.

"I don't know what you're trying to tell me," Fiona finally said, feeling hopeless and angry at the cove – at the bloodline that had given her these gifts. The water had shone once for her – for the true love of her life. It wasn't supposed to shine again for Aiden.

Confused, a mix of sadness and anger making her feel a little sick to her stomach, Fiona turned her back on the cove and followed Aiden, Ronan at her side.

And vowed to follow a dying man's wishes to a T, irrespective of what the cove was trying to tell her.

CHAPTER 44

"*I*'VE GOT THE Yule log started," Aiden called.

Fiona had gone to the guest room when they'd returned. She'd needed to change and shake the chill from her bones that had followed her from the cove.

"Would you like a tea? Another Irish coffee?" Fiona asked as she came into the main room.

Aiden saluted her with a glass of whiskey from where he sat by the fire, a pretty Yule log just starting to burn in the fireplace. He pointed to another glass with whiskey by the overstuffed armchair next to him.

Fiona took it and curled up in the chair, sipping the whiskey slowly as she watched the flames. So much of life was contemplated over the flames of a fire, she thought.

"You'll keep this going for me? After? The whole twelve days?" Aiden asked.

"I suppose I can manage that," Fiona said with a smile.

They passed the afternoon there, trading stories of times past, before Fiona finally grew silent and just listened to Aiden talk about his life with Serena and all the things he was looking forward to about seeing her again. It made her heart sad, and filled her with loneliness for the first time in a really long time. A part of her desperately wanted to say she would be seeing her love soon as well.

As the shadows grew longer and the light outside grew dim, Aiden turned to her.

"It's time."

"I think I will stay out here. Take comfort by the fire," Fiona said softly, sadness already seeping through her.

Aiden stood as did Fiona and wrapped her in his arms. She leaned into his comforting weight, his arms around her feeling solid, and pressed her face to his chest. They stood like that for a moment, no words needing to be said, as love surrounded them both.

Fiona desperately wanted to reach out with her hands and heal him. Instead, she stepped back and looked up at him.

"Safe travels, my friend," Fiona whispered, her hand to his cheek. He turned to kiss her palm lightly – almost as a lover would.

"You've honored my life greatly by being in it – as well as allowing me to end it on my terms. It's been a pleasure and an honor to have been graced with you in my life," Aiden said, bringing his fingers up to his forehead in a salute.

Fiona smiled and watched him turn, her eyes on him the entire time as he walked his last steps and closed the door to his room.

"And now, we wait," Fiona murmured down to Ronan, her eyes once again back on the fire.

Time seemed to draw out and suspend in the air, and soon Fiona found it almost impossible to keep still. Her whole life she had been a doer – someone who took care of others. To sit by a fire and just wait for someone to die – well, that was virtually impossible. She looked around the room, but it was spotless, as was the kitchen. She'd already cleaned obsessively earlier today.

"Let's take in some fresh air," Fiona decided. Aiden didn't need her to sit here – he'd only asked that she not bother him until she was certain he had passed on. There had been no outward indication that he had passed – and a quick scan with her mental senses showed there was still other life in the cottage.

It was the winter solstice after all, Fiona thought as she tiptoed to her room and grabbed a thick sweater, her coat, and a few of her crystals and magickal tidbits. It would do her well to honor the solstice in the ancient tradition of her people.

"Come on boy," Fiona whispered and padded softly to the door where she slipped on her Wellies and slid the door open quietly. Ronan walked out next to her and they stood in the darkness for a moment, the only light spilling from the front window.

"Let's walk this way, Ronan, away from his bedroom window. I don't want to bother him if he is staring out of it," Fiona decided and hung a left.

The cold pressed at her, and Fiona tugged her hat lower on her forehead to ward off the damp chill of an Irish winter. Her feet made no sound as she walked through the hills, and she could barely see a flash of the white in

Ronan's fur as he raced ahead over the hills. The moon was low, but at least the stars were bright.

Fiona froze.

CHAPTER 45

A TREMBLING BEGAN to overtake her body – Fiona didn't know if it was shock or if it was an understanding that seemed to seep through her, causing her body to shake in wonder.

Could it be? Would it be possible?

Fiona searched her brain, thinking about the Winter Solstice and everything that it stood for. The Winter Solstice was when the wheel of the year revolved past death and towards lightness and life. The Winter Solstice was about seeds and the path towards new birth – new life.

Fiona crouched, huddling her body against the brisk wind that buffeted her, and pulled out a few crystals. She drew a circle in the ground and set her crystals at the direction points. She stepped into the middle, but stayed silent for a moment as she turned in a circle to look all around her.

Darkness completely enveloped her – the only light coming from the window of the cottage far down the hill, and the few specks of bright stars in the sky. The moon was but a sliver, and hung low on the horizon. Fiona turned away from it and lifted her head to focus on one star – the one that shone the brightest of them all.

"THE MAGICK of solstice lingers on,
  Though childhood days have passed,
  Upon the common round of life,
  A holy spell is cast."

FIONA CLOSED her eyes as she cast her ritual and prayed. She made her wish – just like John had asked – and prayed that everything he had been trying to tell her was right. Opening her eyes, she looked around.

Everything was still the same.

"I wished, John! The moon is low and the stars are bright! I wished, damn it!" Fiona screeched, her words torn away by the wind that had picked up, tears beginning to stream down her face. She'd been stupid to think there was a glimmer of hope in her impossible plan.

Served her right for drinking whiskey by the fire this afternoon.

Fiona wiped the tears from her face with the back of her hand and willed them to stop, but they kept flowing, blinding her vision. Her grief and loss seemed to reopen inside of her, shattering her strength once again.

"I wished, John," Fiona whispered miserably.

Ronan butted his head against her knee, then pressed his body into her leg, offering her his comfort. She closed her eyes and forced herself to breathe steadily. Loss was a part of life. These were just her feelings about losing Aiden.

Ronan emitted a sharp bark, causing Fiona to open her eyes.

A light, white-hot in its intensity, hovered over the cottage – as though the very star that she had wished upon had fallen to float gently above the roof. Her heart skipped and Fiona knelt to put her arms around Ronan, hugging his furry body to hers. He turned once to lick her tears away.

"You love him," said a voice to her right, and Fiona almost jumped out of her skin.

She turned to see a man, dressed in regal court attire, looking at her. He glowed lightly – nothing like the white ball that hovered over Aiden's cottage, but just enough that she could easily make out his features. Fiona squinted at him.

"Aiden? Yes, well, he's my friend," Fiona said, continuing to hold Ronan in place even though the dog's fur now stood on end.

"Not that one," the man waved his hand dismissively, "The other one. Your husband."

"Yes, I love him with all my heart," Fiona's voice cracked.

"Ye've done good work in this world. Helped many," the man said, as he began to walk in front of her, his hands at his lips as he considered.

"I'm sorry – but – do I know you? I've only been visited by Grace before," Fiona admitted. There was something vaguely familiar about the man's features, but she couldn't quite place it.

"Ah yes, my lovely mother. She was quite the spitfire, wasn't she?" The man grinned and Fiona almost fell over in shock.

"Murrough," Fiona breathed in shock.

"Sure and you won't be confusing me with that traitorous half-brother of mine," the man swore, his features suddenly livid.

"Theobald?" Fiona gaped. Theobald had been borne from Grace's second marriage – she was famous for birthing him at sea immediately before going into battle. Fiona could only imagine what a fierce one he had grown up to be.

"Aye, 'tis I, pretty kin of mine. I've come to bestow upon you a favor – perhaps a favor for a favor – I haven't yet decided."

"You need me to do something for you?"

"Yes, or perhaps one of my kin. I see that young Morgan is a mighty one," Theobald raised an eyebrow at Fiona.

"Aye, she's quite talented. More gifts than the other girls." Fiona wasn't sure what to look at – Theobald or the glow that was hovering over the cottage.

"Well, while your line is all descended from Maeve, there's more of us that you seem to have forgotten about. I suppose my kin would be cousins of yours," Theobald said, and Fiona simply went still.

"More of us," she breathed, her arms tight around Ronan.

"Aye, there's more. Plenty, actually, though only a few are touched as your family is," Theobald shrugged.

"Something about the feminine goddess and power passing woman to woman."

"Yes, I suppose I could see the powerful magick in that," Fiona agreed, unsure of where he was going with it all.

"You've made a wish tonight – and a grand one at that. I'm considering granting it – but I'll have a promise first," Theobald said, turning to meet her eyes.

Fiona paused. Making promises to ghosts was a tricky business, and for all she knew it could be dark spirits that were glamouring her at the moment. She decided to proceed with caution.

"My kin are on a quest of sorts. I only ask that you – or Morgan – assist them on their path."

"Define assist," Fiona said immediately, feeling uncomfortable about making promises on Morgan's behalf. The girl had just recently grown comfortable with what she was.

"Ah, blood of my blood, I won't ask too hearty a boon. I just ask that you find them. Offer some of your knowledge to them – or pass it along through Morgan. They could use some guidance, 'tis all."

"What is the quest they are on? Where do they live? What are their names?"

Theobald laughed.

"I like you, Fiona. I've always admired strong women. How about this – you'll be given the information when the time is right. I'll stop in to visit," Theobald smiled at her. "Your great uncle coming to call, so to speak. As Grace has moved on to experience earthly pleasures and all."

"I knew it," Fiona breathed. "She's in Baby Grace, isn't she?"

"Leave it to her to pick dying and being reborn at the cove. My mother was a strong woman – a prideful one at that," Theobald's features flashed with joy and pride when he spoke of her.

"I will promise to assist however I can so long as it doesn't put me in harm's way – or those I love in harm's way," Fiona said sternly, "And I can't speak for Morgan. It's unfair of me to promise on behalf of someone who isn't here."

Theobald sized her up and then another smile broke out on his face.

"Good, that was just a test. I wanted to see if you were strong enough to stand up to me and not throw someone else in the line of fire for your own wants. I'll be seeing you soon, Fiona O'Brien." Theobald tipped his head at her and in an instant, he winked out of sight.

"Did that just really happen, Ronan?"

Fiona jerked back as the light hovering over the cottage flashed, a thousand times brighter than the sun, illuminating the world around them before it winked out of sight. It should have blinded her, and yet Fiona could still see. She'd thrown her hand up instinctively, but now lowered it to look around.

Darkness greeted her.

"Could it be?" Fiona wondered, jumping to her feet – her heart in her throat. She raced down the hill, Ronan at her side, until she reached the front door of the cottage. Pushing the door open, she pounded down the hallway until she stood in front of Aiden's bedroom door, gasping for breath.

Fiona reached out and put her hand on the doorknob. She paused, her entire body shaking.

He'd told her not to come back here until she was sure he was gone. The brilliant flash of light had to have been his soul leaving. Praying she wasn't making a mistake, Fiona twisted the knob and pushed the door open.

CHAPTER 46

"*T*HERE'S MY FIONA – with the pretty smiling eyes," Aiden – no, not Aiden, but still Aiden, rasped from where he lay on the bed, the soft light of the table lamp shining on him.

"J...J... John?" Fiona stuttered, rushing forward until she hovered over the bed, afraid to touch Aiden/John, unsure of what to do.

"You wished," John said, smiling up at her.

His eyes had changed. No longer were they Aiden's eyes, but John's brilliant blue ones looking back at her from Aiden's body.

"John," Fiona breathed, frozen in place, unable to process the implication of what she was seeing.

"We switched places, my love. He wanted so desperately to be with Serena and I wanted so desperately to be with you, that we were given this gift. Though it feels a little strange to be in this body, I'm sure I'll get used to it," John said affably while Fiona just stared at him, completely in a daze.

"John," Fiona breathed again.

"Well? Are you going to say my name all night, or come over here and give me a kiss then?" A grumpy expression, much like John's, crossed Aiden's face and Fiona felt herself go dizzy.

"I think I'm going to faint," Fiona said distinctly.

"We won't be having any of that," John said immediately, jumping from bed and catching Fiona as dizziness overtook her. His arms felt strong and real around Fiona and she hoped against hope this wasn't a crazy whiskey-fueled dream she was having. John laid her gently on the bed.

"Let's get you out of this coat," he said, quickly unzipping the coat and pulling her limp limbs from the sleeves.

"This sweater is pretty bulky too," John murmured and proceeded to pull off most of her clothes until she lay on the bed in just a thin shirt and her pants.

"There, much better," John said, coming to lie next to her. Fiona felt like she was in shock or in one of her dreams as she watched him prop his head up on an elbow and smile down at her – Aiden's face with John's eyes. It was a strangely surreal experience.

"Am I dreaming?" Fiona finally whispered, lifting her hand out to trace his cheek, but stopping before she actually touched his face.

"Does this feel like a dream?" John asked, quirking an eyebrow at her before he leaned forward and slid his lips over hers, searing her with his heat, as his love rose up and enveloped her. She knew instantly then that it was really him. Much as she had felt their DNA weave together during their handfasting, she felt him now – in this kiss.

Fiona sobbed against his mouth, suddenly ravenous for his kiss, his touch, his nearness. She didn't know what magick this was – but it didn't matter, if she got to have John back in her arms.

"Wait, wait," Fiona pulled back and searched his eyes – eyes that were burned into her memory and now back in real life again. "If you took Aiden's body does that mean you also took his cancer?" Fear rose up in her that it would be too late to heal him – that the cancer had advanced too far.

John smiled at her.

"They healed him – the angels did – when they brought me in. It's part of a ritual they do. You wished though – you didn't believe me at first – but you wished. I watched you wish," John said, his eyes warm with love.

"I didn't know this was possible," Fiona admitted, "It's all so crazy to me – so farfetched."

"We had a love for all time, Fiona. Through other worlds and back," John said.

"Is that why the cove glowed today?" Fiona perked up in excitement.

"Aye, I was there. I've been staying close to Aiden – hoping against hope you would make the wish and that I would be close when Aiden left this world."

"Did… did you see him? Is he okay?"

"Aye, he's happy as can be. He wanted this gift for you, knew what was coming. It seems he got to meet Grace," John said, his eyes dancing.

"Aye! I knew it! I knew Baby Grace had a talk with him," Fiona punctuated her words with her finger.

"Aiden said he'll stop by in your dreams tonight to say a proper goodbye," John said, pulling Fiona close to him.

"That's right kind of him, though I don't know how I'm going to sleep with you here now! I want to cherish every second," Fiona exclaimed.

"We've time, my love, plenty of time. I've negotiated it myself," John laughed at her and Fiona gaped at him. "Consider it an – I'm sorry I've been gone for so long – gift."

"That's the best gift ever," Fiona said, and soon they no longer talked, losing themselves in the nearness of each other as their love swelled up and surrounded them – everything right in their world once again.

CHAPTER 47

"*Y*OU AND JOHN keep that Yule log burning – you hear? That's my gift to you – my blessings for a new year."

Aiden stood before her in her dreams. John had been right – she had been able to sleep, once she was cocooned in his arms again. Already the shock of seeing John's eyes in Aiden's face was beginning to wear off and he was seeming to look more and more like John by the minute. Though that was probably just her imagination – a way to cope with what had happened to her this night.

"Aiden – are you with her? Did you get to see your Serena?" Fiona breathed, hoping against hope that he was as happy as she was. Aiden grinned and turned, holding his hand out to someone that she couldn't see behind him. In a moment, a smiling dark-haired beauty – his Serena, though years younger than she had been – curled into the crook of his arm and wound her arms around his waist.

"Thank you for taking good care of him – you have been a good friend," Serena said.

"Thank you for lending him to me. I think we both needed it. And thank you for the gift of John back," Fiona whispered.

"It's time for us to go, Fiona. I promised I would check in with you, but I see you're as right as rain. Sláinte, my good friend, sláinte." Aiden mimicked holding up a whiskey glass and saluted her before they faded away.

Fiona saluted him back, snuggling closer to the warm body pressed at her back, and fell into a peaceful dream-free sleep for the first time in years.

EPILOGUE

"I HAVE TO ADMIT, I think this might just be the best Christmas in the history of time," Fiona observed over the conversations that ranged through the large living room at Flynn's house. She leaned into John's side, barely able to stay a few steps away from him over the past few days, and smiled contentedly at the room.

The few days since the Winter Solstice had been nothing short of miraculous. Fiona had dutifully kept the Yule log burning as she'd promised Aiden, and she and John had spent their time reconnecting over whiskey and the fire. It all felt like a dream to her and one Fiona hadn't been willing to part with until John had insisted they tell her family what was going on.

Officially, the story they had shared to the village was that Aiden had decided at the last moment he wanted Fiona to heal him and luckily, she'd been able to do so. The goal would be to somewhat limit John's interactions with the villagers so things didn't seem too weird when he didn't remember the things that Aiden should know.

They'd already decided they were going to take a tour of
Ireland and all of Europe over the next year, so Fiona
wasn't too worried about people suspecting anything
different.

Her family, however, was much smarter than that.
Keelin had shown up at the cottage the day after the
Solstice, demanding to help Fiona with Aiden's remains.
Instead, she'd found a very healthy Aiden cozied up to
Fiona by the fire. It had taken a moment for Keelin to wrap
her head around what had happened – but miraculously
she'd taken it in stride. The rest of her girls had followed
suit and now they were all spending Christmas together at
Flynn's house.

Fiona looked over her pretty girls – Keelin, Margaret,
Aislinn, Cait, - Morgan was there but at the stables - and
positively radiated with happiness at having them all close.
They'd all grown and learned so much over the past few
years and it was as though everything had lined up and all
was at peace.

Finally, Fiona had the true Christmas gift she had
always wanted – peace and happiness for those she loved.
Including herself, she thought with another giddy laugh as
she looked over at John. Fiona was quite sure that the
smile hadn't left her face for days now.

"Fiona, this was at the back door for you," Morgan
said, coming into the room and pulling off her coat. She'd
gone out to say goodnight to the horses as she always did
when she was here. Morgan had a special connection with
all animals, and they all preened and jostled for her attention when she went into the barn.

"What is it?" Aislinn asked from where she was curled

up on the floor in front of the fire, leaning back against Baird.

"It's an envelope – maybe a Christmas gift?" Morgan said, her eyes alight with delight.

"I guess we'll see," Fiona remarked and took the envelope from her. Power shot through her as soon as her hand touched the paper and Fiona raised an eyebrow at Morgan.

"You didn't feel anything different when you touched this?"

Morgan's eyes widened.

"No, I didn't at all."

"Which is highly unusual. They must have blocked the power," Fiona murmured. Morgan was one of her most attuned girls, having multiple extrasensory abilities. It surprised her that Morgan had been unable to feel the power radiating from the paper.

"Is it bad?" Cait asked, tilting her head as she watched Fiona.

"I don't think it's evil. But there's power here," Fiona said and then slid her finger under the flap to pull the paper out. The paper, creased in threes and of a thick stock, looked empty at first.

"There's nothing on it," John observed and Fiona shook her head as she turned the paper away from him so that only her eyes could see it. As soon as she moved it from his view, words appeared on the page.

"I'll be damned," Fiona muttered, "There is an invisibility cloak on this. As soon as I turned the page, I could read it."

"So you'd think she'd be reading it then," Cait

muttered and Aislinn laughed at her, instructing her to shush.

"'My dearest Fiona,'" Fiona began and the room grew quiet – the only noise that of the wind outside and the flames crackling in the fireplace.

"'As I said, I would be requiring a favor of you in exchange for John's life,'" Fiona glanced at John and his look of surprise. "It's all right, my love – anything was worth having you home."

"I hope the price isn't too much to pay," John muttered, running his hand down Fiona's thigh.

"Let's find out, shall we? 'As you've been informed, there is another branch of this family you know little about.'"

A collective gasp echoed around the room and Fiona held her hand up for silence. "I've just learned of this, ladies. I've been meaning to fill you in but I've been a bit busy – what with being reunited with the love of my life. Let me finish and we'll discuss."

The murmurs quieted down and Fiona turned back to the letter, the words forming again when she focused on the page.

"'My descendants know little of who or what they are and I'll need one of yours to go find them and instruct them on their path. A few of them have started to research – as it is virtually impossible for them to ignore their magick. I've been content with not interfering in their lives – but dangerous times are ahead and you must go to them and help,'" Fiona said.

"This is ridiculous. Dangerous times? Who is this from

anyway?" Cait exploded, pushing her hand through her short hair in frustration.

"Theobald. Grace O'Malley's son from her second marriage. Born at sea in mid-battle. I'm assuming he holds powerful magick as well," Fiona murmured and then raised her hand to silence the room.

"'I'm sure you're familiar with the Four Treasures creation myth. Except it isn't a myth, and there really are four treasures that must be recovered by the four women whose destiny it is to hold them and keep them from falling into the wrong hands. Each woman a daughter of one of the great cities ranging along the Danube – must be found and instructed.'"

The room exploded.

"What cities?"

"What myth?"

John cleared his throat and held up his hands – the room immediately quieted.

"I've spent a few years on the other side, you know, so I'm sure I'll be able to shed some light on this story," John said quietly.

"Go ahead, love, tell them about the creation myth," Fiona said wearily. There was more on the letter, but it was best that they got through this part first.

"When earth first came into being," John began, and everyone settled down to listen, "There was but dirt and dust. Danu, the divine goddess, allowed water to drip onto earth to form the sacred oak from whence two acorns sprang. These acorns – one male and one female – turned into God Dagda and Goddess Brigid. Their job was to populate the world. In doing so, they created many children of Danu who all lived in four cities that ranged the now-flowing waters of a river. The river is now known as the River Danube," John said and Fiona saw more than a few eyes widen at that. "Four cities – Falias, Gorias, Finias, and Murias, lined the banks of the Danube. Each city had a great treasure that was given to them by Danu. Falias had a stone called Lia Fail – otherwise known as Stone of Destiny."

Flynn cursed across the room.

"Sure and you're kidding me right? Isn't that supposed to be the Scottish throne?"

"There's more than one stone," John said evenly and Flynn swore again. "This stone is meant to shout in right-eous joy when the person who is meant to lead sets foot upon it. It also has a delightful twist of being a lie-detector of sorts. Gorias, the next city, had a treasure that was a very mighty sword. This sword was often referred to as the Retaliator and it shone with great light when given to the right warrior. Famous god Lugh wielded the Retaliator in many battles. It was known to strike down enemies in its path, for people became entranced by its glow."

The wind picked up speed outside as the room remained silent.

"Finias is the next city and was gifted with a magick spear – often referred to as the red javelin – it was known to always find its enemy. Once it was pulled out – it could not miss – no matter where the enemy hides."

"Sure and that's impossible," Aislinn breathed – her eyes wide.

"And finally, we have the city of Murias with the caul-dron of plenty. It was said that nobody could go to the cauldron and leave unsatisfied. It could feed the world if need be – but it also has a power of satisfying people's needs or wants. It is exceptionally dangerous for any of these weapons to fall into the wrong hands," John said, the flames of the fire reflected in his eyes.

"So what happened? How did these weapons get lost?" Keelin asked tentatively from where she cuddled Baby Grace in an armchair.

"Goddess Danu asked her children to go to the Island of Destiny. Also known as Innisfail," John said.

Flynn swore again and Keelin looked at him in confusion.

"Isle of Destiny, Innisfail, or as we know it, Ireland," Flynn muttered.

"Once the children reached the Isle of Destiny, great wars were fought between Danu's children and her sister of the earth's children. Eventually, Domnu, her sister, won and Danu's children were driven to the hills. They would be what we consider the fae now," John shrugged.

"So, um, there really are fairies?" Keelin asked, her gaze swiveling across the room.

"Yes, there are," Fiona spoke up. "And this letter is suggesting that we identify the women whose destiny it is to wield and protect these weapons – in order to keep them from falling into the wrong hands."

"And who are the wrong hands?" Cait demanded.

John cleared his throat.

"Ah, well, I suppose if you wanted to voice it in the most basic of terms – the Children of Danu are the children of Goddesses and represent light. The Children of

Domnu come from the earth and they are drawn to the dark."

"And it appears that we must find these treasures in order. I've been given a name," Fiona said, holding the paper up.

"What is it?" Margaret asked.

"Clare MacBride."

As soon as she uttered the words, the letter imploded in a brilliant flash of light, leaving nothing but a layer of dust on Fiona's slacks.

And a thousand unanswered questions in its wake.

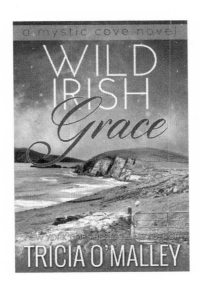

Available now as an e-book, paperback or audiobook!!!

Available from Amazon

The following is an excerpt from
Wild Irish Grace
Book 7 in the Mystic Cove Series

CHAPTER 1

*H*e'd come to her once again, in her dreams, as he had since she'd come of age. A man she'd loved across centuries, for lifetimes, and yet had known so very little of in real life. Her love for him was like a star, each evening searing her soul with its heat, night upon night, until she could only hope that one day the star would collapse in on itself, leaving her dreams finally free of the one man she measured all others against.

Dillon Keagan.

Frustrated, and very aware of needs unmet, Grace sighed and pulled a pillow over her head, running a small spell in her mind to charm herself free of the dreams. They had increased of late and had robbed her of any peaceful moments of sleep over the past several months.

Her power carried her only so far, drifting softly in the grey in-between of awake and dreaming. Then, once more, she found herself walking on the shore, irresistibly drawn to the man who laughed to her from where he stood knee-deep in water, a fishing line in hand, the ocean breezes kissing his curls.

"I've a mighty feast for us this evening, Gráinne, that I do," Dillon called to her as he added another fish to the almost-full basket that lay wedged between two rocks on the shore. Grace smiled at him, battling a shyness so unnatural to her that she wanted to overcompensate by coming up with a bawdy joke to tell him. Instead she caught her toe on a rock and let out a stream of curses usually reserved for sailors as she hopped on one foot, her cheeks flaming in embarrassment.

"You've a mouth on you, that you do, my pretty Gráinne," Dillon laughed, coming to her and sweeping her up in his arms, dazzling her with his charm and the way his eyes crinkled at the corners when he laughed. Blue as the sea when the first rays of sun streamed across its surface in the morning, Dillon's eyes captivated her with their warmth, laughter, and how they spoke of worlds unknown.

Grace wanted to know those worlds, to hear him tell tales of cities both near and far, and to know who this man was and how'd he'd come to land on her shores. Shores she guarded fiercely and had made a name for herself in ruthlessly protecting.

Oh, but she never wanted to leave this place, Grace thought as she nuzzled into his neck, allowing him to carry her like a helpless maiden to the abandoned hut they'd commandeered, where they had spent the last few weeks hopelessly lost in each other's arms. Dillon had been as much of a surprise to her as she to him: he a shipwrecked sailor clinging to the tatters of his boat, and she – an unexpected woman captain of a sleek little sloop – his rescuer. She'd spared him her usual treatment of the vagabonds she'd discovered on the water, whether it was because of his striking good looks – sun-kissed curls and dancing blue eyes – or the fact that she'd known since the moment she'd laid eyes upon him that their lives were somehow inextricably connected.

Grace had docked near a small village on the west coast and sent her crew on home to their families. There had been too many battles and her men were weary. A good leader knew when her crew was spent, and it had been months since many of them had slept in a bed or known the warm arms of a lover. They'd return in a month's time, replenished and refueled, and ready for whatever battle they'd next need to fight.

But for now, in this moment, this part of the world was hers and Dillon's alone. It was their own little island of discovery and exploration, and they dove into it with delight, exchanging stories of battles both won and lost, and sights seen across the seas.

They made love with abandon, late into the night, while the fire burned low and their bodies burned hot, each touch an exploration, an awakening. When Grace looked into his eyes, the edges of her world and his blended to become one.

It felt like coming home.

After hours spent exploring each other, she lay liquid and supple, her eyes on the light that just creased the horizon of the water. The fire was long dead and Grace shivered.

"What worries you, my love?" Dillon's voice, sleepy

and sated at her ear, sent warm tendrils down her neck as he pulled her back close to his chest, his body cradling hers in warmth.

"I can't stay here – in this moment with you. I have children who need me, tenants who depend on my lead since my husband has passed, boundaries to defend, and treasures to preserve. How am I to stay here – tucked away in this hut – forever?" Grace said, her eyes heavy with sleep and something more, an ache of knowing that this moment of pure joy was not to be forever.

She'd had many highs and lows in her short but fiercely-lived life, and a realist she was – Gráinne O'Malley, the great pirate queen of the Irish seas. But buried deep beneath her warrior's shell was a fiercely romantic heart that cherished love in all its forms. It was both her greatest strength and biggest weakness. Her gaze landed on the stone they'd engraved together, branding the cottage as their own.

My heart for yours.

Dillon turned her so that she met his eyes, the sun's light just enough so that they shone intensely blue in his face as he gazed down on her, his look both a caress and a promise. Raising her hand to his lips, he first kissed it before bringing both their hands to her heart.

"You'll have this moment, forever, here in your heart. Once a love like ours is known, it can never be taken from us, and transcends all barriers – those of mortal law, those of time, and beyond what most can comprehend. It's an endless love, one that grows through the ages, and we'll meet, time and time again, our souls knowing each other, our love binding us for centuries. Be it but weeks of time in this life, know that we're promised for more, Gráinne O'Malley, for it is written in the tapestry of the universe."

Grace lost herself in his words. She'd heard them time and again in her dreams, and yet each time he uttered his promises of a love that knew no boundaries she was sucked back in, the pain of love and loss a bittersweet taste in her mouth.

Sighing, Grace pulled the pillow from her head and sat up in bed, annoyed with herself for wanting both to weep in longing and to laugh for the sheer joy of having felt such a love fill her soul. Granted, it was only in her dreams – dreams where she walked as Gráinne O'Malley and not as herself, Grace O'Brien, in the now – but to know that such a love existed was like being in the desert and seeing the hint of water on the horizon.

Try as she might, Grace had never found out what happened to Dillon or how he and Gráinne had parted ways. Though she had many gifts of magick, remembering all the bits of her past lives was not one of them. Some historical records reported that Dillon was a shipwrecked sailor Grace had taken as a lover before he'd been murdered on Donegal land. Gráinne had spent her life avenging his murder, even after she'd taken a new husband; she'd never forgiven the Donegal clan and had gone on to seize their castle and make them regret the day they'd ever wronged Gráinne O'Malley. A part of Grace hoped the story was true, for she was known to have a fiercely vengeful side that rarely forgave a grievous slight, but the part where Dillon was murdered made Grace hope that the threads of time had come unwoven and a happier ending had come to her love.

Grace tugged her hair and ran her hands over her face, taking a few deep breaths to calm herself. In the past few months the lines between the worlds had begun to shift and blur even more than was natural for her, an exceptionally powerful healer and practitioner of all things magick. With this shift in energy, Dillon had begun visiting her in her dreams nightly, causing her to ache each morning as though she'd lost the love of her life once more.

It was a decidedly uncomfortable way to wake up.

"Enough of that nonsense," Grace said to Rosie, granddaughter of Ronan the Great, who wagged her tail at the foot of the bed, her eyes alight with excitement over her impending breakfast.

"Come on, Rosie, let's have ourselves a day off. We haven't had a day of fun in a while," Grace decided, and the dog did a spin of joy at the end of the bed. Looking at her iPhone, Grace reminded herself of the date and what year she lived in.

For though she'd once walked the shores as Gráinne O'Malley, her soul lived in the here and now, and she would do well to remember that. Lover or no, Grace had a life to live and a destiny to fulfill.

Read Wild Irish Rebel today.
Available from Amazon

AUTHOR'S NOTE

Ireland holds a special place in my heart – a land of dreamers and for dreamers. There's nothing quite like cozying up next to a fire in a pub and listening to a session or having a cup of tea while the rain mists outside the window. I'll forever be enchanted by her rocky shores and I hope you enjoy this series as much as I enjoyed writing it. Thank you for taking part in my world, I hope that my stories bring you great joy.

Have you read books from my other series? Join our little community by signing up for my newsletter for updates on island-living, fun giveaways, and how to follow me on social media!
http://eepurl.com/1LAiz.

or at my website
www.triciaomalley.com

I hope my books have added a little magick into your life. If you have a moment to add some to my day, you can help by telling your friends and leaving a review. Word-of-mouth is the most powerful way to share my stories.
Thank you.

MS. BITCH

FINDING HAPPINESS IS THE BEST REVENGE

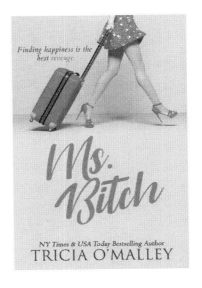

Available as an e-book, Hardback, Paperback, Audio or Large Print.
Read Today
New from Tricia O'Malley

From the outside, it seems thirty-six-year-old Tess Campbell has it all. A happy marriage, a successful career as a novelist, and an exciting cross-country move ahead. Tess has always played by the rules and it seems like life is good.

Except it's not. Life is a bitch. And suddenly so is Tess.

"Ms. Bitch is sunshine in a book! An uplifting story of fighting your way through heartbreak and making your own version of happily-ever-after."
~Ann Charles, USA Today Bestselling Author of the Deadwood Mystery Series

"Authentic and relatable, Ms. Bitch packs an emotional punch. By the end, I was crying happy tears and ready to pack my bags in search of my best life."
-Annabel Chase, author of the Starry Hollow Witches series

"It's easy to be brave when you have a lot of support in your life, but it takes a special kind of courage to forge a new path when you're alone. Tess is the heroine I hope I'll be if my life ever crumbles down around me. Ms. Bitch is a journey of determination, a study in self-love, and a hope for second chances. I could not put it down!"
-Renee George, USA Today Bestselling Author of the Nora Black Midlife Psychic Mysteries

"I don't know where to start listing all the reasons why you should read this book. It's empowering. It's fierce. It's about loving yourself enough to build the life you want. It was honest, and raw, and real and I just...loved it so much!"

– Sara Wylde, author of Fat

THE MYSTIC COVE SERIES

Wild Irish Heart

Wild Irish Eyes

Wild Irish Soul

Wild Irish Rebel

Wild Irish Roots: Margaret & Sean

Wild Irish Witch

Wild Irish Grace

Wild Irish Dreamer

Wild Irish Christmas (Novella)

Wild Irish Sage

Wild Irish Renegade

Wild Irish Moon

"I have read thousands of books and a fair percentage have been romances. Until I read Wild Irish Heart, I never had a book actually make me believe in love."- Amazon Review

Available in audio, e-book & paperback!

THE ISLE OF DESTINY SERIES

ALSO BY TRICIA O'MALLEY

Stone Song

Sword Song

Spear Song

Sphere Song

"Love this series. I will read this multiple times. Keeps you on the edge of your seat. It has action, excitement and romance all in one series."- Amazon Review

Available in audio, e-book & paperback!

Available Now

THE ALTHEA ROSE SERIES

ALSO BY TRICIA O'MALLEY

One Tequila

Tequila for Two

Tequila Will Kill Ya (Novella)

Three Tequilas

Tequila Shots & Valentine Knots (Novella)

Tequila Four

A Fifth of Tequila

A Sixer of Tequila

Seven Deadly Tequilas

Eight Ways to Tequila

Tequila for Christmas (Novella)

"Not my usual genre but couldn't resist the Florida Keys setting. I was hooked from the first page. A fun read with just the right amount of crazy! Will definitely follow this series."- Amazon Review

Available in audio, e-book & paperback!

ALSO BY TRICIA O'MALLEY

STAND ALONE NOVELS

Ms. Bitch

"Ms. Bitch is sunshine in a book! An uplifting story of fighting your way through heartbreak and making your own version of happily-ever-after."

~Ann Charles, USA Today Bestselling Author

One Way Ticket

A funny and captivating beach read where booking a one-way ticket to paradise means starting over, letting go, and taking a chance on love...one more time

10 out of 10 - The BookLife Prize semi finalist

Firebird Award Winner

Pencraft Book of the year 2021

AUTHOR'S ACKNOWLEDGEMENT

First, and foremost, I'd like to thank my family and friends for their constant support, advice, and ideas. You've all proven to make a difference on my path. And, to my beta readers, I love you for all of your support and fascinating feedback!

And last, but never least, my two constant companions as I struggle through words on my computer each day - Briggs and Blue.